Oldham
Council

LEES
Lees

Please return this book before the last date stamped.
Items can be renewed by telephone, in person at any library or online at
www.oldham.gov.uk/libraries

Also Available

Our Doris

INDiSPUTABLY DORiS

Charles Heathcote

VA

VARIOUS ALTITUDES
Cheshire

www.variousaltitudes.com

1

COMMUNiTY

Our Doris is in peril of the Queen. She's been given community service for attacking Janice Dooley of Little Street with a set of scales at the local Bulge Busters meeting. The official Doris press release states that she's cleaning up council estates for the underprivileged children of Partridge Mews. She could have stuck to that story if it weren't for the viral video and our Doris's face on the front of the Gazette wearing a high-vis tabard.

The first time she went to perform her duties, she said to me, she said, 'I am a victim of circumstance, our 'arold, unable to live in respectable society as a heterosexual British woman in a monogamous relationship with no mortgage.'

I said, 'You assaulted someone, our Doris.'

When the Look reached nuclear levels I decided to keep quiet. She left and I had to figure out how to get burnt chicken chasseur off a casserole dish before she got home – I'd been in the midst of cooking it the night before when Granada Reports came on and I was caught in the powerful allure of Lucy Meacock's gaze as she talked about sewage trouble in Salford.

Our Doris came home eight hours later, her Laura Ashley all covered in muck and her M&S absent. She didn't give me time to speak before she began her tirade: she said to me, she said, 'A council estate, our 'arold. They want me to spend one hundred hours on a council estate. We went up one street – a man and something resembling a pitbull with hair extensions were screaming at each other. I approached them and intimated that we were in a public place and could they please show some decorum. Honestly, they had more curses than Tutankhamun's tomb. I considered violence but my probation officer pointed out that I could end up in prison.'

'What happened, our Doris?'

'As you know, our 'arold, I am quite approachable to the underclasses and this poor unfortunate girl, I cannot for the life of me repeat her name, inferred that the gentleman - and I say that in the very loose sense of the word – was involved in an illegal horticulture operation. The shrubbery had overgrown into her half of their shared loft so I approached him and said that if he didn't keep it down and get his garden out of the loft the only plot he'd be seeing is a prison yard.'

'Did it work?'

''arold, do you not know me at all? And did you clean my casserole dish? Mrs Stonesthrow has had a hip replacement and I want to show her what a real beef bourguignon tastes like.'

I said to her – and I've no idea where it came from. It might have been one too many episodes of The Sweeney but I said, 'I'd watch out if I were you, our Doris.'

She were a bit shell-shocked if I'm honest. I had given her a warning. In fifty-four years of marriage my warnings were as infrequent as the buses. Our Doris didn't know what to do with her face. She said to me, coming over all Penelope Keith, 'Why, 'arold, whatever do you mean?'

And here I felt mischievous. I felt the familiar sensation creep into my chest like a bluebottle under a lampshade. I were practically intoxicated on the thrill as I said to her, I said, 'They'll have you as a Gangland crime lord. You'll end up with young men in low-waisted Hollister jeans at your front door. We'll speak to Alf, get it all sorted.' And I settled back into my chair.

Our Doris's bottom lip trembled as she shot the Look at me. Her teeth looked to be testing to see if they could swallow me whole as she gritted them and said to me, she said, ''arold Copeland, I have put up with your funny comments and witty repartee for over half a century. If I wanted to be a Gangland crime lord I could but I will not be attacked because I committed my civil duties.'

'Are you turning over a new leaf, our Doris?'

'I am Doris Copeland, I don't need to turn over a new leaf, I'm practically Mary Poppins. I am the interim chairwoman of the Partridge Mews Women's Institute.'

Two months down the line and our Doris developed something of a following on social media. Some young lad took a photograph and uploaded it to Instagram, our Theo showed us on his iPad.

I have to say that if there were a best dressed award for community service our Doris would win hands down. She's developed something of a uniform for herself: beige Bon Marche cardigan with a Tie Rack scarf – light pink with butterflies. She tells anyone who'll listen she bought it at Manchester Piccadilly in her efforts to appear like a high-flier.

Our Doris has always had a thing for a butterfly print. I've never understood it myself. If a moth gets anywhere near the bedroom she quarantines herself in the bathroom and I have to catch it in the glass for my dentures and deposit it in the back garden because she can't have it getting around that she doesn't treat her Lepidoptera with anything but the utmost respect.

She doesn't choose the best shoes for picking litter does Doris. I said to her, 'You can't wear high heels on grass, our Doris.' She told me that they were Debenhams and that's all they were fit for.

Now that one Instagram photo led to a group of teens, twenty-somethings and funny Hubert with the gammy leg following our Doris around photographing her and putting her pictures all over the internet.

She thinks she's a local celebrity.

When the Gazette got in touch for a Twitter interview she said she wouldn't go so far as to debase herself by constraining her great British eloquence to one hundred and forty characters when the same paper themselves had used their precious column inches on her minor law-breaking.

I said, 'Where did you learn about Twitter, our Doris, you had trouble enough with Teletext.'

She came over all sincere and every bit as menacing as she said, 'The interim chairwoman of the Partridge Mews Women's Institute must understand all reasonable forms of modern communication in order that she may correspond with the truly diverse population.' This were news to me as our Doris never went in for new-fangled technology after a mishap with an electronic till in nineteen eighty-four.

There were a twitch at her lips, imperceptible to most but when you know someone as long as I've known our Doris you get used to their most minute of movements. I said to her, I said, 'And?'

The twitch inched towards a smile as she said, 'Janice Dooley of Little Street believes she can spread idle gossip on social media but she hadn't banked on me discovering she's been corresponding with the former Colonel Watkins of Lipton Avenue, Wren's Lea.'

'What did you do, our Doris?'

'I did what any concerned matriarch would do. I rang his wife.' Our Doris did her best to conceal a smirk as the phone rang.

As she scuttled off to answer, I took my Daily Mirror from behind the cushion covers and skimmed the pages. I'd been hiding copies of the newspaper in the house ever since I caught bronchitis from spending too long on a Sudoku in my shed – I'd put three nines in one line when this fit of coughing burst from my chest as though a cactus were scouring my lungs.

Our Doris found a copy once and brought it into the lounge coming over all General Zod as she said to me she said, 'Can you tell me how I came to find this drivel beneath the potted fern in the dining room?'

'You were taught by Sherlock Holmes and by the sheer process of elimination you came to deduct that the potted fern had developed a longing for the classic red top.'

'You can stop that right now, our 'arold, I did not raise a facetious husband.'

'I'm not keeping the Daily Mirror in my shed any longer, our Doris.'

Now I'm not about to make a habit of standing up to our Doris. It isn't safe. She stopped talking to me for three months in nineteen seventy-five and I didn't notice until she got a cashew caught in her throat at the new Indian restaurant on Manchego Crescent. If our Doris isn't speaking she's liable to do herself a mischief.

Yet I stood my ground this time and said to her, I said, 'I were laid up in bed for months with that bronchitis. I like the Daily Mirror – I've kept it hidden for that long and you haven't noticed so I'm going to keep hiding it and you can do what you will.'

Our Doris's cheeks flushed, there were a rosy glow the likes of which I hadn't seen since she drank too much sweet sherry at Mavis's seventy-sixth birthday party. She said to me, she said, ''arold, you know that I cannot possibly allow those of our social circle to discover such a foul spectacle as this our house. However, if it were say, part of a sociological experiment to discuss how our media is no longer shaped by politics or socio-economic circumstances, I suppose I could allow it to remain hidden, as long as all copies are dispensed of in Number 42's recycling – she's just the type to read such a rag.'

I looked at our Doris flabbergasted and said, 'All right, our Doris.'

And then she did something she hasn't done in the day time since the nineties, she giggled, all flirtatious, and I can't pretend that my heart didn't start beating that fast I couldn't be sure if it were a cardiac arrest or the allure of our Doris but lord does that woman know how to warm a man's cockles.

Since then she's kept to her promise. I keep my Daily Mirrors hidden and she pretends that she doesn't mind. It might have taken fifty-four years, but it's progress.

As Andy Capp went about his business I could hear our Doris's muttering become more pronounced. There's this edge to her voice, as though her words are bullets and she's perfected the art of shooting them down the phone. She must have had her teeth gritted, I don't know, but if she went any more high-pitched the only folk able to hear her would have been of the canine persuasion.

She said down the phone, she said, 'Oh, I understand perfectly, I do thank you for the phone call, common courtesy is so often forgotten nowadays.'

The phone were slammed into the cradle with more aggression than when they cancelled Bruce Forsyth's the Price is Right and she were laid up in bed with gout.

She scurried back into the lounge and I slipped the Daily Mirror back behind the cushions. She looked at me a bit funny but said nothing about it.

I said to her, I said, 'Who were that on the phone, our Doris?'

And she gave me a look, not the Look, not the one that she's the fury of seven Hells in her, no, this were a much simpler anger. I could tell by the Clint Eastwood set of her jaw, and the way her fists clenched, tight enough to make light work on a jar of pickled onions. And her eyes, well, her eyes were maniacal as she said to me, she said, 'You won't believe it, our 'arold, I tell you, you won't believe it. I'm still in shock myself. I mean I'd expect this sort of thing off Mrs Brady – ever since she had her bladder stretched she's been more bumptious but this is someone I saw as a close, personal friend.'

I put my cup of tea down because I could tell it

were getting serious. Our Doris only starts repeating herself during times of dire emergencies, like the time the nets weren't dry and the vicar called around to see if her mother had recovered from vertigo.

Our Doris still weren't letting on who'd phoned so I repeated my question, I said to her, I said, 'Who is it, our Doris?'

Our Doris collapsed into her chair, something she'd never usually do because her spine wasn't developed for something as lower class as slouching. She took hold of the bridge of her nose and said to me, she said, 'It's Pandra O'Malley. She's decided to run for chairwoman of the WI. I should have known there was something up when she went back to Derek.'

I were flummoxed. 'But you've only just got the job.'

She nodded once, curt. 'Oh, I do forget you don't understand politics, our 'arold. Since Violet left me in charge, my official title is interim chairwoman of the Partridge Mews Women's Institute. Any candidate who wishes to put their name forward for the position may do so before the AGM in June.'

'June's ages away.'

'I know that, 'arold, this isn't just an announcement, it's an outright threat. Pandra O'Malley believes she can take the position without a fight.'

'Well then,' I said, 'what are you going to do about it?'

That's when the sharp glint appeared in her eyes. She sat up straight, removing flecks of lint from her shirt as she said to me, she said, 'arold, I'm going to do what I do best. I'm going to throw a fundraiser.'

'Well, I'll get off down the pub then.'

Our Doris let me have a smile. 'I knew you would

understand your place sooner rather than later, our 'arold. Do let Alf know that I will be holding a Bring and Buy sale to raise money for the lesser educated, wording to be confirmed.'

I met Alf at the Hare and Horse. He's become a bit more sensible since our Doris's conviction, says as the world has changed if the elderly are now fair game. He still steals pork pies, but only if they're past their sell by date. I think his Edith is happy if nothing else: she doesn't have to keep explaining his thieving as a nervous tic.

When we'd assembled ourselves with bitter – pint for him, half for me – I said to him, I said, 'Pandra O'Malley's running for chairwoman of the WI.'

He slurped his bitter, smacked his lips and said, 'You've only just found out?'

I looked at him gone out and said, 'What do you mean, only just?'

"arold, she started on about this months ago. Our Edith wouldn't hear anything against Doris so we've only heard whispers.'

'Why didn't you say anything before?'

'It's Pandra O'Malley.'

'Still,' I said, 'our Doris is holding a fundraiser at the church hall. You might want to let the lads know.'

"arold, my old son, you're well and truly beggared.' He hissed through his teeth and said to me, he said, 'This is going to end up costing you pints of ale and tons of pork scratchings, you'd be better off running off to Whitby with Mrs Pemberton.'

'Why does she want to be chairwoman anyway? It's not like she's the most dedicated member of that WI.'

Alf shrugged, halfway through his pint before

saying, 'Our Edith says as she wants to truly ingratiate herself into Partridge Mews.'

'She's lived here since the seventies.'

'Exactly. She's been in this country forty years and the ladies still haven't forgiven her accent.'

'You have a point there.'

We spent the rest of our time talking about Bertie Sterling's latest attempt at growing rhubarb and whether there were anything in that Magic Trowel he bought from QVC.

When I got home I found our Doris buried beneath a pile of address books, Yellow Pages and assorted stationary, as though she'd ram-raided Staples. I said to her, I said, 'You're after an industrial paper cut there then, our Doris?'

She gave me the Look and said to me, she said, 'If I'm organising a fundraiser, our 'arold, that means inviting people, especially when you consider the possibility of a local celebrity attending.'

'Local celebrity?'

'Don't look at me all gone out. A celebrity adds an air of prestige, it gives them some good free publicity as well.'

'Well, who are you after then?'

'That's where I ran into a problem. Do you honestly believe I would make this much mess if I knew who to invite?'

I shrugged. 'I suppose Partridge Mews doesn't really have many celebrities.'

'You're correct in your assumptions, Harold Copeland. Partridge Mews is woefully lacking in people who should be celebrated for their talents. The most we have is Henrietta Rowbotham who appeared in the audience of Trisha Goddard in two thousand and three.'

'If there aren't any celebrities you want, why are you looking for one?'

'Because of Pandra O'Malley. Honestly, I thought you'd understand this. I need to set aside any differences I have ever had with the liberal media and create a spectacular event never before witnessed in this town. Pandra O'Malley is on the planning committee for the Greenfields Fete. They have celebrities and fairground rides. I cannot fit a waltzer in the church hall, our 'arold, but that is just the sort of thing the surrounding underclasses have come to expect – all of the glamour without any thought as to what health and safety might think.'

I didn't respond to this. Our Doris has never been one for health and safety herself.

For Angela's seventeenth birthday she decided to take us all clay pigeon shooting. Our Angela could invite a select group of friends – the impressionable ones who looked to be moving in the right social circles.

Now our Doris never showed any inclination for clay pigeon shooting before, she got it into her head after she discovered Janice Dooley of Little Street had been invited to the shoot by Reginald Humphries of Lavender Close. He'd recently divorced his fourth wife and wasn't after anything serious.

I can't say our Angela wanted to commemorate her seventeenth in a cold, wet field with four of her chosen closest classmates learning how to fire a gun but that's our Doris for you.

Anyway, we were into the third hour of what had been the dullest, dreariest day of my life, and I've been to Grimsby, when who were to emerge from the bushes but Janice Dooley herself. She were having a bash at readjusting her skirt when old Reginald followed on after her, tucking in his shirt.

Our Angela and her friends knew what had been going on, they just couldn't let on to our Doris they knew. Instead they sniggered to each other and got on with their business.

If only our Doris had been so nonchalant about the entire enterprise.

I murmured, 'Looks like we're not the only one shooting hollow birds.'

Our Doris seethed. 'How dare they?' she said as she stormed across the field, and ducked under safety wire, all the time a gun cocked over her arm like a handbag.

And Janice knew better than to run. She stepped from foot to foot, eyes wide and a skirt covered in foliage.

No one expected our Doris to trip.

We all watched in horror as she lost her footing, one foot sinking ankle deep into a rabbit hole.

We couldn't help, did nothing as the gun went off and shot a bullet straight at the branch above Janice's head.

Our Doris didn't mind getting banned from the club for breaking health and safety regulations. She said to them, she said, 'Guns were meant to be fired – clearly the instructor did not train me adequately enough to understand the sheer necessity of the safety on a gun.'

No, getting banned didn't bother her.

Being sent to the same Accident and Emergency Ward as Janice Dooley of Little Street caused her blood pressure to raise that high the doctor questioned if there were lava in her veins.

That's how I know that if she wanted, our Doris would put Dodgems in the church hall and beggar anyone who misplaced a finger.

I left our Doris pondering whether she could find any more celebrities and went to make a brew. I'd barely set the kettle onto the base when our Theo ran into the house and headed straight for our Doris's alcove. 'Nan, you are not going to believe this,' he said to her, the only one allowed to interrupt her during one of her reveries.

'Unless you've found me a local celebrity it won't do me much good.'

'It's you, Nan. Someone retweeted a picture of you with the dead leaves at Number 42.' Theo looked as enthusiastic as a chimpanzee with a banana.

Our Doris, despite her previous claims, clearly had no idea what he were on about. She bobbed her head and said to him, 'That's nice, dear, but you know I am getting tired of being photographed – I considered taking out an injunction against funny Hubert after his last attempts with a zoom lens.'

'You don't understand. You're trending on Twitter. Somehow the picture reached Lucy Meacock and she found out your story.'

Our Doris couldn't hide the smile on her face, nor the twinkle in her eye as she said to us, she said, 'This is it. I can call myself a spokeswoman for the older generation as verified by the most discerning television journalist I ever had the pleasure to watch.'

'I thought you said as Lucy Meacock was eye candy for the man in fear of cardiac arrest,' I said, fetching them their brews.

'That was said in haste – the sheer worry of losing

a Pyrex dish because of your infatuation.'

'You do know how to spin a yarn, our Doris.'

'I do. Now we best get organising the fundraiser. I should ring Mavis, see if quiche really is making a comeback.'

There was only one day free for the church hall.

Actually, there were quite a few days free but our Doris didn't want to take any chances. She didn't know when Pandra O'Malley would make her announcement, but the sooner she held the fundraiser, the better.

That's why she gave herself ten days.

Ten days in which to invite all those who needed to know, all those she didn't want there but would look good in the Gazette's write up, and all and sundry: those our Doris has often sought to call the underclasses, for want of a better word.

I said to her, I said, 'I know you can create splendour at short notice, our Doris, but how are you going to get anyone in to see the bleeding thing?'

This is one of the many moments of my married life where I wish I'd kept my mouth shut. I could have continued watching This Morning, admiring Holly Willoughby but silently wishing for Ruth Langsford, congratulating Eamonn Holmes on the luck of the Irish, but instead I chose to speak to our Doris, the same Doris who once had me wallpaper the landing at one in the morning so as none of the other ladies would have chance to guess at her new colour scheme and claim it as their own. The very same Doris who offered me one of those looks she saved for flirting – or getting hairs out of her eyes – and she said to me, all husky and Mae West, she said, 'I'm glad you asked, our 'arold, because that is where you fit ever so neatly into the arrangement. I've organised for some flyers to be printed – nothing too gaudy or professional – I believe they'll highlight the parochial nature of the fundraiser.'

I nodded my head, pretending I didn't know where this were going, the cogs whirring in my mind like Hickory Dickory Dock on three pints of Lucozade and espresso drip. I said to her, all thoughtful, I said, 'Who's printing them?'

She said to me, she said, 'Lorraine Minchin met a new woman on her last cruise around the Med. She works in graphic design and offered to help the WI with any of its advertising needs. Of course she just wished to sweeten up Lorraine's friends but I'm not about to look a gift horse in the mouth, I was the first in line when Waitrose offered me a free coffee.'

Choosing to get it out of the way sooner rather than later, I said, 'How will you be distributing these flyers, our Doris? The council doesn't look too kindly on fly tippers.'

The smirk became a smile. She knew she had me. 'As my husband, and therefore the spouse of the Partridge Mews Women's Institute's interim chairwoman, you have a few responsibilities to which you must adhere, otherwise the very sanctity of the WI will fall apart, and we can't have that happening now, can we?'

I were too flabbergasted to answer. Not that she gave me much chance to speak as she continued her tirade, she said, 'The flyers will be with us within two days – delivered by a reliable courier, of course. I will then entrust the flyers to you so that you may travel throughout the town and spread the word.'

'I suppose you'll be telling all the others on community service? Try and get some time off for good behaviour.'

I thought the Look were going to come with a desk lamp thrown at my head but she went back to trying to locate last Christmas's paper garlands. She planned on repurposing them as artisanal jewellery.

Next day, with our Doris that deep in planning, I slipped back to the Hare and Horse for a drink with Alf. He'd spent the best part of the morning hiding from Mrs Yearly after he took half a dozen eggs and left nothing in her honesty box.

I bought him a pint and said to him, I said, 'What do you need them for anyway? Your Edith won't be too happy to hear as you pilfered some eggs.'

'This weren't owt to do wi'eggs, 'arold, my old lad. This were about principle.' He folded his arms here.

Alf's principles have got him into a lot of trouble over the years. He once masterminded the theft and subsequent trip to Wales of Albert Butterworth's sheep after he made advances towards Alf's sister behind the Co-Op and didn't walk her home. Alf were never prosecuted but Nancy found it difficult to find a man afterwards. She ended up moving to Halifax.

It were with a heavy heart that I said to him, I said, 'What principles were these then?'

His brow furrowed, as though his eyes had been swallowed by his forehead and he said, 'She offended our Edith's culinary skills.'

Now, his Edith isn't renowned for her cooking – she once pan fried a mango in her efforts to be multicultural – but I wasn't about to say this to Alf. Instead, I said, 'So you stole half a dozen eggs.'

'Because of principle. You know me, 'arold, I never do dirt on my own doorstep, but when Mrs Yearly offends our Edith action must be taken.'

'Just how did she offend your Edith's culinary

skills?' I said to him, wishing I'd had whisky instead.

'Our Martin took egg sandwiches to work.'

'At the charity shop?'

Alf nodded. 'It didn't work out at the Cash and Carry, too many brands of broad beans. Anyway, Heather Yearly volunteers at the shop, and she said to our Martin, and this is what got me because Edith works hard on her meals, she said as Martin's sandwiches would be much better if the eggs had come from her chickens.'

'And that caused you to steal them?'

'She asked me to, bragging about her stock and belittling our Edith's cooking.'

I knew I wouldn't get anywhere so I said to him, I said, 'Our Doris's fundraiser is in ten days. Do you fancy helping me hand out flyers?'

Alf squinted at his pint, scrutinising the head as though assessing each middling bubble before he said to me, he said, 'What's it worth?'

This were no surprise. I said to him, going through the motions, I said, 'What're you after?'

'Three pints of ale, four bags of pork scratchings, an alibi if needs be, and a dirty magazine.' He sat back, pleased with himself.

'You know I can't be seen buying a dirty magazine, our Doris would kill me. Besides, you're seventy-five, what can you possibly want with a dirty magazine?'

'I'd settle for two thousand and two's Kay's summer catalogue. There were a lass in there that used to get the rum rolling.'

I eyed my drink and said, 'I'll see what I can do.'

I found the catalogue in the loft. Our Doris has them all dating back to nineteen seventy-three, in the hopes that they'll become collector's items, hopefully she wouldn't notice one missing.

Once Alf had his payment we were underway. Whilst our Doris set about gathering resources throughout Partridge Mews, Alf and I went handing out flyers and making general nuisances of ourselves.

A week down the line and Friday were upon us.

Our Doris left me in bed whilst she went to make last minute touches to the church hall. She'd spent the best part of Thursday organising trestle tables and trifles and where to hide Gwyneth Miser's guacamole. I'm not sure what she had left to do ... apart from get tangled in paper garlands and fall off a stepladder.

I'd only just parked my car when this young man – reminiscent of Mole in *The Wind in the Willows* – came barrelling towards me like I was a toilet and he'd just sampled Mrs Gilchrist's chilli.

He said to me, all wide-eyed, he said, 'Mr Copeland, you better come sharpish, your missis is in a bad way.'

It's a good job I had my new knee, the rate at which I sped towards the church hall. I barged right past all the folk outside, milling about like ducks after bread, didn't acknowledge Eleanor Stockwell, which I hope folk noticed because that would earn me brownie points with our Doris that would.

And as I huffed and puffed my way into that church hall, certain I were on the brink of an heart attack I saw her.

Our Doris lay on the linoleum, her body entangled in paper garlands, a veritable snake in all the colours of the rainbow were wrapped around her legs.

I hurried over and knelt down. I said to her, and I could sense the panic in my voice, I said, 'What happened, our Doris?'

She groaned like something out of a Hammer Horror film and said to me, she said, 'I asked two young lads to help me and they said as it were against health and safety. I said to them, I said, "Health and safety? You're climbing a stepladder not the Blackpool Tower." but they were having none of it.'

'Maybe you should've listened to them, our Doris.'

'There's no such thing as health and safety in this day and age, 'arold Copeland.'

The fundraiser went ahead thanks to Alf's Edith. She weren't about to let Pandra O'Malley take her chances – she's never been a lover of the Irish, not since her cousin ran away with a market trader from Donegal, giving up his promising career at the building society.

Meanwhile, I got to sit at the hospital with our Doris. I've never been a fan of hospitals but it's worse when I'm there with her. The paramedics had barely wheeled her through the doors before she piped up with, 'If you could please make sure I am seen by an actual doctor – not one of these namby-pambys who went to a polytechnic.'

'All of our doctors are trained professionals,' one of them reassured her.

'But where were they trained? If it were Birmingham I'd rather take my chances with Julie Walters and get a laugh out of it.'

They fixed our Doris up with a cubicle and disappeared before she said anything else. She said to me, she said, 'We'll be getting a visitor in a minute, our 'arold, I saw her pulling up in the car park.'

No sooner had she said this than who should walk through the door but Pandra O'Malley herself. She wore a pale yellow suit that some would call daisy but looked closer to bile, and her handbag were slung over her arm as though it contained top secret MI5 files. I said to her, ignoring her new beehive, I said, 'How do, Mrs O'Malley?'

She ignored me and went straight to our Doris and I knew this wasn't concern, it were politics. She said to our Doris, she said, 'I was so sorry to hear of your accident, Mrs Copeland, and all in aid of the WI as well. I only hope that when I become chairwoman, I don't continue until it becomes a risk.'

'Oh, it was no risk, Pandra. I knew that if I fell you could convince people I was infirm and ought to be ousted or you could be the better person and wait to announce your candidacy.'

Pandra offered an uncertain smile as she said to our Doris, she said, 'You make it sound as if you fell on purpose.'

'Of course I didn't fall on purpose, but like any chairwoman should, I weighed up all possibilities before making a decision.'

'I didn't announce my candidacy, if you must know. Now, I'm going to go and get us some tea. We can discuss these matters when I return.'

And with that she scuttled off down the hall.

Our Doris's eyes were like beetles as she watched Pandra go. She said to me, now sure of her new-found nemesis, she said, 'Did you hear that, 'arold? Be prepared and don't get complacent, we still have a fight on our hands.'

2

CHARITY BEGINS

Our Doris has decided she's going to help people better themselves. This comes after her first day at the Cheshire East Relief Fund for the Bewildered Elderly. Since the fall that saw her relocated from the streets of Partridge Mews to safer premises, she thinks herself fully ingratiated with the staff.

I had to go with her for her induction. She said as it was purely as spousal support but the official legal documents called for a witness.

I said to her, I said, 'You're one step away from an ASBO, our Doris.'

I perhaps shouldn't have said this during her interview with the charity shop manager but the judge says as we have to be perfectly honest with folk.

We were in a stifling hot cellar at a plastic table that looked as if it had been pulled straight from a school examination hall. I had flashbacks to nineteen fifty when I were taking the eleven plus, unable to concentrate due to the millipede Alf had dropped down the back of my polo shirt.

My mother never let him around for supper after that, said as he had nearly ruined my chances of getting into grammar school. Not that I wanted to go there myself but they breed a different kind of woman in Partridge Mews and my mother had her heart set on Saint Ormerod's C of E Grammar School for Intellectual Boys.

Alf ended up at the local secondary modern – I don't know that they knew it, he spent most of his time stealing lead off the church roof with his Uncle Jim. They always put it back again, but only on receipt of payment.

Alf's grandson works for the charity shop. We came here on the recommendation of his Edith who maintains that she's done a turn or two in the shop. The way I heard it she beat a would-be shoplifter around the head with a taxidermied feline and they had to replace the changing room door. Either way, the thought of our Doris and Alf's Edith working together should be enough to put the fear of God in anyone.

They were both office girls for Gadsden and Taylor back in the day and everyone knew that if you wanted your wages paying on time you didn't mess with those two. It were worse if they fell out – there's still talk of the great slanging match of nineteen sixty-three that resulted in three broken boot straps, a dozen squashed vol-au-vents, a severe case of laryngitis and a lifetime ban from Greenfield's Summer Fete. Well the old lord's lifetime anyway – they let them back two years later. It may have also been the result of the entire WI boycotting the event and you can't go around upsetting the WI, it's like setting fire to a hornet's nest and expecting them to sit still.

Well, we were sat across from the manager of the

charity shop. She's a string bean of a woman, looks like she hasn't seen a slice of good bread since the eighties and she had those big glasses so that she looked like a cross between Deidre Barlow and Eli from *Last of the Summer Wine*. I didn't say anything but our Doris piped up with, she said, 'Cosmetic or medical?'

The manager, Evie her name is, said, her eyes wide and magnified by her lenses, she said, 'Sorry?'

'It's your optician who should be sorry,' our Doris said, 'letting a woman in the prime of her life leave with glasses only fit for anorak wearers and perverts.'

Evie looked taken aback. 'Mrs Copeland!'

'Please call me Doris, dear,' she said, a smile curling up the corners of her mouth so that she looked like she were chewing a dried prune. 'And don't you worry, that is a mere glimpse at the fashion advice I will be able to offer your less discerning customers.'

'That wasn't advice, it was plain offensive.'

And our Doris straightened her spine here, shoulders back, and I knew she were going in for the kill as she said to Evie, she said, 'People are so easily offended nowadays. As a white, heterosexual female living in the twenty-first century I am quite aware of the trials and tribulations faced by those the world over. I have an acid tongue and it is this talent that has helped me reach my position as interim chairwoman of the WI. Sometimes my advice may seem offensive, but it is the truth, and the truth is that those glasses wouldn't suit Kate Middleton, let alone the manager of a provincial charity shop.'

Evie sat, bewildered as she said, 'Shall we get on with the interview?'

'Here I was believing this part of the interview process, how very presumptuous of me.' Our Doris removed a packet of Fox's Glacier Mints from her handbag and offered one to the manager who declined. I saw the cogs whirring in our Doris's head – she was interviewing Evie as much as Evie interviewed her, testing to see whether she wished to offer her services as a volunteer.

Not that she had much choice. She no longer had to pick up litter on the streets of Partridge Mews but she still had a few hours of unpaid work to do before they'd let her off the hook for assaulting Janice Dooley.

Eventually, after a few more fashion tips and advice on how to make the most of tiramisu, they offered our Doris the volunteer position. Every Tuesday from nine till one she wouldn't be home. I could watch all the episodes of Rosemary and Thyme I had recorded to see how Felicity Kendal is getting on. I was in the midst of a dream about hot, buttered, English breakfast muffins when Evie sprung it on us. She said to me, she said, 'Of course your husband will be attending the first few weeks so as you become properly ingratiated.'

Our Doris looked at me as though if I put one foot wrong she'd be adding hours to her community service and said to Evie, she said, 'I'm sure 'arold would like nothing more than to gain a better understanding of the inner workings of charitable organisations. He listens to Radio 4.'

And that's how I ended up sorting through folks' unwanted detritus, the stuff they deemed too good for the bin man. I'd never given much thought to the things people donate to charity shops. I envisaged stacks of newly ironed clothes with a spot of Febreze for added freshness. When I were elbow deep in my third bag of soiled ladies undergarments, I knew how wrong I'd been.

Our Doris fared better than me. She'd been assigned to the till. As I were only volunteering for a few weeks they didn't want me anywhere near the cash.

It's a smart move, really. Our Doris is good with money. She never loses track of mine. It's as though her ears are tuned to the frequency of my wallet opening – I can't buy a half of bitter without our Doris sensing the money slipping from my grasp.

That's how I knew our Doris wouldn't let anyone get away with short changing her. When she were still at the Co-Op, someone tried to get away with putting their shopping on the slate. It just so happened that our Doris had the key to the shop and the knowledge that said customer, a Mr Alan Jenkins of Pickford Street, had won on the horses the prior weekend and she wasn't about to let him leave without paying when he was a proven risk to throw his money away.

He paid her and left.

Carrie Marshall never forgave Doris after her waters broke in aisle three and she had to struggle with the worry that her daughter would be born under tinned goods.

Either way, Evie thought our Doris would be a good fit for the till and tasked another volunteer to mentor her. I wonder that Evie didn't know about the history between our Doris and Erin Beaumont because whoever thought those two could work together either knew nothing about local politics or had a death wish.

I'm still not sure what Evie's motives were.

Erin Beaumont was the victim of the WI's biggest intervention since Seraphina Hogarth flashed her midriff during the Christmas Pageant of nineteen seventy-four. For Erin had committed one of the greatest misdeeds known to man: she didn't take the advice of the Partridge Mews Women's Institute.

When the poor lass was pregnant the WI began to badger her. Mrs Patel offered her a recipe for haemorrhoid treatment and the name Sanjeev. Pandra O'Malley went around with biscuits and the suggestion of Alby. Eventually, she must have spoken to each and every member, her stomach growing by the day and her mind fit to bursting with the constant meanderings of the great WI.

And she ignored them all.

Her son was born and she called him Red, after her favourite football team.

I imagine she thought it the end of the matter entirely. She'd be sat there, enjoying her well-earned maternity leave, completely oblivious to the outside machinations that continued until she agreed to change the name of her firstborn.

And the one who spearheaded this campaign, who took her letters to the Gazette and spread rumours through town faster than nits through a crèche, was our Doris.

Personally, I think Erin knew Red to be a stupid name for a child but it can't have been good for her, being scrutinised.

Now they had to share the till together, our Doris and Erin. I spent the morning in fear, wondering when the pottery were going to start flying, one barbed comment from our Doris and Erin would be throwing the Royal Worcester.

I didn't hear a peep out of them, save for our Doris's titter. She's perfected a chuckle for when she's out in public. It happened after she saw our nephew's wedding video. The reception were in full swing, they'd arrived at the speeches and our Doris may have had one too many glasses of sweet sherry – she since maintains she was out of sorts due to a migraine from the DJ's cheap lights – and the best man gained control of the microphone and after one joke about the vicar and the bride's mother, our Doris laughed. No, she howled. Her laughter reached decibels Andrea Bocelli would be thankful for.

When our Doris heard her guffaws she taught herself a new laugh, little more than a high-pitched cough really. She sounds something between a chipmunk and a popped balloon. And our Doris, listening to the words of Erin Beaumont, used this titter now.

I couldn't ask her about it until we got home and even then we had to contend with an intruder. We pulled into the drive only to find Pandra O'Malley on the doorstep. She'd changed her style somewhat in the last few weeks. Gone were the jeans holier than the Sabbath, gone were the mayonnaise-stained blouses bought on sale from TK Maxx, they had been replaced by a two piece suit the shade of lemon and a top that clean I wondered that she hadn't started wearing a bib. She'd done something new with her hair. Not that I notice these things normally, but when someone who usually looks like they've spent their life in a barn shows up looking mildly presentable you take note of the pixie cut where a beehive should be.

She had eyes only for our Doris. As we approached she reached into her purse and removed a stack of brightly coloured flyers expounding on the need for a new church roof, and how she, as a concerned citizen, had taken it upon herself to hold a fundraiser.

Pandra said to our Doris, she said, 'Doris.'

Our Doris's eyes squinted that much she could've

had a bee trapped in them as she said to Pandra, 'Please, call me Mrs Copeland, commonplace niceties are so often lost nowadays. Through no fault of our own, of course, what with the advent of email and with your heritage you're bound to misunderstand all the finer details of polite conversation.'

'I'm Irish!' Pandra protested.

'I know, but please, do not fret. We are a multi-faith, multicultural society and wouldn't dream of holding it against you.'

'Dori – Mrs Copeland, please, if you'd just allow me to speak.'

'I don't believe I've stopped you from speaking. I've merely highlighted a few issues with your vocabulary.'

'I didn't know you were an English teacher.'

'Apparently I'm as much an English teacher as you are a comedian.'

'I wanted to let you know I'm raising money for the new church roof by holding a sale of baked goods, would you like to contribute something?'

Our Doris gave her the Look and said to her, she said, 'Of course I will contribute something, I've been contributing cakes and pastries since before you got off the boat. Now, if you will excuse me, I must get inside and find the insecticide. There's a great, blithering pest on my garden path. Come on, 'arold.'

And with that we entered the house, leaving Pandra O'Malley to stalk off down the street.

We'd barely stepped across the threshold before I said to her, I said, 'I thought you and Erin didn't get on. What were you using the titter for?'

Her shoulders went up at this and she headed off into the kitchen. She said to me, all of a mumble, she said, 'I don't know what you're talking about.'

I followed her – that's one of the good things about my new knee, I can keep speed with her as she tries to avoid awkward conversations. 'You can come off that, our Doris,' I said, 'you said as you wouldn't spend two minutes in the same room as a young girl who didn't know the difference between a colour and an appropriate moniker for her firstborn.'

She hid her face behind the mugs and said, 'Did I?'

I said, 'You did.'

And here's where she thought she'd figured it all out, that she was being smart because she said to me, she said, 'Clearly you're misremembering, it can happen in a man of your age, I've been meaning to say something for quite some time, but a wife cannot really bear the reality of such a situation.'

'You and Erin got on then?'

Our Doris busied herself with the tea and said, 'She's quite a charming girl who had the misfortune to make a drastic mistake so young as it coloured society's view of her. It is ever so sad to see in this day and age, but that is the world we live in.'

'I'm not getting a straight answer out of you, am I?'

'Miss Beaumont expressed a wish to go back to college, twenty years old and the community has already washed its hands of her.'

'And how are you going to help her?'

We sat ourselves down at the table before our Doris continued, unveiling the cake tin, she said, 'This community order is nothing short of an imposition. It will remain as a blemish on my character from now until the end of time. This means that Pandra O'Malley is already a step ahead of me.'

'But she's Pandra O'Malley, she's not got much

about her.'

'Exactly. She doesn't stir the pot – remember the hubbub caused when I added raw courgette to salad?'

I couldn't forget, I spent days cleaning green gunk from my dentures, only to find that my Fixadent had glued it to the roof of my mouth.

'None of this tells me what you're planning with Erin Beaumont.'

'Well I was getting to that, our 'arold, but you will interrupt me with your nonsense.' She gave me this withering gaze and folded her arms, ever the headmistress.

I weren't about to argue and ruin my chances at a slice of Battenberg so I said to her, I said, 'All right then, our Doris, I'll stay quiet. Why don't you tell me your plans for Erin Beaumont.'

Our Doris settled into the role of storyteller immediately. If she had a campfire and some undercooked sausages she'd have been set. Instead, she set about unwrapping the cake. My eyes were focused on the pink and yellow checkered squares – much more fulfilling than a game of chess. And my mouth had fallen open – I could have resembled an asthmatic goldfish and I couldn't care less because the icing on the cake, the marzipan, sang to me. It were like the Battenberg were Marilyn Monroe and I were JFK. I am a firm believer that although Victoria sponge will remain the great British staple, it has a much more attractive cousin in the form of Battenberg. Not that I'd ever say that to our Doris.

She must've seen me gawping because she cut a thick slab and, all dainty-like, passed it to me on a Royal Worcester china saucer.

And I knew to savour it. I let it linger as she poured

the tea into porcelain so fine the cups were practically translucent.

Our Doris behaved like the first lady of afternoon tea. It's a wonder pigeons weren't nesting in her perm she kept her head that aloft, and she cradled the teapot with such aplomb she could've been an Italian fountain.

Once all this was sorted, she regaled me with her intentions towards Erin Beaumont.

She said to me, she said, 'Erin Beaumont is a young woman who has made some poor life choices due to the lack of a strong role model growing up.'

I hurried the chewing of my cake to try and get a word in edgeways but our Doris steam-rollered on, stirring her tea with all the vigour of a tornado after Dorothy and she said, 'It is my belief that with the correct education, from one such as myself, there is no reason Erin couldn't become a respectable member of polite society.'

'And just what sort of thing will you be teaching her,' I said, swallowing hard. Our Doris had already brainwashed our Angela with her fuddy-duddy ideas about Quiche Lorraine, I didn't want to see some unsuspecting so-and-so go the same way.

Our Doris appeared pensive, all thoughtful like, holding her china cup in the bowl of her left hand. She said to me, words all breathy, she said, 'How Caesar salad has lost its place at the middle-class dinner table and to never overuse prawn cocktail as a starter.'

Ordinarily, a husband may have been flabbergasted by his spouse's comments on the social standing of something as simple as a prawn cocktail, but most husbands haven't had to sit through a lecture on the implications of cheese straws only to miss Kim Tate check her make-up.

But I knew that our Doris wouldn't just help Erin Beaumont become a better class of citizen out of the kindness of her heart. When you've been married for fifty-four years you get to know a person and I said to her, I said, 'What's in it for you, our Doris?'

And this is when she got that smile, that supercilious little grin like a child just gifted with a crate of Mars bars and she said to me, she said, 'It's no secret that I have had my fair share of misdemeanours in the past year, our 'arold, but with the support of my friends I have managed to uphold a social standing Pandra O'Malley seeks to usurp. In helping Erin Beaumont on the path to bettering herself, I emphasise my wish to give back to the community and show Pandra O'Malley just where she can put her fundraiser for the church roof.'

Our Doris decided Erin needed a more presentable wardrobe. She said to me, she said, 'If Erin had the opportunities that I had, our 'arold, then I'm perfectly sure she would dress like a model citizen. Much of the problems with today's youth are down to jogging bottoms. It's the loose gussets that do it.'

Now I've known our Doris since my trousers still showed the scabs on my knees. I said to her, I said, 'And where do you plan on taking her for these new clothes, our Doris? I'm guessing the charity shop isn't your port of call.'

'Although the East Cheshire Relief Fund for the Bewildered Elderly does have a wide range of clothing donated by the veritably brilliant donors in Partridge Mews and the surrounding areas, Erin is going to require something a bit more upmarket, as I'm sure you can understand.'

When she starts talking to me as though she's the

Queen come to tea I know that the joint back account is going to be diminished in good time. I always thought that when we retired we might spend our savings on posh holidays, cruises and the like, only to discover that our Doris's ambitions stuck closer to home: John Lewis and Bon Marche.

With our Doris off gallivanting about town I made my way to the Hare and Horse. I was midway through a half of bitter when in walked Alf looking like he'd been dragged backwards through a gorse bush and buried in cement.

He sat down as Linda rushed over with a pint of Carling and a few packets of cheese and onion. Her eyes were wild as she said to him, beating me to it, she said, 'Bloomin' heck, Alf, what the devil's happened to you?'

The entire pub were watching at this point. Alf looked completely shell-shocked, it were as though he'd just been told the brewery had closed and the butchers had been sold off to a vegan bistro. I hadn't seen him in such a state since his wedding day and even then he'd managed to stay clean throughout the ceremony.

No, although Alf can be a filthy beggar he knows not to get himself so dishevelled that folk start questioning his Edith's skills as a housewife.

He reached for his pint, and even this caused a tremor through his hand. Once he supped his drink, he settled back into his chair and he did this face – like a gargoyle on the brink of a sneezing fit before he said to me, he said, ''arold, I think I've just been mugged.'

Well you'd have had more luck hearing a pin drop at a haberdashery. It were then that the holes in his clothes looked all the more prominent, this wasn't untidiness, his coat had been torn until it looked more like Maypole ribbons than an anorak.

I said to him, I said, 'By who?'

He shrugged his shoulders, his eyes were drawn and his face looked ever more like a collapsed turnip. He said to me, he said, 'Some young lass, young to me in any case, probably best just to forget the whole thing.'

'You should go to the police, Alf,' Linda said, her fists clenched, skin mottled the colour of beetroot.

'It's not like I had anything worth nicking,' he said, 'and don't go telling our Edith, she'd only worry.'

'And rightly so, just wait until I get my hands on the beggars.' Linda clamped her hand on Alf's shoulder in what she probably imagined to be a consoling gesture, but looked more like she wanted to cut circulation to his arm.

I said to him, unsure of the proper procedure, I said, 'Let me take you down the police station, it'd make a change you reporting a crime rather than committing it.'

This earned me a smile and I could see his eyes begin calculating like a dazed hawk after a dormouse before he said to me, he said, 'I'll have to finish my pint first, wouldn't like to see good ale go to waste.'

I knew we were joking because the alternative was too much to contend with but at that point I were hopeful that Alf's spirits hadn't been dampened too much.

Whilst I waited at the police station for Alf to finish giving his statement his grandson arrived. Now, Martin is a smart lad, usually, what had caused his latest lapse in thinking was beyond me, but as he walked in with Edith I did begin to question his sanity.

I said to him, I said, 'What have you gone and brought your grandmother for?'

'Don't you shout at him, Harold Copeland! Alf is my husband, I have every right to know when his life is in mortal peril.' Edith had this ferocity about her, something akin to a lioness with a perm.

I felt myself shrink until I were certain I had no more substance than a slug. I said to her, I said, 'I'm sorry, Edith. It's not Martin's fault but Alf didn't want you to know.'

'It doesn't matter what he wanted. As his wife I should be informed when he gets himself into stupid scrapes.'

I didn't take it any further. Edith had tears in her eyes and looked as though she'd tear your arm off as soon as look at you.

We sat in silence. Someone brought Edith a cup of tea and she threw out all sense of decorum and swigged it like a builder with a pint mug.

Eventually a police woman led Alf out to us. He looked as downtrodden as a donkey carrying a thirty stone man up a mountain. When he saw his wife he straightened his shoulders and added a jaunt to his steps but the damage had been done, Edith crumpled.

She bawled that loud she could've been a hippopotamus with bronchitis. She stormed across the room, wailing, 'I'll kill them, Alf, I'm going to find out who did this and bleeding well kill them.'

'Careful what you're saying there, Edie, you never know who could be listening,' Alf warned her, his arm around her shoulders.

'Let them listen. I want the world to know what happens when they cross Edith Simpson.'

Once I knew they'd be all right, I left them there and made my way home. I knew there were something awry as soon as I walked through the front door. For one thing, our Doris and Erin were tittering that much they could've been hyenas and the door to the kitchen was closed. Our Doris never closes that door, she says as it is the one door that should always be left open for the kitchen is the heart of the home.

Well, when I walked in the kitchen no longer looked like a kitchen. A coeliac could have walked in and been dead in seconds. Every surface, the table, the counter, the side cabinet, they were all coated in a layer of self-raising flour. It was as though there'd been an explosion at Mr Kiplings' – fingerprints all over the show – and I had no idea what to say.

Our Doris stood beside Erin at the counter, the burnt carcasses of several earlier attempts upended onto cooling trays. Their hair looked like it were covered in ash, as though they'd seen a dead bonfire and thought to roll around in it.

Erin said to me, she said, 'Sorry about the mess, Mr Copeland, only I've never made a cake before.'

And I know I should've been sympathetic but I said to her, I said, 'How the heck did you get it over everything?'

This is where our Doris stepped in. She had this glower I hadn't seen in about three hours and she said to me, she said, 'Don't you come in here throwing your weight around, 'arold Copeland, I am your wife. This is my home as well.'

I nodded, thought about arguing but for some reason, rather than ask about the state of the cakes I said, 'Alf's been mugged,' and there were something about seeing our Doris dusted in icing sugar that made it more palatable. I could see the ire rise in her like boiling water and so I said, a bit hasty but I said it, 'he's fine, a bit shaken but he's fine.'

What I hadn't anticipated, what I hadn't really given much thought to, was Erin. Of course, I knew she worked with Alf sometimes down the charity shop. I knew Alf had a certain charm most couldn't get away from – it's one of the reasons he's never been formally charged with pinching pork pies – I didn't know that Erin cared enough about Alf to smash a Pyrex bowl full of cake mix against the kitchen counter.

She stormed past me, all fired up, fancying herself a cannonball – as she shot out the front door without passing comment.

I said to our Doris, I said, 'If she ends up with community service you're beggared if you think I'm driving you both about.'

Our Doris didn't speak much as I helped her tidy the kitchen. Clearly her plans for the Bake Sale had been put on hold, that was to be expected, and after fifty-five years you get used to your wife's silences. They can range from being quiet because you've said something wrong, all the way through to her knickers being in knots Boy Scouts would be proud of. This were a different silence than I was accustomed to. This isn't to say it were a silence I hadn't met before, mind. No, I knew just what cogs were turning in that mind of hers, going faster than hamsters on hamster wheels.

Our Doris were calculating, as stoic as Churchill in a gentleman's club.

After three hours in that she started muttering to herself, mere hushed whispers tickled her lips but she were muttering all right, I felt like I were trapped in the kitchen with an anaconda and only a cup of sweet tea to save my life.

I let it go on for fifteen minutes before I said to her, I said, 'Will you give over with that whispering, our

Doris? It's getting right on my last nerve.'

Her head snapped back at this. She gave me the Look and satisfaction swelled in my chest as though we'd just got amorous.

She said to me, she said, 'That smile better not have any dubious intentions, our 'arold, I've had just about enough of that for a married woman.'

I couldn't contain my grin. I tried, but it were like locking a moth in a dog cage as I said to her, I said, 'You're giving me the Look. I can contend with the Look. I know what's coming with the Look.'

'Yes, the Look,' she said, 'because I wasn't bleeding muttering. Do you think I'm on the edge of senility, our 'arold, because I'll have you know I am one of only four members of the Partridge Mews Women's Institute who can recite Mrs Burr's rock bun recipe from memory.'

'Aye, and maybe you'd be best to forget it.'

'I'll have you know my rock buns are the staple at my afternoon teas.'

'They taste like bloody staples and all.'

'Honestly, I could spiflicate you.'

'Oh, I look forward to it, I haven't had a good spiflicating in a long while.'

Our Doris's cheeks went rosier than that time she tried cross country to impress the Shahs of Palmer Street. She said to me, she said, 'Honestly, 'arold, talking like that, anybody could have been listening.'

I said to her, unable to contain my excitement, I said, 'I got you to stop muttering though.'

She gave me a different look then and let me hear her real giggle as she said to me, she said, 'I think we should try that new bistro on Grimshaw Lane tonight, what do you think?'

I said, 'I'll finfish the washing up whilst you get your glad rags on.'

I knew I were on to a winner when she said to me, giving her best Bette Davis impression, she said, 'Leave the washing up.'

I tell you, I gave Mo Farah a run for his money on the way to that bedroom.

Next morning, I woke up with the need to relieve my bladder whilst contending with a blinding headache. When you're young no one bothers telling you how easy it is to get hungover once you hit your seventies. I thought my head might explode, the pain compounded by our Doris's foghorn snoring. I love her, but the noises she makes whilst she's sleeping give me flashbacks, it's like being stuck in bed with an air raid siren.

I wish I'd taken her snoring as a warning in any case. No sooner had I passed enough water to fill Lake Windermere than there came an almighty pounding on the front door. I'm surprised it didn't come off its hinges. It were just my luck that I'd have one night of frivolity, take my mind off everything going on with Alf, only to be sent more chaos than pandemonium to make up for it.

I offered a feeble shout of, 'Hold on a minute!' before opening the front door, completely forgetting I were in my pyjamas and our Doris would throw a fit if they were ever seen by the general public. As I looked through the slits of my eyes at the two of them, decked from head to toe in black, I said to them, I said, 'What're you doing here this early? I am geriatric, you know.'

Alf and Erin pushed past, shutting the door behind them.

'It's eleven o'clock, 'arold,' Alf said, 'you and Doris aren't the type to sleep in.' He cocked his head at me, a grin setting on his face like something out of a Carry On film, he said to me, he said, 'Wild night was it? Get in there, my old son. Were you unable to resist the call of Doris?'

'I'll have you know, Alfred Simpson, that such business is between a man and his wife and certain men should be careful what they say if they ever want such business to happen again. Isn't that right, our 'arold?' Our Doris sauntered downstairs bedecked in pink dressing gown and house shoes. 'Now, to what do we owe this pleasure?'

Erin chimed in here, as excitable as a fox amongst hens as she said to us, she said, 'We've only gone and found her.'

'The mugger?' I said. I were a bit dense at this moment in time, but my head felt worse than the time I mistook absinthe for crème-de-menthe.

'They were stupid enough to go back where they got me,' Alf said.

Our Doris didn't allow us to go any further as she said, 'It is much too early for me to contend with this situation. 'arold and I require time to make ourselves properly presentable as we are not accustomed to stepping out in such disarray. Please wait in the lounge whilst we get ready.' With that she turned around and flounced back up the stairs. I followed her, not nearly as hopeful as the night before.

Once we'd washed and changed and, in our Doris's case, added a layer of daytime make-up – a selection of shades and tones she deemed appropriate for entertaining house guests – we made brunch and settled in the lounge to hear Alf's tale.

He and Erin sat on the edge of the settee, as ravenous to tell stories as a Weight Watcher over a steak dinner. Erin were the first to speak, she said to us, she said, 'When you told me what happened to Alf I were furious, sorry about the bowl, I hope it wasn't antique.'

'It was Pyrex,' Doris protested.

'Yes, but nowadays there's plastic,' said Erin before she continued, 'Anyway, I were proper angry like and I had to do something. I wasn't sure what. I've never gone in for decking people, that were more our Elaine's thing, but she's calmed down since she met Sasha. Anyway, I started walking about town – I nipped into the Hare and Horse and that's where I met Alf.'

Alf looked at me and said, 'I needed a bit of something. You know what Edith gets like – she was all for packing our bags and running away to Whitby.'

'You have your grandson to thank for that.' I slurped my tea, wondering just how much alcohol there really is in Theakston's Old Peculiar – bleeding heck was that hangover making me wince.

Alf shrugged and said, he said, 'Well we can't blame the lad – he were only looking out for me after all – if he hadn't told Edith she'd have skinned the both of us.'

Our Doris piped up at this and said, she said, 'Can we please stop making unnecessary diversions? I must be coming down with something of a virus and simply do not have the patience for long-winded trivialities.'

With all the thought I'd given to my own struggles I had completely forgotten all about what our Doris had put away. I know that we ordered a bottle of Pinot Grigio because our Doris says as it's a true rival to champagne without all the pomp. I'm just not too confident of our choices after the event.

Either way, she spurred Alf on to cut to the chase. He bit off the majority of a ham sandwich triangle in one bite and washed it down with his tea. Sated, he said to us, he said, 'Well Erin here met me and I told her that I'd been walking down Barnaby Road when out of nowhere this girl jumped me. Now, I've had a bit of rough and tumble in my time – I landed in a hedge – but she tore at my coat, took my wallet and the like, if she finds any money in there, good luck to her, I've been looking for about forty years. But the mouth on her, I tell you, it were as foul as sewage. I told her, I said to her, "And who do you think you are out robbing the elderly because you're too dozy to find the dole queue." Well it turns out –'

' – when Alf mentioned Barnaby Road I knew who he were talking about,' Erin interjected, she'd helped herself to a fair number of finger sandwiches, I'd noticed. She went on to say, she said, 'She's done it before. Her name's Ruby Shaw. If the police caught her, she'd deny everything and remind them that her mother ran away to Tunbridge Wells with a German detective sergeant and she'd get off. And we couldn't let that happen.'

Our Doris raised her hand here and said, 'Please if you've brought crime into this household I can't let you go on.'

'It wasn't crime really,' Alf said.

'I mean, more of an inconvenience than anything.'

'Erin had the idea because of your baking.' Alf's eyes had a twinkle I knew only too well, like when he hide tadpoles in Mr Higgins's desk and they ruined his cheese sandwiches.

Erin said, 'Ruby lives on the estate up near me. She doesn't lock the back door at night in case the dachshund needs to go out. So Alf and I took a trip over there after we'd been to the supermarket – just for the essentials like icing sugar, self-raising flour, honey.'

'Whipped cream,' Alf added before they chorused 'Jam!' and fell about chuckling.

Throughout this tale our Doris remained as placid as ever – being a bit addled will do that to a person. Although I caught sight of something resembling a smirk, she still wouldn't allow herself to properly smile. She sipped her tea before saying to them, she said, 'Am I to be lead to believe that whilst this young woman slept you emptied these "essentials" all over her house.'

Alf and Erin nodded, unable to contain their excitement, 'Yes,' they said.

'As concerned citizens I am sure you only wished to help her redecorate, I'm confident that colour scheme is most tasteful.' Our Doris sat back in her chair and tittered, then I joined her, soon the titter grew louder until all I could hear was our Doris's real laugh, the one she kept hidden for so long and we knew revenge isn't always the answer but this time it were certainly sweet.

For the remainder of the day, me and our Doris pottered around the house like a pair of old sots. We didn't stomach much apart from toast and the odd cup of tea, we didn't even stay up long enough to watch Emmerdale, and our Doris hasn't missed an episode since they brought in Cain Dingle.

It's why I were so gone out the next day when who should appear at our door but Pandra O'Malley.

Our Doris had nipped out to see the vicar so I had the misfortune of having to greet her. This time she'd had something done to her face so that she looked like a cross between Lulu and Rose West. She said to me, attempting a smile but settling for a pout, she said,

'Good morning, Mr Copeland, I do hope I'm not intruding, only I've come to pick up a cake.'

Our Doris materialised that quickly she could've been an understudy in I Dream of Jeannie. She had recovered that well from the previous day you'd wonder if she'd ever been drunk in the first place. She came down the drive with all the confidence of a Head Girl, her hair perfectly curled for the occasion. Once she reached us both she said to Pandra, she said, 'I am ever so sorry, Pandra. We have had something of a crisis and I haven't been able to produce a cake worthy of my own high standards and therefore must withdraw my previous offer.

'I have, however, made a donation to the church roof fund.

'You must work on your advertising skills though, as the vicar had no idea about the Bake Sale. In fact, and you must forgive idle gossip, he is a man of the cloth and not as up-to-date with social convention – but he intimated that the last he heard you were planning for a Caribbean holiday. I have to say, this struck me as rather odd as you've only just paid for your new conservatory and you're not made of money, but I wouldn't speculate as to just how you planned to procure such funds.'

'These are some very serious accusations you're making, Mrs Copeland,' Pandra said, eyes a bit wider but attempting to look as cool as a salad drawer.

But our Doris has never been one to back down. She said, 'Now, Mrs O'Malley, we have known one another for how long now? Thirty, forty years – decades. You can't bake to save your life or have you forgotten the rum cake debacle? Mrs Owens' eye-brows never grew straight after that. I'll admit I was mildly dubious when you announced the sale but for the vicar not to know – a Caribbean holiday, Pandra.'

'Just because you haven't stepped foot outside Partridge Mews since the Stone Age.'

'Maybe if I'd diddled folk I could've done. Who else knew about the Bake Sale?'

Pandra shrugged, looking more like a chastised schoolgirl and said, 'Only the WI, a few friends.'

'If you tell them the Bake Sale is cancelled we'll speak no more about it. If I find out you've had money off anyone I'll make your life so difficult you'll question whether there is such a thing as the luck of the Irish. Are we on the same page?'

Pandra offered a shaky nod.

'Good. Can I interest you in a cup of tea and a slice of my famous Battenberg?'

She considered the offer for a moment before saying to our Doris, she said, 'Could you stretch to coffee, I've had something of a morning.'

Our Doris, ever the hostess said, she said, 'I'll see what I can do.'

They moved into the kitchen, chatting like long lost friends, leaving me to shut the door, completely and utterly flabbergasted.

3

STOWAWAY

Our Doris has gone away with the WI. They left last Saturday.

It's part of her new initiative as interim chairwoman. She wants to rebuild the sense of community she believes lost since she joined in the sixties. We were in the middle of changing the bedsheets when she told me. She said to me, she said, 'I've arranged a trip to the Cotswolds for the WI to boost morale.'

I said to her, I said, 'Do you mean the morale that went down when Janice Dooley of Little Street was in control of the garden safari?'

'I've maintained that next time we should not allow corruption to strike the heart of the WI.'

She slipped a new pillow case over her pillow.

It's always easier for me to change the pillow cases because I'll turn them inside out and flip the pillow upside down but our Doris says it's too lower class for her to entertain the idea. As I watched her struggle, I said to her, I said, 'Or could morale have been lost when Violet Grey, long-standing, former chairwoman, revealed her husband's affair with the aforementioned Janice Dooley that led to the departure of Violet and you gaining the position of interim chair?'

Our Doris were on the verge of the Look but I continued to tease, 'Or was morale lost when you chucked a pair of scales at Janice Dooley for which you're currently serving a community order?'

She dropped the pillow and fired a Look that vicious I were almost vaporised on the spot. She said to me, she said, 'Is there a reason you feel the need to bring up my minor indiscretion at every given opportunity, 'arold Copeland? It's not like you never made a mistake. Or have you forgotten the Bonfire Night of nineteen ninety-four. Keith Armitage nearly lost an eye.'

'Not because of me!'

'Yes, but you were meddling in the vicinity.'

I had to keep her away from Nerys Armitage as she spread the rumour our Doris purchased a Value margherita pizza from the Bramhall Tesco Express.

I had spent three weeks watching our Doris's movements, fielding every facial expression just in case she decided to go nuclear and catapult Nerys to Kingdom Come. I got the neighbours to keep an eye on her – I've questioned whether that's why she doesn't get on with her at Number 42 but it's too late to worry about it now.

Everything was going well until the fifth of November.

Of course, I'd made plans for the eventuality that Nerys would be there. I checked our position in the crowd for the fireworks, steered our Doris clear of the Tombola where Nerys were stationed but it were no use.

Our Doris offered a child some treacle toffee and out of the shadows I heard this whiny drawl of a voice, not unlike a balloon deflating, and she said to us, Nerys said, 'I do so wish the supermarkets wouldn't get us with their advertising – all that store-bought rubbish – our children could be eating the waste of marsupials and we would be none the wiser. I suppose one must save money at every given opportunity, I cannot judge, Mrs Copeland, but I do ask, for what cost do we threaten the future of our children?'

That bag of treacle toffee were nowhere to be seen as our Doris spun around and said to Nerys she said, 'You'd know all about tight purse strings, Nerys Armitage, the way your knickers are knotted – it's like you let the Boy Scouts loose in a lingerie factory.'

Nerys gave our Doris this smirk, the likes of which I hadn't seen since Robin Hood. She was on the verge of saying something when an almighty drunken wail roared across the churchyard.

I spun around to discover Nerys's husband sprawled over Mrs Cockermouth's grave, his head caught between two wrought iron fence posts.

News of Keith's inebriated escapades soon spread throughout town and although he maintained I had tripped him, folk saw it as a vendetta against our Doris, who had only ever offered the most gracious advice to Nerys regarding undergarments. Mrs Armitage would always be Nerys Butler to them, and they all remembered the summer of nineteen fifty-seven when she had more pine needles in her hair than bobby pins.

Our Doris usually falls back on the Keith Armitage argument. When she broke my toe with a Goebbel lamp she said as I should think about Keith Armitage's head – never mind that it was twelve years prior and he'd emigrated to Rhyl.

Either way I left our Doris in the bedroom and went downstairs to make a start on elevenses.

It may have only been an hour since breakfast but elevenses are a great British pastime and our Doris likes us to strive to be quintessentially British – it's the reason she still buys Spam.

I'd just finished pouring the hot water into the teapot when I became aware of this figure at the backdoor. I didn't dare look. At my age anything can be a portent of doom and I didn't fancy staring the Grim Reaper in the eye, especially when our Doris had an event planned.

I let the tea brew and went in search of the biscuits, certain our Doris had hidden all-butter shortbread in the salad drawer. I'd nearly made it to the fridge when he started knocking. I would've avoided looking if our Doris were out but she weren't and if word got out that I were inhospitable to guests she'd have me sectioned faster than a hamster on Lucozade.

I knew that knock like I knew I'd best get out the pint mug our Doris pretended was a quirky plant pot when the ladies were around, because at the back door, in desperate need of his eyebrows trimming, stood Alf.

He came in and said to me, he said, 'Bleeding heck, 'arold, what're you doing leaving me out in the rain like yesterday's washing?'

I told him, I said to him, I said, 'I thought you were some sort of waif, out on the rob, you can't be too careful nowadays.'

'Are you referring to my mugging?'

I nodded. 'I am.'

'Because that Ruby didn't nick anything and we got

her in the end.'

'It's not Ruby I'm worried about. It's our Doris,' I said. Alf had ingratiated himself at the kitchen table, his boots left by the back door. I brought the tea over and said, 'If anything happened to me, how would she react? She already has that blasted community order.'

Alf said to me, he said, 'I've never seen your Doris as the vigilante type, she's too many blouses.'

I said to him, I said, 'If I were to die before one of our Doris's dos she'd kill me. She'd put me on life support just so as she could pull the plug.'

'Aye, that she would,' Alf said, and slurped his tea. He has this way with his tea does Alf, the way he clamps his mouth around the mug and practically vacuums his drinks leaves you questioning whether his father might have been a Dyson.

I said to him, I said, 'And you can't deny this business with Ruby hasn't affected you. Ordinarily on wash day you're down Saint Jude's scrounging a hot dinner.'

If ever someone had looked more incredulous I didn't know about them. Alf gave me a Look our Doris would be proud of and said to me, he said, 'It's vegan lasagne. I'd sooner gnaw on a postal tube than eat vegan lasagne.'

'I've never known you pass up food before, even if it isn't fit for purpose.' Alf once consumed a jar of pickled onions three years past their use by date. Apart from halitosis he was completely unaffected – he's always been a bit waste not want not.

He said to me, all calm-like, he said, ''arold, it's vegan. Now I have no problem if you want specially prepared food – kosher, halal, coeliac – it's all gravy to me but lasagne wasn't made for vegans. It is Italian and they know a thing or two about animal produce.'

'So you protest veganism?' I said.

Our Doris slipped into the room, perm recently brushed and said to me, she said, 'Of course he does, our 'arold, if you want to be vegan it's fine but don't butcher proper food whilst you're at it.'

'Exactly!' Alf beamed. 'If you want a lasagne, eat a lasagne, don't swap out Béchamel sauce for guacamole.'

Our Doris sat herself down and poured herself a cup of tea. She said to me, she said, 'I'm glad you found the shortbread, 'arold, but you could have brought me a dark chocolate digestive in the meantime.' I got up to collect her chosen biscuit and listened our Doris as she regaled Alf with her plans for the WI. She said to him, she said, 'Could you let Edith know I'm arranging a week long excursion to the Cotswolds. We will be staying in a four star hotel and on our final evening there will be a gala with a complimentary glass of pink champagne.'

Alf looked at her like a goldfish, completely stunned, as he said to her, he said, 'You'll ring her though won't you, Doris?'

She smiled and said to him, she said, 'Of course I will, though it would be an insult for me to invite you into my home and not offer you the knowledge of your spouse's forthcoming departure.' I set down her biscuits as she went on, 'A few husbands may organise their own time well so as they enjoy themselves in their wives absence without letting their reputations fall into disrepute.'

I swallowed my tea, more to get my words together than anything, and said to her, I said, 'Are you suggesting we have us a lad's day out, our Doris?'

She did that thing with her eyelashes where you're

not sure if she's blinking or having a seizure and said to me, she said, 'Certainly not – you're neither of you lads, you are distinguished older gentleman and shall hold yourself in such a manner.'

'So we can go away as long as we're respectable?'

'Do you know, Alf, it's taken fifty-five years but I think our 'arold is finally listening to me.'

Over the next few days, me and Alf met up to scheme about what we would do whilst our wives were away. They were leaving on a Saturday – to any sane person the worst day to go, all those folk wanting weekends away, clogging up the motorway, leaving you to sweat worse than It Ain't Half Hot, Mum.

I said to our Doris, she were in her cubbyhole and I were in the hall checking the junk mail, I said, 'Why're you going on a Saturday, our Doris, you'll spend all day in traffic – that won't illicit much camaraderie in the WI will that.'

She stopped writing to her cousin in Whaley Bridge who'd just broke their ankle avoiding a Pomeranian in Age UK and gave me the Look. Our Doris said to me, she said, 'One, we are staying just outside a quaint little village that has the most wondrous market on a Sunday. The ladies wish to acclimatise first. And two, this coach cost that much I want to make sure I get every pennies worth. Besides, it has a lavatory.'

And that was all she had to say on the subject. She went back to accosting her cousin and I read about recent research into cancer and how with just three pounds a month they'd investigate whether pineapple juice was a cure all.

That Saturday, I drove our Doris, Edith and Alf down to the church hall. The coach were gargantuan – if King Kong were the driver I wouldn't be surprised. I said to our Doris, I said, 'No wonder it cost so much, it's the size of the bleeding Titanic.'

Our Doris gave me the Look and said to me, she said, 'The price of the coach needn't worry you for the WI had enough funds to cover such costs. I can commend your concern for the environment for that is the only criticism I will accept, but what you must deign to remember is that I have the ladies to consider and there are a few who will benefit from the extra leg room. Now, 'arold, you bring the suitcases, Edith and I will introduce ourselves to the driver.'

As I strained my new knee lifting our Doris's case out of the boot Erin arrived. She offered a hand and we both struggled to get the case to the pavement. 'Bloody hell,' Erin said, 'What's she got in there? We're only going for a week.'

'You managed to arrange childcare then?'

She said, 'It were a struggle at first because he said it would get in the way of his time at the bookies. When I told Mrs Copeland she stormed off to Ladbrokes and I got a text saying he'd have Reuben for the week.'

Alf sniggered behind us and said, 'Do you always travel light then, Erin?'

She spun around and grinned. The suitcase looked as light as dryer lint. She said to us, she said, 'One pair of jeans, some tops and enough underwear to fill a nunnery, what more do you need?'

I didn't know how to break it to her. I thought long and hard about how to approach the subject because our Doris made plans and she likes her plans to go unhitched. I sighed and said to Erin, I said, 'Have you forgotten the gala?'

Erin looked all gone out. She said, 'Have you met your wife, Mr Copeland? She's been on the phone everyday asking me about colours and shades and silhouettes – I felt like I were auditioning for The Chase.'

'So what're you wearing then, Erin?' Alf asked, unwilling to rid himself of his wolfish grin.

'Mrs Copeland has a gown in her bag for me. She said as I wouldn't know how to pack it to make sure the fabric is properly protected.'

I said, 'That's our Doris,' and we approached the coach.

Our Doris greeted the ladies as they arrived. She wasted no time in telling them she'd had a local deli owner provide lunch. She said to them, she said, 'I have managed to obtain a lunchtime meal for us all. Ann Walton's dear sister-in-law has baked us a few bespoke quiches to share with seasonal salad and locally produced bread.'

Pandra O'Malley's face could have been replaced with an old potato she had that much of a grimace. She said to our Doris, she said, 'And what of the coeliacs amongst us, or those who prefer a diet free from gluten?'

'Oh, Mrs O'Malley, I do thank you for reminding me,' she said, shooting Pandra a look that could snare pigeons, she said, 'Due to the eclectic dietary requirements of our numbers I have made sure that all foods are gluten free and abide with strict religious doctrine.'

Pandra traipsed onto the coach and our Doris tried hard to hide her smile. She hadn't looked so smug since Anton Wainthrop burst a button during his paso doble. He tried to call it artistic but we all knew it were sausage rolls.

An hour later and we were waving the ladies off. A

few of the other husbands showed up, if anything to make sure their wives actually left. It had been a while since the WI last had a break and as that coach started up I felt this wave of relief rush over the husbands of Partridge Mews.

Once our wives were out of sight we did what any sane men would do, we went to the pub.

Thus began the week. Saturday we stuck to the Hare and Horse – the rugby were on and even though it's not a sport our Doris approves of – she says it reminds her of Conan the Barbarian and she's never forgiven Arnold Schwarzenegger – I sat and watched and Alf managed to wangle a free dinner for us both when he caught Bertie Sterling up to no good in the ginnel.

When our Doris goes away she has to have an itinerary, everything is planned down to the last letter – it's why I saw the Whitby Cathedral three times in one week and never set foot on the beach. It's the way she runs her life really. I'll decide the hyacinths need pruning but our Doris will have made plans for a trip to locate plimsolls in Chester and mapped out the best time to hit Bon Marche so as to leave a lasting impression.

Sunday arrived and me and Alf decided to relax. We were like young lads on half term. Alf stayed in the spare bedroom and we ordered food in – for breakfast we had bacon, sausage and egg barms from the greasy spoon across town. It's a bit of a risk really but at seventy-five the auctioneer on Bargain Hunt could slam his gavel too hard and cause cardiac arrest so you don't mind eating a heart attack on a bun.

We tidied the house a bit. Our Angela rang to check up on me and I conveniently forgot to remind her I'd invited the lads around. They showed up ready for a feast. I couldn't see the kitchen for Theakston's and Marston's and Robinsons, the odd Captain Morgan, a few Famous Grouse, Neville donated a bottle of twenty-five year old Glenfiddich to celebrate his third decree nisi – he's had terrible luck with women has Neville, but I suppose that's what happens when you never look further south than Hurdsfield.

If our Doris didn't like rugby for its barbarism I'm glad she couldn't see our house that night. Alf used the television to hack into his grandson's Netflix account and after a mishap that saw us watching an Asian documentary on southern-fried noodles we settled for Dad's Army. Personally, I was all for finding my old tapes of Charlie Dimmock but the film's getting a bit worn so that you'd have more luck with Alan Titchmarsh.

I never thought you could get steak pie stuck in a letterbox but Ronnie made the discovery after exploring several cans of Carling.

I should have learnt after last time, only last time hadn't been planned and without the threat of our Doris over them, we went as wild as vegetarians in an abattoir.

Someone kidnapped the cat from Number 42 and fed it whisky. An inebriated feline is something no man should have to contend with, especially a man who is just as, if not more drunk and has no way of stopping the cat from climbing the net curtains and leaping onto the head of a comatose Mark Chaplain.

Mark bellowed and threw the cat to Tim who caught the thing and stumbled back into Aunty Sylvie's vase. The vase so precious our Doris brought it on our honeymoon. The vase that now toppled to the ground with all the aplomb of a dead budgerigar.

And shattered.

Now, a proper Doris-fearing husband would have yelled at them and made them leave, bemoaning the consequences but I had inhaled my fair share of steak and kidney pie and wasn't fully aware of the situation. The ale probably fuelled me somewhat because I said to them, 'Bleeding heck,' I said, 'it's finally gone – I've hated the sight of that pot since our Doris brought it back from the wake.'

The Glenfiddich was opened and the rest of Sunday and most of Monday remain a blur.

Over the next few days we steered clear of the rest of the lads. Theo came around and helped us with the tidying. He's sworn to secrecy. I'm amazed what three bitter shandies and a lager top will get you, not that I endorse underage drinking, it's just proven a more effective bribe than Haribo.

Meanwhile, me and Alf made plans for our last day of freedom. We'd had a postcard. Angela must've telephoned her mother and informed her of Alf's whereabouts. Our Doris were pleased about the idea. She wrote in her most professional handwriting, no doubt worried it were going to be intercepted by some ne'er-do-well who'd auction it off to Janice Dooley of Little Street or the Gazette. The postcard were a watercolour of a valley with white smudges that could've been sheep or clouds or something and on the back she wrote, 'I am most pleased to discover you used your initiative and invited Alfred to respite in our home. It is no secret we have faced struggles these past few months and apart from saving on his bills he is also safe in the knowledge that his friends will always be there for him. Don't forget to record Emmerdale.'

She made no mention of camaraderie in the WI, save to say as Pandra O'Malley behaved most graciously and had organised a trip to a flower garden for afternoon tea. I could tell our Doris were seething through the ink.

Either way, she'd be home Saturday night and thus me and Alf thought it the best day to have a run out.

There weren't really that much we wanted to do.

Our wives want us to be more cultured and although I can tell my Vivaldi from my Vimto I'm not about to book a ticket for the Bridgewater Hall.

Alf brought up going to Chelford but you can't take him near an auction. He once bought three hundred Texel ewes when the auctioneer mistook his swearing for a bid.

We've known each other since milk teeth have me and Alf, we're quite content to spend our days down the allotment but our wives won't be happy unless we prove that we're sociable creatures making the most of our retirement. Not that you can do much anyway, once you're over seventy folk just aren't inclined to insure you for go-karting.

We ended up at the Hare and Horse trying to think up ideas. I said to him, I said, 'Is there anything at all in the last seventy-five years that you've wanted to do and haven't?'

He said to me, he said, 'I've always wanted to climb Ben Nevis but I've never got on with Welsh rarebit.'

'And once you've done Shutlingsloe is there much point in anything else?'

'There is that,' he said and we were no closer to figuring out what to do.

Until we saw the advert.

Game and Country Fair, Knutsford, practically on

the doorstep and not likely to feature much hillwalking. It were the beer tent that sold it for me. I'd never claim alcoholism but at my age you're happier when the shakes are drink-related.

We made sure the house was tidy – that all the crumbs were out of the letterbox – and we were on our way.

I'd only just pulled up to the end of the road when it happened. And I knew. I knew that this were some form of karmic retribution for breaking Aunty Sylvie's vase – that awful, blue-green ceramic horror would drag me to my doom because as we stopped at the give-way line I caught sight of a man rush past us.

The back passenger door was torn open.

Before I could protest, Derek O'Malley sat there, heaving breaths like he'd left his lungs two streets back.

He said to me, he said, 'You have to help me. My life's in danger.'

I stared at him and then across at Alf and said, 'Can you believe it? He hijacks my bleeding car and expects me to listen to his demands.'

'You need to drive,' he said, he practically pleaded with me, his face red, sweat pouring down his face faster than Niagara Falls on Imodium.

'Get out of my car.'

''arold, listen to me.'

'No. Get out of the bloody car!' I were yelling now, I sounded like my father, you can't just surprise a man and expect him to act all reasonable. Copeland men are notorious for responding poorly when shocked. My Dad once thumped a DJ when he played Mambo No.5 instead of That's Amore.

Still Derek persisted with, 'Our lives are in danger.'

'Yours might be if you don't get out the car.'

Derek exploded at this point, spit sprayed against my cheeks as he said to me, he roared, 'Pandra is going to announce her candidacy.'

I said to Derek, I said, 'And why can't we just telephone? Why do I have to drive I don't know how many bleeding miles to let our Doris know in person?'

He looked at me all gone out, as though he were the last rational being in Partridge Mews and said to me, he said, 'We know what your wife did to Janice Dooley. Do you really want to risk the same thing happening with Pandra?'

We were silent. My eyes went from Alf to Derek back to Alf and back again. Alf gulped and said, he said, 'Right, 'arold, we'll have to make a detour.'

I nodded and said, I said, 'I know. Seatbelts on.' I pressed my foot down on the accelerator. Our Doris had her heart set on going away for a fortnight on a cruise not six months in Styal prison.

On the way Derek explained how Pandra had rung him at breakfast to give him the news. She'd been planning for that long now she thought our Doris's event would be the perfect spectacle to showcase herself to those who don't know who she is.

If I were an Irish ex-pat with a history of defrauding people I wouldn't be looking to showcase it. My cousin married a Vauxhall salesman he knew how to keep quiet about creative accounting, and it didn't involve becoming chairperson to a small town WI.

I thought that we'd take a few hours to get to the Cotswolds, warn our Doris, and be on our way home in time for Casualty. I never thought I'd have to contend with Alf's bladder. We'd only been travelling for fifteen minutes when he announced that he needed to use the facilities. He said to me, he said, 'I could do with going, 'arold.'

I slowed the car down and pointed out a problem to Alf. 'We're in the middle of the countryside. Didn't you think of going when we were back at the house?' I knew that I sounded like a parent on their way to the seaside but no one warns you about bladder shrinkage when you're younger, or that it's always that urgent you never know whether you've a pond or an ocean making you sweat.

Alf shrugged at me and said to me, he said, 'Just pull over – I'll go in one of the fields.'

I said to him, I said, 'It's not like when we were lads, Alf, you can't go for a country one without being done for indecent exposure nowadays.'

He gave me this surly grin I know only too well and said to me, he said, 'It's my right as a British citizen to piddle in a policeman's hat if I'm pregnant, I'll go in that field, just pull over. If anyone asks I'll say I'm checking on the herd.'

Indeed there were a great many sheep in Alf's chosen field. I don't know why he had to choose that field but I've learnt never to question his antics. He's a bit like our Doris in that respect - you let them get on with whatever they're doing and sort it out afterwards, like potty training toddlers.

I pulled the car in as far as I could to the grass verge. Alf hopped out and headed towards the gate.

For the next few minutes there was an uncomfortable silence between me and Derek.

After what seemed like hours I fixed him a look in the rearview mirror and said, 'You can't just jump into someone's car and expect them to listen to what you have to say.'

He looked about to reply when we heard this

almighty yell from outside. Alf swore like a trooper as the car was surrounded by a great woolly army.

Alf had left the gate open.

I couldn't open the door for sheep surging in the opposite direction down the road. The air filled with ululating baas as though the ewes were screaming a battle cry.

Alf came hobbling across the field, doing up his fly. He called after the sheep but they paid him no mind.

Out of nowhere there were the sound of a tractor blaring its horn as it trundled down the road behind us. The sheep turned around in the opposite direction but Alf were prepared. As lads we'd had a few summers helping the Sterlings on their farm to earn pocket money and Alf had clearly remembered a few things. He threw himself in front of the sheep like something from the deep, splayed his arms, his eyes that wild he could have been Wuthering Heights and he roared, practically tore his vocal cords as he sent the great vile beasts back into the field.

I knew not to bother getting out of the car. Sheep like nothing more than to take down the weakest link - I still recall sheep biting into the back of my thighs after a taste of beet pulp.

Before we knew it the sheep made their way back into the field, the tractor leading them with Alf bellowing a few choice phrases. He closed the gate and the tractor slowed to a halt. Alan, the farmer jumped from his cab. 'What do you think you're doing?' He looked murderous. It were like showing a lettuce leaf to a Weight Watcher, his fists clenched, his face looked like it had been boiled for three hours and his eyes were that wide I wasn't sure if it were anger or conjunctivitis. He advanced on us and said, 'Letting a man's sheep out all over the road. I could understand it if you were senile, heck I'd give you a lift back to the home but when a perfectly sensible man does something so stupid you can't help but question his intentions. Did the Butterworths send you?'

I must've looked a bit gone out as I said to him, I said, 'No. It's our Doris - Mrs O'Malley's about to announce she wants to be chairwoman.'

Alan nodded. 'I'm a reasonable man, I can understand the need to get wherever she is but she's not in my field so what the devil were you thinking?'

'Alf needed to pay a visit.'

'In my field?'

Alf piped up here with, 'No, I just picked a field, when you feel the need you can't be dithering about trying to figure out whose field it is you're going in.'

'Right.' Alan shook his head, looking no less murderous. At least a farmer were going to kill me because when our Doris found out Pandra's intentions she'd eradicate anyone within the immediate vicinity.

Derek got out of the car and said to Alan, he said, 'You can't pretend that you haven't gone in a field before now, Alan. The sheep are all back in the field, nothing's been lost, why don't you let us on our way and go about your business?'

Alan breathed, calculating Derek's words. He looked at the three of us, a sorrier trio never before seen, and said to us, he said, 'You best be going on with yourselves then.' As Alf got back into the car he added, 'And make sure you choose another field next time – I hear the Butterworths wouldn't mind their fields watering.' He banged his hand on the roof of my car and stepped back, watching us leave.

'Blimey, 'arold!' Alf exclaimed, 'That were lucky.

The fizz went out of him faster than a bottle of pop.'

Derek said to us, he said, 'That's the thing about farmers. They're always ready for an argument – you would be, too, if all you had to do was sit around watching sheep all day.' And no more was said about it.

Now, me and our Doris have been to the Cotswolds a few times in the last fifty-five years and we have always made the journey with just the aid of Radio 3 and a map. Our Doris says as classical music is the only option worthy of eliciting the quaint atmosphere one associates with the Cotswolds.

I think they must have added a few more lanes and tributaries since I last made the journey because after three quarters of an hour I had no choice but to admit that we were lost.

I'd been down D-roads and motorways, country roads and town centres and somehow ended up in Sandbach.

Sandbach.

I wanted the Cotswolds and I ended up in Sandbach, a town that may as well be Crewe with a shampoo and set.

I pulled up on the library car park and Alf said to me, he said, 'You'll have to use the Sat Nav, 'arold.'

I groaned but let him get the blasted device from the glove compartment.

I've never got on with Sat Nav but our Doris made me get one as soon as Sadie Davenport called Tom Tom a lifesaver on her trip to Hull. I said to her, I said, 'What's wrong with a map, our Doris?'

This earned me the Look and she said to me, she said, 'We are in an advanced technological age, our 'arold, manufacturers spend their days looking to make our lives easier, yet you choose to spend hours perusing the A-Z only to realise you forgot your spectacles, mixed up Margate and Marple and I miss Meredith Weaver's piano recital.'

'That were twenty years ago,' I protested but it didn't matter. Meredith Weaver's recital is renowned for being the worst rendition of Bach ever performed – the Gazette said as she was Quasimodo at a Kemble and our Doris will never forgive me for making her miss it.

I knew I had no choice but to use the Sat Nav. I got Derek to key in the address and we were off.

There's something about the dulcet tones of a Sat Nav that had me yelling at her several times. First, she kept telling me to turn right when I were stuck at some traffic lights. Then, the Sat Nav thought it would be entertaining to send me three miles home before I realised we were going in the wrong direction.

But the thing that really frustrated me, that ground on my very last nerve was when the Sat Nav decided I'd taken a wrong turn.

It began with a robotic 'turn around'.

I carried on to hear a more forthright 'turn around' a moment later.

I carried on, only for this roar, this veritable banshee wail to exclaim from the speakers, 'Turn around!'

I roared at her then, my eyes bulged, I were certain I looked crazed as I said to her, I said, 'I'm on the pigging motorway, I can't very well turn around.'

The Sat Nav either heard me or gave up because after that we were on the right track.

Eventually we reached the gala. We tumbled from the car like rusty springs uncoiling, my bones creaking more than Moll Flanders' mattress.

The hotel was huge. It looked like something pulled

straight from an Agatha Christie. A long drive wound its way through a golf course so that you had the constant threat of a shattered windscreen.

I didn't run over any pensioners and circled around a water feature the likes of which wouldn't look out of place in Rome, or the Trafford Centre. It had some sort of humanoid fish spitting water into a bowl and bathing itself. Alf said it were a gentleman's shower but I were too busy staring at the hotel.

It were immense. It must've been a manor in a previous life, with great stone columns and the entire place were sandstone. That's how you can tell the standard of a place is the sandstone – our Doris would have had a sandstone façade put over our house if she could've got the planning permission.

We climbed the steps and entered through arched double doors. The place was that upmarket I thought I'd entered Buckingham Palace itself. With its parquet flooring in the foyer and a chandelier I were waiting for Alexis Carrington to walk down the stairs.

Erin stood by a pair of white doors. We hurried over, Derek rushing straight past her.

'You all right, Erin?' I said to her as we approached.

Erin were the most enthusiastic I'd ever seen her, like a schnauzer after a sausage roll. 'You should see it, Mr Copeland. Mrs Copeland got them to let her have the ballroom. It's great. Did you see the chandelier? I bet it's real crystal.'

'Is there any grub?' Alf asked.

Erin nodded. 'Mrs Copeland hired caterers for a banquet. I'm all right with a fish supper from Gav's Chippy, but you should see the size of those prawns.'

We followed Alf as he rushed straight into the ballroom.

Our Doris had outdone herself again. She'd used fairy lights and candles so that the place had an air of Midsummer Night's Dream. There was an almost hazy glow to the room and a light tinkling of classical music in the background, our Doris has always had a thing about Mantovani, ever since our days down the dance hall.

I sensed that the joint account would be a lot lighter than it had been so said to Erin, I said, 'Just how much has this set me back?'

Erin shrugged and said to me, she said, 'I got sent a voucher to get the rooms on the cheap. Something to do with late rooms. And the ladies paid for themselves.'

Something like relief soothed my heart and I knew I were no longer on the verge of a cardiac arrest.

I caught sight of our Doris making small talk with some of the ladies. They'd have been talking about the feast – our Doris has a knack of making sure you notice her achievements, at her Aunty Gwen's wake she bypassed checking on her cousin to tell folk all about her Quiche Lorraine.

She met my eyes and I watched as recognition settled over her face – it were either that or an ingrown toenail.

Our Doris excused herself and approached me, the merest hint of a smile upon her lips. This were the smile she used to hide her frustrations. This were the smile associated with that time Linda Metcalf drank too much babycham and revealed just what happened between her and Monty Phillips in August nineteen seventy-three.

When she reached me, she said, 'What an unexpected surprise, our 'arold. Most husbands would follow their wife's advice and visit elsewhere but not my 'arold, not when he can meet me one hundred and twenty miles away from home.'

I said to her, I said, 'You can blame the O'Malleys. That Pandra is going to use the gala to announce her candidacy.'

Our Doris were astonished. Her face did things faces aren't accustomed to doing and she said to me, she said, 'What the beggary are we going to do, our 'arold?'

We didn't have time to formulate a plan. A microphone whistled and we all turned around to find Pandra O'Malley stood on a platform. There were a few murmurs about her pairing a Basler jacket with Tu trousers but folk mostly remained silent as she began her speech. She said, 'Good evening, ladies. Before we get too tipsy, I just wanted to say a few words.

'First, thank you to Doris, our interim chairwoman, for organising this week away – the bargains you can find on the internet – and this get together is really *swish*.

'Anyway, even with a criminal record Doris has shown us what can be done in our golden years and it's because she's such an inspiration that I have decided to put my name forward to be the next chairwoman of this accepting group.

'Thanks everyone, do enjoy yourselves.' She fired a winning look in our Doris's direction and stepped off the platform.

Our Doris were seething. She were more gobsmacked than when Deirdre Barlow had her fling with Mike Baldwin. Her fists were clenched that tight Mike Tyson wouldn't stand a round with her. She were positively murderous as she said to me, she said, 'Did you never think to use the bloody telephone, our 'arold?'

I said, 'Derek convinced me not to.'

'Of course he did, you great lumbering oaf. Pandra is his wife – she will have told him exactly what to do, make no mistake.' Our Doris pulled at her bracelet like it were a rosary and she needed divine intervention as she said to me, she said, 'I've no choice. I'll have to make a speech. Did you hear hers? She's as common as muck on a potato is that one.'

She set off to the microphone and was once more beaten to the platform.

Erin stood there as uncomfortable as a cat in a kennel. She spoke into the microphone all soft at first and said, 'Sorry to disturb you, everyone. I'm not good at these things – speeches – I had to do one as my sister's bridesmaid but I told everyone about her psoriasis and that were the first Pete heard about it. He's with that Shannay Cooper now – she's a right – sorry, got a bit lost.

'Right, so some of you know that Mrs Copeland is helping me out a bit. In return I do some admin for her. Well Aimee Sprink sent me the link for a trip to the Cotswolds and I knew Mrs Copeland wanted to take us all away. We all know about saving pennies here and there – my Grandad always said that even with rationing he still went to Blackpool – that Mrs O'Malley brought it up just goes to show how Mrs Copeland helped us enjoy ourselves and not put ourselves in debt. And I got to go on my first holiday with some great friends.

'This is also a personal thank you to Mrs Copeland who apart from being awesome is going to help me re-enrol in college this September. And all as she performed her community work and fulfilled her role as interim chairwoman of this great WI. Thank you.'

Erin scuttled off like a nun caught in a brewery. If it hadn't been for the fairylights I could've sworn I saw a tear in our Doris's eye. I handed her a napkin and we went over to Erin who had buried herself in a pint of Stella, a concerned Edith at her side.

'Erin, you were brilliant,' our Doris exclaimed, 'the mention of frugality and rationing – I'm not normally one to use online vouchers as they do nothing more than emphasise the opinions of those who feel entitled to more than their share but Erin yours was a stroke of genius.'

'Mrs Simpson helped.'

Our Doris beamed at Edith and I left them extolling the virtues of online shopping. I found myself a quiet corner to enjoy a pork pie because if our Doris had another war on her hands I'd need all the strength I could get.

4

EDUCATING ERIN

Our Doris is at war with the local college after they rejected Erin's application. They say as she doesn't have enough GCSEs, our Doris says as if the college administrators had a qualification between them they'd be dangerous.

I blame the WI. If Pandra O'Malley had kept her mouth shut about becoming chairwoman our Doris would never have got involved with folk she's always described as so close to the gutter they may as well be the kerb.

Erin's a nice girl, it's just that she didn't consider her future when she bunked off school in favour of hanging around the off-licence. I think she's helped our Doris see past a few of her issues with the underclasses in any case.

I knew something were up as soon as our Doris walked into the house. I were sat watching Homes Under the Hammer when she burst into the living room like a Jack Russell over a hose pipe. She had this murderous look in her eyes, not dissimilar to when she sees the price of a train ticket and she does her pacing across the carpet – I question why we didn't just go for lino the amount of pacing she does over the carpet.

I paused the television and said to her, I said, 'What's the matter, our Doris?'

She really glowered at me then. She could give Medusa a run for her money with that Look. And she said to me, she said, 'Never before in my life have I questioned our nation's educators but I'm beginning to wonder at the sanity of those in charge of the establishment. It's all because they got rid of the eleven plus. I knew there was something not-quite-right but did I say anything? Did I heck as like.

'I thought, "they're our government they know what they're doing." Well I was about as right as lapsang souchong.

'Erin, a woman who actually wants to be educated. Who only wishes to enter a better career to provide for her son has been denied a place on a course because she doesn't have the desired qualifications. Qualifications? Who do they think they are? I wasn't trained by RADA but I'm still the best soprano this side of the Pennines.'

And that's when she stopped to breathe and I stared at her completely flabbergasted.

Ordinarily, I would've been down the allotment but I chose not to in favour of catching up with my television programmes.

Our Doris likes me to keep track of the home design shows so that I can properly acquaint myself with modern soft furnishings. I said to her, I said, 'I'm too old to be the next Lawrence Llewelyn Bowen.'

She gave me the Look and said, 'It's been fifty-five years, believe me, I know.'

If I'd gone to the allotment I wouldn't have had to contend with her tirade. She were like something out of *The Exorcist*, I kept waiting for her head to spin around and for her to start climbing the walls – see how much she cared about her soft furnishings then.

I said to her, I said, 'Can you appeal the decision?'

'Of course I'm going to appeal the decision, our 'arold. I've booked an appointment with the college headmistress tomorrow and I expect you to accompany me.'

Which is how I ended up sat on a chair so rough it could've been made from sandpaper in a claustrophobic hallway, on a day when I could've been starting a jigsaw or some other equally tedious activity.

I were more bored than when I were in hospital and the televisions were down. At least there were always the chance I'd see something out of *Embarrassing Bodies*.

Our Doris had dressed for war – lemon blazer, Marc Cain skirt and a blouse that expensive she made sure to leave the price tag in the shop.

I were just grateful my trousers had an elasticated waist.

Eventually, we were allowed entry into the headmistress's office. It looked like an office – MDF desk, mahogany bookshelves with framed photographs and potted plants and a view over the car park. If she'd worked at a morgue she'd be spot on.

The headmistress, Mrs Porter, was built like a bricklayer. She towered over me and our Doris like a bungalow over a dormouse. Her suit were pinstriped and she'd tied her hair into a bun. This was her first misstep.

Before she had time to speak our Doris said to her, she said, 'Mrs Porter, I must apologise for this meeting to discuss Erin Beaumont's education. Now I understand the reason you've behaved so erroneously the entire situation seems easily corrected.'

Mrs Porter had a chance to look perplexed before saying to our Doris, she said, 'I've no idea what you're talking about, Mrs Copeland.'

Our Doris tilted her head to one side. The head tilt is almost worse than the Look. It means our Doris is calculating, planning something, and no one ever came out of an our Doris plan unscathed.

She said to Mrs Porter, she said, 'Why, isn't it obvious?'

When Mrs Porter shook her head, our Doris said, 'The bun in your hair is that tight it clearly cut off circulation to your already taxed brain. The impeded blood flow lead to your completely ludicrous suggestion that my good friend Erin Beaumont isn't qualified to attend your social work course.'

'That's because she doesn't,' Mrs Porter stated, matter-of-factly, 'I've spoken to admissions and Miss Beaumont doesn't have the required grade in mathematics.'

Our Doris offered a smile, looking something like a cartoon villain and said, she said, 'Mathematics, you say? Please could you inform me as to how mathematics has anything to do with social work? Will Erin need to know the value of pi to see if Mrs Higginbottom requires a stairlift?'

'It's the college's policy.'

'It's discrimination.' Our Doris stood up and said, 'Miss Beaumont had an unfortunate upbringing and as such you are stigmatising her. I will be writing to my MP and if you are unwilling to find a way to allow Erin onto the course I will take matters further. Good day to you, Mrs Porter. Never before has the phrase "let your hair down" been more pertinent.' She swept from the room and I followed.

Our Doris has always been a formidable force. When our Angela didn't get the part of Mary in the school nativity, our Doris had the entire production shut down in case of religious offence. It didn't matter that Sunjeev Smith had the part of the Angel Gabriel, our Doris didn't stop until our Angela were in that blue frock.

That's how I know to be wary.

I dropped our Doris off at the house and went to visit our Angela. With Theo off school for his summer holidays, she'd taken some time off work.

She were in the garden when I arrived. It were hot enough to melt a Tory in an icebox. I made myself a brew and joined her. I said to her, I said, ''ow at, Angela?'

She said to me, she said, 'Sweltering — it's no better inside. If I were anything like Mum I'd have forced Neil to pay for air conditioning.'

'If you were anything like your mother you'd have forced the council to do it.'

She looked at me aghast and said, 'Don't be a fool, Dad, we own our houses.'

I nodded and said to her, I said, 'Exactly, she'd have charged them a consultation fee.'

'Now you're just being ludicrous. Honestly, Dad, she's not that bad.'

I shrugged at that and said, I said, 'I suppose you're right.' I didn't mention that our Doris once funded a new sink with her knowledge of what Councillor West had been doing at that duck pond. He wasn't feeding anyone bread in any case. I slurped my tea and said to our Angela, I said, 'Besides, I think your mother might be getting a bit senile.'

'Don't let her hear you saying that. She's still convinced she's shielded herself by eating that many prawn cocktails in nineteen seventy-two.'

'The seventies were full of prawn cocktails – same with avocado. You couldn't go anywhere without someone shoving a Dartington glass avocado dish in your face and calling it a starter.'

Our Angela said to me, she said, 'Anyway, how's Mum going senile?'

'Well not senile ... more so round the twist she could be a pipe cleaner.'

'All right – well what's she done?'

'Erin hasn't got the qualifications for her college course so your mother stormed down to see the headmistress and demanded Erin be allowed to join.'

'I have to say I'm surprised at you.'

'With me?' I must have been incredulous. I was trying to be incredulous but it's difficult to do after seventy, you always end up resembling a Doberman.

'Yes,' our Angela said, 'with you. I'm surprised that Mum's behaviour surprises you.'

I said to her, I said, 'Where's Theo? He'd agree with me.'

'It's midday in the middle of the summer holidays. Where do you think he is? In bed. He stays up till three in the morning and sleeps through the day – it's like living with a flatulent vampire.'

'That's another thing we shouldn't let your mother hear.'

Angela shrugged and said, 'I've already told her. She's going to have a word.'

'You're your mother's daughter, our Angela.'

'It's a trick I learnt from you – how to weaponise Mum.'

'It can't be that bad, him sleeping in.'

'He's so loud when I'm trying to sleep. Usually I wouldn't mind having a lie in but sometimes you want to be awake with Eamonn and Ruth.'

'Your mother's going to love this. She's getting Erin into college, stopping Theo from being idle and fighting for her place as WI chairwoman. It'll be like all her Christmases have come at once.'

A few days down the line the first of our Doris's letters regarding the exclusion of those of lower-class households from further education appeared in the Partridge Mews Gazette. Our Doris could have been a writer – she'd crafted Erin's biography into such a tale filled with enough woe and catastrophe to make Catherine Cookson jealous. She likened the college to jumped-up caviar eaters excluding those who have to be happy with tuna mayonnaise. At times it tugged at the heartstrings before returning to the family angle and emphasising how Erin only wished to make her son proud.

We were sat at breakfast when I read it. I said to her, I said, 'You've outdone yourself there, our Doris.'

She offered me a smirk as she smeared jam on her toast and said to me, she said, 'If only Mrs Porter had heeded my words rather than write me off as a demented old biddy I wouldn't have had to resort to such drastic measures. Her failure to act has meant I have no choice but to wage war on the Partridge Mews College.'

I said to her, I said, 'What's next?'

'I've already penned a missive to our MP regarding the situation and a few written in case I must take it further and contact the media. I've even included Channel Five.'

'I didn't know it was that serious.'

'The day folk decided that I was nothing more than a pensioner with a community order, it got serious. I'll even take this to Sky News if needs be.'

I ate the rest of my poached eggs in silence before heading down to the allotment. I'd got some geraniums I wanted to share at the Poynton Show and had to keep a close eye on them. Alan in the next plot has got himself a new fella and he'll stop at nothing to impress him.

I arrived to find Alf buried beneath a tarpaulin in my shed. His snoring were louder than Mrs Drummond's screaming when she mistook a kite for the Luftwaffe in August nineteen eighty-three.

He'd clearly spent the night. There were the tell-tale odours of sleep and Boddingtons Finest ale.

I managed to rouse him with the threat of his Edith.

He shot from under the tarpaulin faster than Eddie the Eagle, his eyes wide.

I said to him, I said, 'What the devil are you doing here?'

He rubbed his eyes looking a bit like a koala with sinusitis and he said to me, he said, 'I've done a bad thing, 'arold.'

I said, 'You're always doing bad things, you're Alf. You spend that much time down the police station they save you a cell.'

He groaned and said to me, he said, 'It's worse than anything I've ever done before, 'arold. And that includes the time I stole an Etch-a-Sketch for mine and Edith's silver wedding anniversary.'

'It wouldn't have been so bad if you'd nicked it from a shop.'

'I was drunk! Who leaves a toddler near a man half-cut? Our Martin's never forgiven me, says as the trauma stopped him from being the next Kandinsky.'

'I thought he was all set on being a drummer.'

'He was until he discovered French women. Now he wants to work for the foreign office.'

'How old is he?'

'Twenty-seven. But listen, 'arold, you'll have to help me. I've made this mistake and I need you to help me put it right.'

'You haven't told me what you did. How am I supposed to help you when you won't tell me what you did?'

Alf swallowed hard and said to me, he said, 'I were playing dominoes and bet my wedding ring.'

I stared at him, I were that astonished. I said, 'You bet your wedding ring? You're right – you did make a mistake.'

Alf groaned, shaking his head and said, 'I know. I know. Will you help me get it back?'

'I wouldn't say I have much choice. If Edith finds out she'll kill you. If Edith finds out I know she'll tell our Doris. Who did you play against?'

Alf looked sheepish as he told me, he said, 'It were Janice Dooley of Little Street.'

I felt the colour leave my face faster than vindaloo and knew that I were right. We were dead.

We found Janice at The Blind Cat, a dingy pub frequented by those from the worse end of the council estate. A few of the windows were boarded over and the general stench of ammonia filled the place as though we'd enter an Olympic-sized urinal.

I said to Alf, I said, 'If your Edith finds out you've been drinking here you may as well move into my shed.'

Alf didn't say anything in reply.

I hadn't seen Janice Dooley of Little Street since our confrontation during the garden safari. She hadn't changed much, had the same wrinkles around her lips from too many cigarettes and not enough hot dinners. Her eyes had this sort of glaze about them, somewhere between cataracts and marbles – they're that beady it's a wonder her father wasn't a crow.

She sat in the corner, sucking on pork scratchings to let everyone know she'd come out without her dentures.

I bought myself a bottle of sparkling water and got Alf a pint of bitter. No doubt his stomach could cope with filthy pumps, it's had to cope with much worse in seventy-five years. I said to him, I said, 'You owe us a lot for this, Alf, it's one thing if you'd played against Moira Janowski – she's top of the league – but Janice Dooley of Little Street? After all she's done.'

He looked down into his pint and said to me, he said, 'I'm sorry, I am, 'arold, I weren't thinking. You know how it is.'

'This is one of the stupidest things you've done, and that includes the time you asked the Methodist minister for a brandy.' I wouldn't usually give Alf a talking down but this was different. Alf's always had something of the ragamuffin about him but he's always had honour. I don't understand what he was thinking playing dominoes with Janice Dooley. 'You should've known how much trouble this would cause,' I said to him and made my way over to her.

She sucked her lips over her gums as we approached and offered this wink. Well, I think it was a wink, it was either a wink or she was in the midst of gastroenteritis. She were dressed in a skirt that high it revealed every purpling vein on her legs and the tattoo of a flower Bob McIntyre gifted her for her sixtieth birthday – an act that saw Ian Coppack jailed for assault because he had been courting Janice for three months at the time.

Janice has always had a reputation.

She said to us, she said, 'Why if it isn't Partridge Mews very own Harold Copeland. Slumming it, are we?'

'I've come to get Alf's wedding ring back,' I said, getting straight to the point. Now that I looked at it there were a layer of dust around the rim of my sparkling water. I wanted to be done as soon as possible.

Janice smirked and tapped her fingernails across the top of the table. She wore the ring on her wedding finger, her nicotine-stained, false-tipped wedding finger. 'I'm not sure I know what you're talking about. Alf would never be seen dead talking to me, why should I have his wedding ring? He's that much of a layabout he could have left it anywhere.'

'But that's my ring,' he said, pleading worse than a toddler before a tantrum.

I said to Janice, I said, 'Does this mean you don't plan on giving Alf the ring back?'

She sat back in her seat and said to me, looking worse than Stig of the Dump after a night on the town, she said, 'I think I'm the sensible one here. I won the ring and if Alf gets caught it'll make a worse situation for all three of us. It seems the only one with a problem here is the old man himself.'

I nodded and said to her, I said, 'That's what I

thought. Come on Alf.'

'I haven't finished my pint.'

'Good – it means you won't be stupid enough to bet anything else. Now come on.' I'd clearly been spending too much time around our Doris because he followed.

We went back to my house where I made a pot of tea and Alf reacquainted himself with our biscuit tin. Our Doris wandered into the kitchen, saw the two of us and said to us, she said, 'What did you do?'

I said, 'What're you talking about, our Doris?' I'd racked my brains on the journey home and couldn't come up with any lies to tell her. She has a knack for knowing when I'm not being altogether truthful does our Doris. I think she must've been fitted with a polygraph test when we got married, had some new hardwire to aid her in her quest to thwart her husband's escapades at every turn.

She gave me the Look, took the biscuit tin off Alf and said to us, she said, 'You look more sheepish than spring, tell me what you did.'

I poured the tea and sat down at the table. I didn't know what to say to her – you can't tell your wife that you've unwittingly invited her mortal enemy back into your lives without threat of nuclear war.

Alf's skin had blanched as he said to her, he said, 'I lost my wedding ring, Doris, it's nothing.'

Our Doris sat down at the table. She set her shoulders back, pursed her lips and took the cup of tea I'd poured in her favourite Aynsley china cup. There were this atmosphere in the air, as though she were a judge ready to contact the executioner. She stirred her tea, all precise, and I could almost feel Alf's trembling across the room as our Doris said, she said, 'That is a rather distressing tale, Alfred. Perhaps we should speak to a certain Janice Dooley of Little Street who has been seen around town sporting a fresh wedding ring. Of course, we know it can't possibly be hers – women like Janice Dooley are not made for marrying – could this be the same wedding ring you are searching for, I wonder?'

The Look reached atomic levels.

A glimmer shone in our Doris's irises, her eyes pinched that tight they looked ready to fire laser beams straight at Alf. I hadn't seen a Look this impressive since nineteen seventy-three when Eleanor Stockwell had one too many at the Christmas party and put the moves on Lawrence Hepburn.

Our Doris were ready to go in for the kill – Alf had raised such ire in her that saw her usually peach-coloured cheeks steam to a shade more tomato. She spoke to him, and lord if her voice didn't sound as though it were filled with acid as she said to him, she said, 'Tell me, Alfred, with all that Miss Shaw business did you perhaps take leave of your senses? Because that is the only reason I can see for you to commit such an atrocity. You have always been a few shillings short of a pound but this has to have been the most stupid thing you have done since you urinated in a souvenir plant pot in front of a party full of under-tens.'

Alf stood at the kitchen counter staring at the floor. He looked like he were about to throw up as he said to her, he said, 'I'm sorry, Doris, really, I am. Please don't tell our Edith.'

'You honestly believe I could tell my dear friend that her husband is nothing more than a drunk plebeian who lost his wedding ring to a woman who has tried to make our lives difficult for the last fifty years?' She knocked back her tea as though it were a glass of bad wine and went on, she said, 'And do you want to know what I find exceptionally stupid? The one thing that has me questioning your sanity more than I questioned net curtains in nineteen ninety-eight? It is a well-known fact in Partridge Mews that Janice Dooley of Little Street has never played a fair game of dominoes in her life. She is at the top of the league because those judging are too drunk to notice when she cheats. This is common knowledge and the reason she only plays against Moira Janowski and her cronies. So please, Alf, humour me. With this information in mind, why did you make such a ludicrous decision?'

Our Doris poured herself another cup of tea and slurped it. The Look had miraculously vanished from her eyes. She settled back in her chair like a politician who knows they have won the election and waited for him to answer.

He looked like a downtrodden Dobermann as he sat down at the table and said to her, he said, 'I'm sorry, Doris. I thought I were on to a winner.'

'You were drunk,' she said, 'of course you thought you were on to a winner. I question whether I was a tad inebriated when I allowed you to remain friends with my husband.'

Alf slumped at this and said, 'You're right there. I'll get off then.'

Our Doris grabbed his arm and glared with eyes that fierce she gave Christopher Lee a run for his money. She said to him, she said, 'You're going nowhere, Alfred Simpson. You came to me with a problem and we're going to solve it – I can't let you go home without a wedding ring, what would Edith say? No, we're going to get it back. Now, stop moping and have a cup of tea – there's bourbons in the tin.'

I sat there, my mouth floundering. I had no idea what to say. I hadn't been able to get a word in edgewise with our Doris's ranting and I knew it definitely weren't my place to start talking but I still ended up saying, and it must've pleased our Doris to hear me say it, I said, 'How's it going with Erin?'

Our Doris beamed at this and said to me, she said, 'We've had some luck. Mrs Porter has agreed to let Erin sit an exam next Monday that should guarantee her the grade required to enrol on her course.'

'Does Erin have the knowledge to pass?' I said, dunking a rich tea biscuit into my now-lukewarm tea.

Our Doris said to me, she said, 'I've decided to kill two birds with one stone, our 'arold. Theo will be here at nine o'clock in the morning to tutor Erin. She'll get onto this course if she has to take every exam in the country.'

Next morning, I came downstairs to find our Theo slumped over the kitchen table, intent on using a box of corn flakes as a pillow. I said to him, I said, 'How do, Theo?' and received something of a grunt in reply. At least our Angela would be happy, she'd finally be able to return to a normal sleeping pattern. I made Theo a strong cup of tea with an extra spoonful of sugar to really get his motor running. I've never known why folk bother with Lucozade – there's no amount of listlessness I haven't found cured with a good cup of PG Tips.

Erin arrived at ten o'clock, shortly followed by our Doris. They'd been out early getting supplies – revision guides, notebooks, stationary, wall charts – their bags were that full I'm surprised our Doris didn't come out with shares in Staples.

I said to her, I said, 'By 'eck, our Doris, Erin's test is only on Monday, what've you gone buying all this for?'

'Sorry, Mr Copeland,' Erin piped up, 'I didn't know what I'd need and I want to do this properly. I can't wait.'

Our Theo were well and truly gone, his snoring that low he could've been a tumble dryer.

I turned to Erin and said to her, I said, 'You don't need to empty your wallet to fill your head, Erin. Don't stress yourself out. Once Theo comes round he'll help you no end.'

Our Doris didn't leave it ten seconds before she yelled at Theo to pull himself together and I took the opportunity to run off into the living room, Rip-Off Britain had an expose on Age UK that I didn't want to miss.

Over the next few days our Theo and Erin squirrelled themselves away in the kitchen. Erin went mad with post-it-notes. I kept opening the bread bin to find colour-coded notecards stuck to my Hovis. Theo made use of our Wi-Fi to show Erin instructional videos he deemed basic and I found so convoluted I went to bed with my Clive Cussler.

Throughout this our Doris fielded queries from the press. Someone from the Partridge Mews Gazette came to interview Erin only to be turfed out when he mentioned our Doris's community order. She's said if that ends up in the newspaper then she'll show him what damage she can really do with a pair of secateurs.

Our house was practically a Buddhist temple that weekend it were that quiet.

I should've known it wouldn't last.

After being in that kitchen for so long together I

ought to have anticipated they'd get some sort of cabin fever. I sat in the living room watching Sunday Brunch when the illusion of silence were shattered like crockery at a Greek dinner party.

'This isn't rocket science, Erin, just answer the question!' Theo roared with all the intensity of a billy goat.

She said to him, she said, 'Of course it's not rocket science – they let you do it, don't they? Call yourself a tutor? I'd have more luck with an aubergine.'

'I never called myself a tutor,' Theo went on, clearly forgetting just whose house he was in, he said, 'Nan asked me to help because you're that much of a lemon you couldn't learn yourself.'

'A lemon? Mrs Copeland asked you to help to stop you being such a layabout.'

I could have intervened. I were just about to rise from my chair when our Doris got involved. She scuttled into the kitchen like she were Apollo 11 on track for the moon, and she said to them, she said, 'Do I look like I'm running a public house? When I purchased a Magnet kitchen it wasn't so as you two could hold slanging matches over my granite work tops.'

Both of them suitably chastised, our Doris returned to her cubbyhole for the remainder of the weekend.

She had been mostly absent since I told her about Janice Dooley. Alf kept himself scarce – hopefully his Edith wouldn't find out about the wedding ring before our Doris had chance to get it back.

Monday morning arrived with little else happening. We dropped Erin off for her test and she were as pale as Casper the Friendly Ghost after a prostate exam. I said to her, I said, 'You've every right to be nervous,

Erin, but I'm sure you'll do great. All the time you've put in revising will be evident today, trust me.'

Our Doris nodded and said, 'There's no harm in failing, Erin. You are well on your way to becoming a model citizen whose worth cannot be graded by a mere mathematics examination.'

'Right, I'm going,' Erin said, 'Mrs Copeland has her posh head on – she must mean business.'

'Good luck,' I said.

She took one glance at our Doris and replied, 'And you, Mr Copeland.'

Once Erin left, I said to our Doris, I said, 'Just why have you got your posh head on, our Doris?'

She gave me the Look and said, 'That is a term of endearment from Erin who doesn't know any better, our 'arold. You, however, have been my husband for well over fifty years and you will behave as such.'

'You're avoiding the question.'

'We're going to the Blind Cat, if you must know.'

'How do you know Janice'll be there?'

Our Doris met my eyes with a look so ferocious she'd make mincemeat of Brunhilda. Her fingers clenched her handbag as though it weren't genuine Italian leather from a small Devonshire boutique. And she said to me, she said, 'When Violet went to the papers with Doug's affair it wasn't just his name she dragged through the mud but everyone who ever associated with him. He is a former councillor – a lot of people have worked with him and because of what he and Janice Dooley of Little Street did, we have all faced consequences.

'Doug had the sense to run off to Madeira and have a heart attack but Janice is still here, lingering like black mould on a wet tile. If there are men with loose morals at the Blind Cat then Janice will be there.'

I stared at our Doris open-mouthed. I'd never seen her so rattled and that included the time on Bake Off when Diana took Iain's Baked Alaska out of the fridge.

I buckled my seatbelt and said to our Doris, I said, 'We best be going then.'

We met Alf outside the Blind Cat. He'd dressed up – wore a navy blue suit that spotless he looked fit for court. He came over and said to us, he said, 'Our Edith thinks that I'm out on a day trip with the old fogies – we'll have to go for fish and chips after – she only gave me enough pocket money for myself though.'

Our Doris cocked her head to the side and said, 'Edith will not find out about today, Alf, for our sake as much as yours. What would people think if they heard that Doris Copeland, interim chairwoman of the WI, was seen entering the Blind Cat?' She bustled towards the front door and we followed.

Alf met my eyes and I shrugged in response. When our Doris has a plan it's best not to question her – she lost an entire group of Girl Guides in Greenfields forest in nineteen fifty-seven and only brought them back once they'd found Mona Whittaker's patent leather pumps.

Our Doris had her nose turned up as soon as we set foot in the place. She avoided looking at the floor, as though one glimpse of the various stains would cause her to go weak at the knees. She made for the bar and ordered herself a bottle of tonic water, leaving me to pay as she surveyed the area, her eyes searching the craggy faces most associated with the Blind Cat. I knew that Norman Turner had a bad divorce but I'd never have thought to see him there. He'd been a greengrocer and now he sat in the corner like something out of

Gremlins.

I paid the barmaid and that's when our Doris clapped eyes on Janice Dooley. I'm surprised Janice didn't melt on the spot – her entire form disintegrated by the sheer intensity of our Doris's glare.

I felt like I were watching a Western, the way our Doris approached her, each step hard against the hardwood floor so that she sounded like she were either determined or testing the strength of her new hip.

Our Doris reached the table and said to Janice, she said, 'I do wish we didn't have to meet under such circumstances, Miss Dooley, our disagreements being so widely publicised, but then you have always been something of a parasite so I shouldn't be surprised.'

Janice were stunned.

I were stunned.

Every customer in the Blind Cat were stunned.

Our Doris had done something never before done by our Doris. She had openly offended Janice Dooley of Little Street.

Usually she minces her words, hides her insults behind veiled niceties but this time she'd gone for straight up insulting.

Janice stammered for a moment before replying, she said, 'Nice to see you too, Doris.'

'I imagine it must be. Now, we have some business to attend to and then I'll take my leave – lord knows there are scents less odoriferous in a slurry pit.'

Janice offered something akin to a smirk and said to our Doris, she said, 'I won that game fair and square – Alf wants the ring, someone's going to have to win it back.'

Our Doris sat across from Janice and said, 'Though I doubt you've ever played a fair game in your life, I'm glad you're willing to relinquish the ring.' She paused for a moment, sighed and went on, 'Very well, Miss Dooley, we will play a game of dominoes.'

Janice chugged back her Carling like it were cough mixture before asking, she said, 'And if I win?'

Our Doris said, 'If you win you keep the ring.'

'And?'

'Surely you can't expect more than that. Need I remind you that I am Mrs Doris Copeland? I once arranged a luncheon for the mayor with a budget of five pounds fifty and a kilo of frozen prawns – not the type of woman you see speaking to women such as yourself.'

'What do you mean such as myself?' I can't say that Janice looked affronted. It's hard to look affronted when you've got that many wrinkles you question the structural integrity of your cheekbones.

Our Doris said to her, she said, 'Janice, you've been with that many sailors the navy call you shore leave. The only reason folk would think we were talking was if you'd stolen something of mine.'

'Like your husband?'

I intervened here and said to Janice, I said, 'I prefer my women with something about them, not those whose only claim to fame is re-enacting the Kama Sutra in a transit van.'

'Can we just play dominoes?' Alf cut in, 'We know Janice is a tart, do we always have to repeat it? It's like flaming ITV3.'

I could see our Doris holding back a grin as she said, 'I do so apologise, Alf. Although the ring is important to me, when I meet Miss Dooley I can't help but be astounded by the fact that she's had more truckers than the Mersey tunnel. Now, shall we get on?'

Janice said nothing as she removed the dominoes

from her bag and set them on the table.

I were tense as anything. My shoulders were pressed that hard against my ears I questioned whether I had any neck left. All the air had fled my lungs so that I watched the game unsure as to whether I'd still be alive to catch the outcome.

As it happened our Doris lost within two minutes, all the time it took for Janice to down another pint.

'Guess I'm keeping the wedding ring after all,' Janice said, her grin wide enough to go spelunking amongst her dentures.

Our Doris remained regal. She sat, ever the lioness, and indulged Janice for a few moments. I could sense it in the air, almost like egg mayonnaise on a hot day without the threat of salmonella – there were this tingling of anticipation as I watched our Doris's smile unfurl like a snake from a washing basket. I swear she could've been an anaconda as she said to Janice, she said, 'Not necessarily.'

Janice's face warped. She'd gone from grinning to questioning in one fell swoop, looking somewhat like a constipated alpaca. And she said to our Doris, ever wary, she said, 'What do you mean?'

Our Doris picked up one of her dominoes and said, 'There are six dots on one half of this domino and five on the other, yet the matching domino, the winning domino I might add is also on the table. How can there possibly be two in a set?'

She shrugged, sighed and refused to let Janice continue as she said, 'It's probably an error on the manufacturer's part. I can't possibly blame you for that. I imagine you only ever play those who are a tad inebriated and unable to notice these things as a sober player like myself can.

'No, I lost. But you're still going to give the ring back.'

'I don't think so.'

This is where our Doris got venomous. She went straight for the jugular, teeth bared, I were surprised her tongue weren't forked as she said to Janice, she said, 'It wasn't a question. Nor, was it a demand. You will give the ring back.

'A few months ago, my dear friend Alf was mugged. He did not notice anything missing at the time but it has since come to his attention that he has lost his wedding ring. The same ring that a certain Janice Dooley of Little Street has been flaunting in this very pub.'

'That's a bare-faced lie.'

'Is it?' Our Doris sipped her tonic water before going on, 'Perhaps you inadvertently came across it in the street where Alf was attacked and never got around to taking it to the proper authorities. Perhaps your niece, Ruby, the perpetrator of such an attack gave you a gift you assumed was perfectly above board.'

'You're getting too big for your boots, Doris. Someone's going to have to knock you down a peg or two.'

Our Doris held out her hand and said to Janice, she said, 'I'm sure they'll try, but let's hope they'll know how to trim their nose hairs. Ring. Now. Otherwise I'll tell the league all about that business with Billy Drayton.'

'Who's Billy Drayton?' I asked.

No one answered. Janice, more cowed than a beef burger handed the ring to Alf without another word.

He were ecstatic. It were reminiscent of when his Aunty Mabel bought him his first yo-yo in nineteen forty-six.

Our Doris stood and said to him, she said, 'You'll want to wash that before you wear it, Alf. You could end up with an infection not suited to a semi-detached household.' And finally, she leant down to Janice Dooley of Little Street and said to her, she said, 'I've been more kind than I had to be here, Miss Dooley. If I so much as hear a whisper of your philandering near my family and friends again I will take this further than I ever have before. I will make things so unpleasant that Guantanamo Bay will seem like Butlins, do you understand?'

After she nodded her head we left Janice seething.

Back in the car, I said to our Doris, I said, 'Who's Billy Drayton?'

She shook her head and absent-mindedly said, 'No idea – she's had that many acquaintances I imagine she couldn't spot a fake one if she tried.'

As promised, we ended up at Pete's Chippy for lunch with Erin and Theo. We assembled ourselves at a table, I were that eager to know the exam had gone I might as well have had a cricket under my ribcage.

I said to Erin, I said, 'How did it go?'

I thought she'd tease us, say as she'd failed before revealing the truth but the smile on Erin's face told us everything we needed to know as she said to us, she said, 'I passed – I can start my course in September.'

Our Doris beamed and said, 'I am pleased – and thanks are also due to Theo for helping you in your endeavours.' She raised her mug of tea. 'I'd like to raise a toast to family – may we always support each other in our times of need, no matter how trivial the problem. To Erin and Alf.'

We toasted the two of them and I saw a twinkle in

Alf's eye that could have been tears or the glint from his reclaimed wedding ring. Either way, he put his cup down and said to our Doris, he said, 'Thanks Doris. I got myself into a mess with Janice Dooley I didn't think I'd be able to get out of. If we should be toasting anyone it's you – you can be a bit pernickety but you still found time to help a drunken lout with a penchant for stealing pork pies.'

Erin nodded at this and added, she said, 'And I thought you'd be asking Evie to move days at the shop but you're helping me get on in life, Mrs Copeland, there's not many as would do that.'

Theo piped up with, 'Stop complimenting her. Nan's got a big enough head as it is – much more and she won't fit through doorways.'

Our Doris's smile couldn't have been wider as she said to them, she said, 'Thank you for your kind words, I am most appreciative. Of course I helped you both – the interim chairwoman of the Partridge Mews Women's Institute cannot be seen to be unsociable. Now, drink your tea before it gets cold.'

Our food arrived and we set about eating, all worries cast aside for the time being.

5

SOMETHING WICKED

Our Doris has gone missing. Once the Partridge Mews Gazette labelled her as a Satanist she disappeared into the ether and I've not seen hide nor hair of her since.

It all started a fortnight ago.

I was in the back garden raking leaves. Our Doris says that although she is a staunch supporter of autumn she believes it to be the underclass of all seasons, leaving its detritus for those of a more tolerable nature to tidy away. Not that she ever rakes any leaves, prunes any flowers, or sprays the drive with Round-Up. No, our Doris freely admits that she's a silent partner in all our horticultural endeavours.

My new knee had just begun to twinge when she appeared at the back door, ever menacing as she said to me, she said, 'I have put the tea things out, our 'arold, do come inside.'

I returned the rake to my shed and went inside. Our Doris had brought out the carrot cake. She wanted to host an authentic autumnal feast with foodstuffs appropriate to the season, I'd had my fill of pumpkins and squashes and fruit breads - minus cranberries in case she invited Mrs Wainthropp with the blood disorder.

I said to her, I said, 'Haven't you held enough dinner parties in the past to know just what to include in an autumnal feast?'

She didn't give me the Look. Not that look anyway, no, she came across all pitying as though I'd asked a question so inept it wasn't worthy of her comment as she said to me, she said, 'But we have been through this, our 'arold, though I love nothing more than when you notice my talents I must remind you that all talents must be practised and honed and in this case although I have held feasts of this ilk before I must still endeavour to impress our guests. Theresa Cadogan would have a field day if I served the same venison casserole I served in nineteen eighty-three.'

I said, 'If you served the same venison casserole you served in ninety eighty-three she'd be dead.'

And she gave me this smile as she said to me, 'Now, 'arold, one mustn't forget the silver lining.'

Which is why it came as a surprise when I sat down at the kitchen table and our Doris said, 'I've decided to replace my autumnal feast with a Halloween banquet, something I've always been against as you and I both know.'

I said, 'I thought you despised Halloween, said as it was a glorification of childhood obesity and gangland crimes.'

Our Doris poured me a mug of tea. I know our Doris is being serious when she gets out the mugs. My Aunty Geraldine collapsed in a Tesco Metro doing the tango and even that wasn't serious enough for our Doris to get out the mugs. She took a great gulp from her own mug, another oddity considering she's spent seventy-three years refining her sips, they must be dainty so as any potential adversaries don't question her status as a woman but also aggressive enough that they know she won't allow any trifling, and she said to me, our Doris said, 'Although it is my firm belief that Halloween is a dastardly endeavour created for the sheer purpose of making money from the more superstitious lunatics on the planet, it has come to my attention that Theo has attended Halloween parties since he was four years old - something our Angela failed to mention - and when I spoke to him he informed me that Halloween is a long-standing tradition that has had the unfortunate fate of being commercialised by big business. And that is why, against my better judgement, I have deigned to hold my first politically correct Halloween banquet free from cultural appropriation and Batman.'

'Why Batman?'

Our Doris said, 'I've never been one for Val Kilmer, even after all that business with Nicole Kidman.'

I said to her, 'So how do you go about hosting a Halloween banquet free of cultural whatchamacallit?'

'Appropriation - and as someone who has steered clear of those wonders too dark and mysterious for mortal minds, I haven't the foggiest, that's why I've invited a member of the local Wicca group to come for afternoon tea today.'

'Great,' I mumbled into my mug. Afternoon tea meant as I wouldn't be getting lunch. It meant I'd have to go hungry until our Doris presented me with cucumber sandwiches cut into triangles, both bread and cucumber sliced that thin it's like eating air, with the cucumber comes the inevitable wind that leaves you unable to get through Emmerdale without belching. At least there'd be cake. More cake. It wasn't like I had devoured enough cake in the last month to solve the world hunger crisis.

Our Doris, on the verge of the Look, some squinting with only a hint of the demonic spark, said to me, she said, 'Please do modify your language, our 'arold. Miss Moonflower shan't be too impressed with mortal folk if you become a monosyllabic grouch at the first sign of scones.'

'You never mentioned scones, our Doris.'

'You never thought to ask. Do scones make a difference?' The spark in her eye had become something of a twinkle.

'Of course scones make a difference. Scones are pure gluttony - if there's jam and cream. Will there be jam and cream?'

'When have you ever known me serve scones without jam and cream? I might be more than experimental with my culinary skills but I still haven't found a better substitute for such a classic dish.'

After that she gently forced me to eat a slab of carrot cake and comment on the use of spices, she nearly decapitated me when I said as her delicate use of nutmeg was about as delicate as Gorgonzola.

We had our tea and the preparations for Miss Moonflower's visit began. Our Doris had me unearth the Bible and stash it in my shed, hide any silver and remove any plants in case they had hidden mystical properties.

I said to our Doris, I said, 'Since when have lilies had hidden mystical properties?'

She came over all proper then and replied, she

said, 'I am planning a politically correct Halloween party with the possibility of a sensible séance. I don't want to offend anyone who could potentially put a curse upon this household.'

I looked at her all gone out and said, 'They're Wiccan, not witches, our Doris. It's a religion. They're not about to arrive on broomsticks, flinging toads at our rhododendrons.'

She held her tongue. I could see her mulling it over, could practically hear the cogs ticking overtime in her head before she said to me, she said, 'That may be so but we'll leave the flowers in the back bedroom – we think we're inviting the next Samantha Stephens into our home but will just as likely end up with Morticia Addams.'

Three o'clock arrived with someone knocking at the front door. I were filled with dread, as though Miss Moonflower's knocking were some sort of death knell. Some might say as I see too many portents of doom in things, I say that when you've known our Doris for as long as I have it's hard not to.

Our Doris opened the front door with a grand flourish, like she were throwing open the doors of Windsor Castle.

Miss Moonflower had stepped out of a medieval tapestry. A veritable giant of a woman, she must've stood about seven foot tall in her fur-lined boots. I'd never seen a Wiccan before but she wore a dark green cloak with pride, looking something like a long lost descendant of Robin Hood, and I couldn't help but question whether this was the uniform.

At least she didn't have a broomstick.

Our Doris beamed at the young woman like it were going out of fashion before greeting her, she said,

'Miss Moonflower, I am most pleased you could join us on this beautiful autumn afternoon. Would you care to accompany me to the lounge where a humble feast of assorted desserts, sandwiches and hot beverages awaits?'

If Miss Moonflower were shocked she did a good job of hiding it. She stepped forward and said to our Doris, she said, 'Good afternoon, Mrs Copeland, thank you for inviting me. So often I find myself shunned by common folk. It is most agreeable to meet someone willing to associate with those of my nature.'

Our Doris nodded sympathetically as she led Miss Moonflower into the living room. They stopped at the door for our Doris to introduce me and I followed them, confident that no amount of carrot cake would make the next few hours agreeable.

Once we'd assembled ourselves – our Doris in her Arighi Bianchi chair and me in the recliner, letting Miss Moonflower have full rein of the sofa – we got down to business. Our Doris has never been one to mince her words, she said, 'So, Miss Moonflower, that's an interesting moniker. I hope you won't be too offended if I ask if it is your given name.'

After helping herself to some cake she said to us, she said, 'I take no offence at all. No, this is not the name my mortal parents assigned me at birth. This is the name I was destined to have?'

'Destined, you say?' Our Doris stirred her tea the way a matchmaker might, studying our guest.

'I embarked upon an online quest. My name was chosen by a website and since then my fate has been sealed.'

Our Doris's voice now tinged with wariness, she said, 'Is this a website your sisters used upon their first foray into the mystic arts? I imagine the naming means a great deal, especially when parents go to such trouble to name their children suitably.'

'My parents never did understand why I wished to change my name, but Emmeline was a cage, it held me back from seeking my true potential as a queen in my own right.' She certainly knew how to feast like a queen, she shovelled those cucumber sandwiches down her gullet faster than Nora Batty after a cream cake.

'One might consider such a thing an affront to one's parents, after all they do to make their child comfortable, for said heirs to be so unbecoming as to refuse their Christian name. Though, I suppose, if it is part of the Wiccan lifestyle I dare not judge for I do not know the various rites of passage within such a unique religion.'

'Wiccan?' Miss Moonflower looked like someone had stolen her last Malteser as she said to our Doris, she said, 'Mrs Copeland, I'm most sorry to say but I am not the woman you seek.'

'Whatever do you mean?'

'I am not Wiccan, nor have I ever been, I am an elf.'

Our Doris's face sank like brick through a blancmange as she finally started to take note of Miss Moonflower's appearance. I'd been a bit concerned myself, it's not everyday someone turns up at your front door wearing a green hooded cloak. I thought she was just a bit eccentric, a tad too in touch with Mother Nature. Everyone wants to be individual nowadays, there's not a week goes by without someone announcing their desire to live as an artisan mung bean in a studio apartment.

But our Doris would have none of it. She's always

been set in her ways, sometimes I think she only accepted colour television because she got to see Ken Barlow in all his glory.

No, our Doris was perfectly offended.

She fired the Look, every bit the frilled lizard as she said to Miss Moonflower, she said, 'You mean that you have been stringing me along this entire time? I wished to hold a party free of racial stereotypes, that politically correct Mary Whitehouse would have me as head of the BBC.'

'She's dead,' the elf pointed out.

And our Doris raged. She bypassed the Look and went straight for the humiliation. She said, 'If I'm to believe that you're a tree-bark feasting elf shouldn't you believe in the powers of the long-since passed? No, don't you dare think to answer. I invited you into my home and you have proven that you are nothing but a charlatan, preying on ladies of a sensitive disposition.'

'I've no idea what you're talking about. You came to our meeting in the library.'

'Because you were speaking in tongues.'

'We were speaking Elvish.'

'To the unsuspecting British person on British shores in these uncertain times of ours it could have been any number of foreign languages. How was I to know you weren't summoning Satan from the very depths of Hell?'

Miss Moonflower glared at our Doris, her face that screwed tight with anger she could have been a gargoyle as she said, she yelled, 'I can't believe I thought you'd be any different than the rest of the people in this town. Your mind has been dulled by consumerism, tainted by the class system so ingrained into this country. Though, I too, was born a mortal, I have grown to accept my heritage. Alas, it may already be too late for you, Mrs Copeland.' She stuffed her pockets full of cake and stormed out.

'Good riddance to you!' our Doris yelled after her, as the front door slammed. If she'd damaged the paintwork her life wouldn't be worth living. Our Doris turned on me and said, she positively seethed, 'Can you believe it, our 'arold? I mean, really, there were no illusions when I set foot in the library. I asked as to the purpose of their meeting – she says as they're a practising religion whose only wish is to get back in touch with nature. I didn't mention there's a perfectly good forest up the road, no, I politely accepted their words and invite their leader around for afternoon tea for a proper consultation. Who in their right mind would believe they were blithering elves?'

I helped myself to a scone and said to our Doris, I said, 'We'll keep her in mind for the Christmas do.'

She calmed down slightly and said to me, she said, 'I suppose she would add an air of authenticity beside Father Christmas. Perhaps I could get Melissa Hodgkinson to dig out her Frosty the Snowman.' Our Doris stood up and set about removing the afternoon tea things and said, 'You deserve that scone, our 'arold, but I can't help feeling rather peckish myself. How about I make some sandwiches fitting for a middle-class home with two televisions?'

I said, 'I'd like that,' and she scuttled off into the kitchen.

Our Doris spent the next few days in search of witches. She rang a number from an old phone book only to discover the Spiritualist church had been replaced by a Chinese. She spoke to fortune tellers and naturalists, herbalists and Methodists and came no closer to finding an answer to her questions.

No one wished to tell our Doris what to include in a Halloween feast.

In the end she got our Theo to come around and use the internet, something she'd never usually do as she says that although the internet was created with the best of intentions it has since become riddled by keyboard warriors and pornography. Either way, desperate times called for desperate measures and our Doris had no choice but to get our Theo to bring his laptop around and scour the world wide web.

He said to our Doris, he said, 'Why do you need witches, Nan? You know we can just research the origin of Halloween instead.'

Our Doris shook her head and said, she said, 'The internet was created by mortal beings such as ourselves, Theo, and we are fallible. Of course we could research the origin of Halloween on the internet, but would we be getting a precise and accurate history or one person's subjective account? The reason I must find an actual consultant in all things Wiccan is because they will know the subtle intricacies that will add a truly authentic feel to my banquet.'

Theo rolled his eyes and set about typing that quickly I wondered that it wasn't an Olympic sport. After half an hour of searching we discovered a self-proclaimed medium who agreed to a consultation that evening.

Our Doris said to me, she said, 'We're going to visit Mrs Wanda Sykes at her home so as she may show us the full extent of her abilities.'

I said, 'I thought you only want to be politically correct.'

'I've made that mistake once. This time she can

prove she's genuine.'

We sent Theo on his way and made our way to Wanda's house. When I think about mediums or witches or anything otherworldly I envisage them living in some sort of Gothic manor. I imagine it to be sprawling, all turrets and spikes with mist and wolves and shadows at the windows. I don't expect to find myself outside a semi-detached council house in need of double-glazing, but this is where I found myself. I could have stayed home and seen some poor beggar bumped off Emmerdale but no, I followed our Doris to the home of Mrs Wanda Sykes, medium and mobile nail technician.

When I first saw her all I thought was red – she had hair such a shade of pillar box red she'd have Toyah running scared.

Our Doris said to her, she said, 'Good evening, Mrs Sykes, my name is Doris Copeland, interim chairwoman of the Partridge Mews Women's Institute, we spoke on the phone regarding your communication with souls long past.'

Wanda looked like the only things she communicated with were sausage rolls, never mind spirits. She wore Tesco's finest jogging bottoms and her vest rolled up her stomach revealing all her worldly cellulite. She said to us, she said, 'We sure did. Come in, the lads are in the living room - I've put them a film on, they won't give us any bother.'

'Will they be part of the séance?' our Doris asked as we followed Wanda into her house.

She shook her head and said, 'No, let me take you through to the retreat. It's in the back garden so I hope that weather doesn't get too bad.'

Our Doris nodded, ever the diplomat and said to

her, she said, 'I am confident that should the weather become too inclement then your retreat would provide adequate shelter.'

Incense sticks burned in the hallway, the odour caught at the back of my throat like bad whisky. Three men in their early twenties sprawled on a well-worn three piece suite in the living room Wanda lead us past to get to her retreat.

When we reached the back garden I knew that Mrs Wanda Sykes of Gaskell Lane could embroider the truth because as I clapped eyes on her retreat I said to her, I said, 'It's a shed.'

Wanda didn't take too kindly to this. She gave me a look our Doris would have been proud of and said to me, she said, 'It's a retreat where the spirits find solace enough to contact me.'

Our Doris spoke up here and said to Wanda in tones that to anyone else would appear mousey but I knew she were as confident as a hare after a tortoise, she said, 'Excuse me for saying, Mrs Sykes, but to the untrained eye it does look rather like a shed.'

Wanda bristled more than a gorse bush here as she said to us, she said, 'You came to me for help. This is my home and that is my retreat, you can like it or lump it.' She folded her arms, giving her the added benefit of looking like the Michelin man.

'It seems we've got off on the wrong foot.'

'No, it's fine. I've dealt with the elderly before – just because you're closer to spirits yourself you think you can say whatever you like.' And she lead us into her shed.

Our Doris bit her tongue as Wanda seated us in deck chairs by an old plastering table. It was that cold I was glad for my thermal socks. Fairy lights hung like disgruntled garlands around the shed, nailed into the rotting wood. This great odour of damp had me on the verge of sneezing.

Wanda said to our Doris, she said, 'Now, Mrs Copeland, I want to make sure you know I'm not a witch but a medium. I am a conduit for spirits to communicate with their loved ones – it is not usually in my nature to converse with the other realm under such circumstances.'

'I understand completely, but I think even the dead can appreciate the need for a politically correct Halloween soiree. I'm planning a pumpkin gazpacho.'

'And the payment?'

'I'm sorry?' our Doris said, looking as though the damp were getting on her sinuses as well.

'Connecting with the dead has adverse effects on the body and it is only natural that I ask for some form of compensation.' This was clearly a speech Wanda had rehearsed and utilised repeatedly.

Our Doris swallowed this down. She seethed – the blood practically bubbling beneath her skin. I hadn't seen her so incensed about paying for something since Mrs Pritchard-Singh tried to charge her for murdering her goldfish.

Our Doris said to Wanda, she said, 'Naturally once you prove your talents I'll be more than happy to offer you some form of recompense. I only wish you had mentioned something on the phone so as I may have prepared for such a revelation. After all, should your services prove inadequate I will not be continuing our business and will seek another professional consultant.'

Wanda looked at our Doris all gone out. I could tell she were trying to figure out what our Doris just said.

She does like to ramble does our Doris. Anthony Green had gone purple by the time our Doris finished lecturing him about pulling his zipper up too fast when she caught him with our Angela in August nineteen eighty-seven.

We got ourselves settled and Wanda began the séance.

Wanda didn't use cards or a Ouija board. She must've worried about potential fire damage to the shed because instead of burning incense sticks she had a Glade air freshener. Perhaps spirits are attracted to the scent of fresh laundry.

Wanda had us hold hands. I knew she'd do something modern and homeopathic the second I met her. Hand holding is such a new-fangled idea. My parents were married for forty years and they never held hands, even with my father on his death bed, Mum sat and read her Rosamund Pilcher.

Wanda's hands were greasy, like she'd dipped her hands in Crisp n' Dry before sitting down.

I didn't sense any change but she must have done because no sooner had we held hands than she proclaimed she had someone ready to speak to us.

I said to her, I said, 'I hope it's not the gas man.'

Our Doris gave me the Look and said to me, she said, 'I'll have you know I've heard quite enough about the gas man and your Aunty Margaret to last me a life time, our 'arold.'

'I don't mention it that often.'

'Good, you'll take care not to mention it again.'

'If you two would stop arguing, you're creating a very hostile environment for the spirit.'

'That's what they said about Aunty Margaret and the gas man.'

Wanda thought she'd caught on to something here. Her gaze calculating as she said to me, she said, 'Now, isn't it strange that you'd mention an Aunty Margaret because guess who just so happens to have something to say to you?'

'It won't be anyone I want to talk to,' I said.

'Not even your Aunty Margaret?' Wanda asked with a smile on her face.

'If that's my Aunty Margaret you're being conned.'

Wanda's face fell. 'I don't get what you're saying.'

'My Aunty Margaret is in residential care in Devon. She might be ninety-eight but she refuses to die until she's got her letter from the queen.'

Wanda shook it off and said to me, she said, 'I must have become confused with all the excitement, I'll just check.' She closed her eyes here and began some strange chanting that sounded like it were pulled straight from The Lion King soundtrack. This went on for a while before she went on and said, 'Does the letter R mean anything to you?'

I shrugged. 'Apart from coming between the letters Q and S, not really.'

'No distant relatives? Childhood friends? Long-lost relatives?'

'I wouldn't know about them if they were long-lost would I?'

Our Doris interjected here with a cry of, 'Harold Copeland! How dare you be so insolent in front of our hostess? Mrs Sykes has given up her evening, the least we can do is be co-operative.'

'Fine.' I turned back to Wanda, and I were moody, every inch the chastised choir boy as I said to her, I said, 'I'm sorry if I haven't been co-operative but there's no one I can think of who'd want to contact me.'

This was clearly the height of entertainment for Wanda who did nothing to hide the smirk on her face. She said to me, she said, 'It's fine, Mr Copeland, most folk get a bit uneasy at the thought of speaking to the dead. Let's channel our energy into calming this spirit down, whoever it may be.'

She closed her eyes again and my spine instantaneously became an icicle, transformed by something I were certain was otherworldly. I thought that was it, that I, Harold Copeland, would die in a garden shed on a council estate. If I did our Doris would never forgive me – she'd give me a poor man's burial and cast herself off to Mavis's to hide her shame.

The air grew thick with smoke. Our Doris stifled a cough with her M&S handkerchief and said to Wanda, she said, 'Must we really endure these theatrics? I'd like to hold my banquet without bronchitis, thank you very much.'

Wanda said to us, she said, 'This isn't my doing, Mrs Copeland, this is a malevolent spirit we're dealing with.'

'And could you perhaps inform me as to why you chose to conjure such a spirit? I had hoped for someone more worldly like Winston Churchill or Clarissa Dickson Wright.'

'I have no control over who wishes to escape the confines of the other realm.'

'I must say that does sound rather like codswallop. You're a medium, surely you have a duty to make sure no undesirables manage to sneak through – what would you do if someone expects their great uncle Albert and ends up talking to a deceased Soviet spy.'

Wanda remained expressionless as she said to our

Doris, she said, 'We are currently being visited by a malevolent spirit, could you please give me some time to get rid of it?' She started chanting again and what small light we had extinguished, leaving nothing but a bright green dot in the corner, blinking through the smoke. If anything were malevolent it were that light, little more than a pin-prick but enough to send fear shooting through me like Tropicana through a toddler.

I were certain my number was up, questioning why I bothered with the new knee because it clearly hadn't covered its running costs, when our Doris said, she said, 'I'm most apologetic to disturb your chanting, Mrs Sykes, but the light from your Wi-Fi router does shatter the illusion somewhat.'

Wanda's eyes flew open faster than pigeons after a Range Rover. Looks can't kill you but hers looked dangerous as she said to our Doris, she yelled, 'What're you trying to say, you daft bat?'

Our Doris held her composure as she said, 'I'm not that up to date with technology but I'm quite confident that all the smoke and tomfoolery is being controlled by a wireless network, meaning that although you put on an excellent show you're not quite communicating with the dead.'

'How dare you?' I noticed that as the two of them conversed, the smoke had dissipated and the fairy lights came back to life.

'I notice you don't deny the accusation. Clearly your only concern is earning money – something to be commended nowadays, but preying on the chairwoman of a provincial Women's Institute is quite unacceptable.'

'I'll have you know I'm a qualified medium.'

'What qualifications do you need to make smoke and scare some older people?' Our Doris took out her purse and place ten pounds on the table. She said to Wanda, she said, 'You've no worry. I won't tell anyone you're a fake – you do put on a good show, you just didn't fool me. You couldn't have if you tried – I was fifth alternate for the magician's assistant in the Greenfields Fete nineteen seventy-three.'

We took our leave, neither of us expecting the repercussions. No, we both went home to bed with no concerns, only to wake up and discover that our Doris had been labelled a Satanist by the Partridge Mews Gazette.

She was front page news with the headline 'Devil in the WI' emblazoned across the photograph taken of our Doris after her infamous Bulge Busters battle with Janice Dooley of Little Street.

Our Doris made us some sausage sandwiches and we sat down to read the article together. She was painted as a geriatric devil worshipper who may also be a member of the Illuminati. The paper questioned whether the WI could be a front for summoning demons from alternate dimensions, and how would this affect immigration laws?

They talked about our Doris's history, dedicating pages four and five to her biography titled 'Portrait of a She-Devil'. The writer questioned whether our Doris's penchant for writing letters wasn't in actual fact Satan's work, if our Doris was trying to sway the public to her way of thinking. He'd even consulted a historian who suggested that due to lack of records there was no way of knowing if she was descended from a long line of witches.

When our Doris read that she yelled, louder than a hippopotamus with a megaphone, she said, 'My father worked in the silk mills – he didn't go around burning black candles and sacrificing livestock.'

And if that wasn't enough, if the paper hadn't delved deeper into our Doris's life than a colonoscopy, they'd interviewed not only Pandra O'Malley but Janice Dooley of Little Street.

I said to our Doris, I said, 'We could sue them for slander. They might have a lot of the facts but they can't legally call your name into question.'

'Did you see the name of the reporter? It's the same one I hit with those secateurs. No, we won't stoop to their level.'

We finished breakfast when someone knocked at the door. I'd just finished putting the pots in the dishwasher as our Doris lead Pandra O'Malley into the kitchen.

'I must say, Pandra, this visit is somewhat unexpected considering you're most concerned about the level of depravity I may be exposing to the WI. Would you care for coffee? Nescafe, I'm afraid, I'm fresh out of eye of newt.'

Pandra remained stoic as our Doris surged towards the kettle. I said to Pandra, I said, 'You'd best take a seat.'

'Yes, do remember to be hospitable to the guest, our 'arold. It's not as though she just stabbed me in the back. Et tu Brutus and all that.' She slammed the kettle with that much force it's a wonder the water didn't instantly boil.

Pandra removed her Florence and Fred beige overcoat and sat down. She said to our Doris, she said, 'Now don't be like that, Mrs Copeland, the newspaper came to me with a question and I answered. You know what it's like.'

Our Doris rolled her eyes and grabbed the mugs

out of the top cupboard, and said, 'Come off it, Pandra, you saw an opportunity to drag my name through the mud and you took it.'

'I believe I am the best person for chairwoman – I don't need to drag anyone's name through the mud to get elected.'

'Are you so sure? Because you did an awfully bad job of it in the article, I can tell you. Please enlighten me, what have I done in the last thirty years to suggest I'm a Satanist?'

Pandra didn't know where to look as she said to our Doris, she said, 'I've spoken to the committee and they believe that the recent revelations may result in an early election.'

Our Doris looked over the dragon with her nostrils flared and a look that vicious I'm surprised her eyes weren't aflame. 'Early election? Of course, I shouldn't expect anything different from you – after all you won't want to give me enough time to redeem myself, will you? I wouldn't expect anything less from a former dinner lady.'

'I was a catering supervisor,' Pandra said, ruffled like a turkey.

'At a private school.'

'I once made dinner for Barbara Knox's third cousin twice removed.'

'I've tried your chicken supreme, you probably served up salmonella on a crispbread.' Our Doris flung the coffee and biscuits on the table in front of Pandra. 'You do look parched. I'm almost reminded of your last Victoria sponge. You understand, don't you, Pandra? Too dry and nobody wants a sample.'

Pandra helped herself to a digestive and said to our Doris, she said, 'I know you're hurt but it's only a bit of friendly competition.'

'Friendly competition? Friendly competition? Since when has friendly competition constituted labelling your running mate as a devil worshipper?' Our Doris snapped a ginger nut in half and threw it into her mouth, not caring that she'd only just finished her breakfast and wouldn't usually allow herself a biscuit for at least three hours afterwards.

'We have known one another for years, Doris. We can't let something as inconsequential as a WI election get in the way.'

'If I remember rightly, you chose to put your name forward for the position.' Our Doris finished her biscuit. These women were clearly mistaken when they called our Doris a Satanist because sat in that kitchen I felt sure we were in the presence of the devil incarnate.

I decided to interrupt them both. I'm not sure why, maybe the blood fled my brain after being stood by the counter for so long but I said to Pandra, I said, 'Before you fling any more insults, why are you here?'

They both looked at me as though they'd forgotten I was there. Pandra looked just like a goldfish, opening and closing her mouth before saying, she said, 'I thought that you'd like to know that the Gazette is planning a follow-up article. They're asking the public for their opinions on Mrs Copeland, Doris, with the intention of making the story known on a national scale.'

Our Doris and I were flabbergasted. I pulled together enough to say, 'How did you find all this out?'

'He rang me this morning to ask if I had anything more to say on the matter.'

'And do you?' I asked.

Our Doris had gone straight for the jugular and

lost any semblance of composure she'd previously entertained, and although I'd love nothing more than for her to let her hair down, I couldn't let her give Pandra O'Malley anymore ammunition.

'I won't say anything else. I'm sorry I hurt you, Doris.'

Our Doris didn't respond. Her shoulders were more rigid than a plasterboard. She clenched her mug like a knuckle duster. She knows how to get angry does our Doris, she's like a milk pan, always simmering but one false move and she'll boil over.

Eventually Pandra left.

I were stuck with a silent Doris. She was a statue. She was stoic. She was ready to take a chunk out of downtown Tokyo.

If we expected things to get better we were mistaken.

Next day, another article appeared in the Gazette this time with a headshot of our Doris beneath the headline, 'I'm a witch!' It turned out that we should never have trusted Pandra O'Malley – she'd recorded the entire conversation and given it to the reporter. If that wasn't bad enough Wanda Sykes had replied to a Facebook thread regarding our Doris's satanic leanings which lead to a subsequent interview in which she relayed how our Doris hadn't been happy that Wanda was unable to open a portal to Hell in time for Halloween. I kept an eye on the lawn, certain that the townspeople would appear with flaming torches threatening to burn the witch.

Still, our Doris didn't speak.

I went out to run some errands and returned to find her gone. I knew I wasn't lucky enough for her to leave me after fifty-five years so I made a brew and found her note. All our Doris's notes are written with a calligrapher's knack for lettering – she took a three month course in nineteen ninety-two to perfect her gs – she does this in case she ends up kidnapped and the note ends up presented as evidence. Her note read, '*Taking Erin out, will be home late, order Chinese.*'

This was a shock in itself. Our Doris always writes in full sentences – says as anything less proves that modern society is in too much of a rush. And she only went and wrote a note that read like ... well, a note.

As a concerned husband, invested in all my wife's worldly pursuits I ordered from Treasure House and sat down in front of The Good, the Bad, and the Ugly to await our Doris's return.

She still wasn't home when I went to bed, nor when I woke up. I rang our Angela but she hadn't heard from her, Erin's phone went straight to voicemail, and no amount of worry would have me ringing Mavis.

I got Alf to come around to the house – there's folk at the Hare and Horse who have said our Doris is in touch with the devil for decades and I wasn't sure I could contain myself if I saw one of their smug faces.

Alf brought a few bottles of Hobgoblin and snuck around the back. He said to me, he said, 'Who's she gone and upset this time, 'arold? Althea Littlewood is telling all and sundry that Doris cursed her Howard to fail his exams.'

'And here I was thinking you had to turn up to fail something.'

We sat down with our ale and I said to him, getting straight to the point, I said, 'Has your Edith heard anything from my wife?'

Alf gave me the answer I should have expected as

he said to me, 'If your Doris is up to something do you think Edith would tell me about it?'

'It was worth a shot. I've no idea where she's gone – the note only said as she was going off with Erin.'

'She can't come to too much harm with Erin around, can she?'

Alf left to go and see Tom about some courgettes and I wondered how long I could make the hoovering last.

Another day passed with no sign of our Doris. Erin telephoned to let me know that she was all right but needed time to put some things together. I said I'd let them get on with it, hoping this wouldn't be a repeat of the great fall-out of April nineteen seventy-one which resulted in several casualties, three broken wing mirrors and the loss of her suede pumps.

Next morning the Gazette landed on my doorstep, a special edition to feature a letter from our Doris. She didn't detail the exact events that led up to the accusations, she didn't call anyone's name into question, she came over all Agatha Christie and revealed the truth would be unveiled that evening at the church hall and all who wanted answers would be welcome.

I spent the rest of the day full of anticipation, restless, unsure of what to do with myself. I made a casserole, I washed the dishes the old-fashioned way and I finished bagging up dead leaves for the compost heap, all before it was time to go.

I put on the navy blue suit and my brown brogues, just in case our Doris happened to be out for blood, and made my way to the church hall.

The car park was jam-packed full of cars. There were a queue out the door – I hadn't seen that much footfall at the church hall since Eleanor Stockwell flashed those toddlers.

I found Alf and Edith and we packed ourselves into the hall like mice in matchboxes. I said to Alf, I said, 'This is cosier than your first flat.'

He nodded and said, 'At least I had space for a bath. They're certainly after haranguing your Doris.'

He was right. They were. Packed in as I was I got to hear everything everyone had to say about our Doris. The heat rose molten in my body as Patricia Dunlop said as our Doris's dinner parties were a front for scoping out who'd make a good witch. Manuela Esperanza joked maybe she wasn't after witches but human sacrifices. Even Joan Heapy got in a dig about the time our Doris pointed out she'd gained four stone at Waitrose in Poynton.

In fact folk talked that much no one noticed our Doris take centre stage until she started speaking. She stood on a small raised platform at the back of the hall with a screen behind her, the overhead projection currently showed a blank screen but it filled me with the sense of dread I usually get when our Doris begins one of her schemes. She has been known to be nefarious when wronged and I knew for certain she wouldn't be any different here.

She said to us all, she said, 'Good evening, ladies, gentlemen, and anyone of indeterminate personage, thank you for allowing me to speak with you tonight regarding something rather close to my heart.'

Our Doris allowed a pause here, making sure she had everyone's attention before she went on, she said, 'Halloween.'

I half-expected a crack of lightning, the rumble of thunder, that the ground would crack around us and we'd plummet into the very depths of Hell. Instead, our

Doris carried on, she said, 'Now, do not fret. My broomstick is in the cupboard next to the Electrolux.'

There were a few laughs but you could cut the tension in the room with a spoon. Everyone was on tenterhooks, some wanting to hear our Doris prove herself a witch, others here simply because there wasn't much doing on the box.

'Back to the topic at hand,' our Doris said, 'Halloween has often been a practise whose association I have refused. It worries me that many use it as an excuse to be mean-spirited, tactless, and downright rude all in the name of trick or treat.

'All publicity is good publicity and this past week has made me feel as though I'm in a Shakespeare production. Macbeth, if you will. I have been visited by three witches who have sought to make my life as uncomfortable as possible, and this is from someone who has spent the better part of sixty years wearing a bra.'

The snickers were louder here but I found myself concerned, our Doris has never been the type to make light of her underwear arrangements. When she goes to get herself measured at Marks and Spencer it's a wonder she doesn't have the girls sign the Official Secrets Act.

Still, our Doris clearly had a point to make and she was going to make it as she said, 'I have been the victim of a vile, cruel prank and although it is my duty as interim chairwoman of the Partridge Mews Women's Institute to retain a degree of aplomb in such situations, my name has been tarnished in such a horrific manner that I have taken the only possible recourse.

'Erin, the first slide please.' Here, I noticed Erin sat at her laptop at the side of the stage, her face illuminated by the blue light so that she looked like some sort of impish assistant. She clicked something and an image of Miss Moonflower appeared on the screen behind our Doris, looking every inch the elf.

Our Doris said, she said, 'This is Emmeline Duvall, otherwise known as Miss Moonflower. She is one of Cheshire East's premier elves – not Christmas elves, mind you, these people will not be making any children happy with gifts. These are fully recognised Tolkienesque elves with a hankering for bathrobes.

'Up until three months ago Miss Moonflower lived a rather sedate home life with a nice little job at Mrs Singh's greengrocers. Most of you will recognise her as the shop girl who wraps your bananas every Saturday for a reasonable price. Erin, the next image.'

Here the screen transformed to reveal grainy CCTV footage with censorial bars covering certain areas of the screen. Miss Moonflower was definitely behind the shop counter, alongside a man who definitely shouldn't have been doing that in a greengrocers.

When the image elicited, 'Oh, Doris, don't do this,' from Edith I knew something had gone terribly awry, that in the grand scheme of things our Doris was committing a social faux pas worse than when she offered Rhiannon Gwyn escargot instead of Welsh rarebit.

Our Doris must've chosen to beggar all consequences because she went on, she said to the crowd, she said, 'Miss Moonflower did well in her job until she was caught with one hand in the till and the other in the trousers of Mrs Singh's son Syed.

'I'm not saying that to have such relations has any negative connotations whatsoever but even I believe that shouldn't happen anywhere near fresh strawberries.

'Subsequently Emmeline, Miss Moonflower, was let go from her position and decided to live her life as an elf. This is a perfectly acceptable practise in this day and age, according to my grandson Theo. It is not acceptable to try and take your former employer to a tribunal citing your alternative lifestyle as the reason for your dismissal. The only thing alternative about your lifestyle was forgetting to put a cushion under your knees.'

This gained a few guffaws from the audience. I stood there and questioned just what effect Erin Beaumont was having on my wife – she'd never been as bawdy before. Beside me Alf's Edith grew more tense, staring at our Doris open-mouthed, shaking her head. I just hoped they didn't fall out – that'd be like firing two torpedoes straight at one another would that.

Our Doris would have continued but for the unrest in the front rows. 'Miss Moonflower, leaving so soon?' She had bundled her cloak around her neck and fled, followed by a group all dressed in elven cloaks, heads down and shoulders hunched.

The image behind our Doris changed to that of Wanda's retreat, zooming in on the wireless modem, including a few screenshots of commands on her computer. The way our Doris were going she might have gone as far as to include Wanda's search history.

'Let's move on to Mrs Wanda Sykes. A self-proclaimed medium and nail technician, she'd do better to take her show to Britain's Got Talent. Myself and my husband attended a séance only to discover it was all a ruse to scam money out of the unsuspecting public. I did not have to break my probation to collect these photographs, her sons were more than happy to send them to me, alongside witness statements – it seems they're quite fed up with their mother's occupation and wish to transform her retreat, as she is want to call it, into a game's room.

'And last but not least we must discuss Mrs Pandra O'Malley, a former friend of mine who has chosen to besmirch my good name in the hopes that she can win favour with our esteemed WI. Sadly, she has made a mockery of something I hold dear and I am left with no choice but to reveal that whilst Mrs O'Malley is not a witch, she is both a fraud and a thief.'

This raised an audible gasp from Edith who grabbed Alf's arm with that much force she nearly tore it from its socket. She said to me, eyes wide enough to be pinned back, she said, 'She should have let this all die down, 'arold. Forgotten the banquet and gone about her business. She is making a farce of the WI and I worry what the committee will do.'

Onstage our Doris continued with her rhetoric, 'Earlier this year Mrs O'Malley began to organise a bake sale to raise funds for a new church roof. Alas, she never planned to host the bake sale. Once she gained all the money she needed she would have put it towards her new Caribbean holiday.

'This may seem like idle speculation from a wronged old woman and because of this I decided to delve into the archives of the Partridge Mews Gazette where I found a rather interesting article. Of course, this was in the days when the Gazette was a respectable newspaper, unlike nowadays when it only seeks to be a slanderous rag perpetuating vitriol towards one of its longest-standing supporters.'

A newspaper clipping from decades ago appeared on the screen behind our Doris. Alf, Edith and I couldn't look away however much we wanted to. It was like watching car crash television, watching one of our own descend into such throes of fury that she had commanded a witch hunt of her very own.

'The font may be too small for you all to read so allow me to elucidate, thirty years ago Pandra O'Malley conned the unsuspecting public out of a few thousand pounds in order to pay for her honeymoon. She did this under the guise of raising money to save the whales.

'It was swept under the rug because we believed she had turned over a new leaf, redeemed herself. She wishes to become the chairwoman of the Women's Institute, and if the events of the last few days have taught me anything it is that she is entirely unsuitable for the role.

'And finally, because I am aware I have gone on for far too long to be anywhere near hospitable, I am not a Satanist. I am Mrs Doris Copeland of Shakespeare Avenue – I have made many enemies in my time but I have never found an ally in the devil. Thank you all for coming and I wish you all a safe journey home.'

There was no applause. Our Doris left us all stunned as she disappeared behind the stage, leaving the crowd to thin as rapidly as it had grown. Pandra O'Malley stood in the centre of the hall, receiving glares, pierced gazes and muttered curses from the people she'd rallied against my wife.

Our Doris was nursing a glass of water when I managed to find her.

I said to her, unable to contain myself, I said, 'What the bleeding heck was that, our Doris?'

She gave me this look like a wounded puppy and said to me, and it is one of those things a husband never wants to hear his wife say, she said, 'I've had enough, our 'arold. I'm constantly fighting a losing battle against people who are nowhere near worth the fight. Let Pandra O'Malley do as she wishes because if I can't be chairwoman I'm going to make sure she can't either.'

I said, 'I'm guessing there won't be a Halloween banquet then?'

'You saw that crowd, our 'arold, we've already raised the dead. They'd never be able to appreciate a politically correct banquet.'

'What will we do then?'

'We'll go to that new restaurant in Wren's Lea, avoid any potential imps after sugar-highs and an obesity ridden future.'

'If you like, our Doris.'

She offered me a smile and said to me, she said, 'Next time your wife considers celebrating such a ridiculous spectacle don't let her.'

I said to her, 'You're never turning over a new leaf are you?'

She shrugged and said, 'Take me home, our 'arold.'

'Gladly.'

We went home, all demons hopefully laid to rest.

6

FLU

Our Doris and I have spent the best part of this week in bed. Sadly, it's not like our younger and more impressionable years when we would explore the length and breadth of one another's bodies, uncovering birth marks, moles and the scar where Ernie Wainwright stabbed me in the leg with a pencil during Mr Cooper's numeracy class. No, if me and our Doris explored each other now we'd need a full archaeological team and a cartographer just to figure out where the wrinkles on my left shoulder are leading.

I wish amorous intentions had left us bedridden, rather than the stinking flu.

I've not been able to breathe properly since Thursday and even then it was only because Ann Hegarty incorrectly answered a question regarding Catherine the Great on The Chase.

The human body is mostly made up of water, mine is mostly made up of snot. I have sneezed and coughed and spluttered that much over the last week I've become a walking ball of mucus.

I blame our Doris, it's not often I can do that but she's practically comatose with this flu so I'm getting it in whilst I can. She got home on Tuesday afternoon having spent the morning performing her duties at the charity shop. She had this look of pure disgust on her face, as though she'd spent most of the day with her head jammed into a dustbin.

I'd been sat at the kitchen table doing the Daily Mirror crossword when she came in. She'd moved that quickly I'd had no choice but to shove the newspaper down my trouser leg. I said to her, I said, 'What's the matter, our Doris?'

I'm a bit wary of her at the moment. Ever since Halloween she's been more high-maintenance than usual, something I hadn't expected as I thought she'd mastered that in nineteen sixty-one.

She paced the carpet like Road Runner and said to me, she said, 'I do not ask for much, our 'arold. Being a white suburban housewife in Cheshire has an air of prestige about it and I want for nothing. I committed an offence and as such partook in my community service today at the charity shop, the same charity shop where an absolute beansprout of a man, waxy, achy, and so close to being a zombie he was practically Frankenstein chose to sneeze on me.'

'He sneezed on you?' I asked, wiggling my leg in the hope the newspaper might fall out onto the floor where I could collect it later.

Our Doris torpedoed towards the kettle and said to me, she said, 'I was on the till, I imagine it's the level of dignity I bring to the role, when this complete plebeian, representing everything wrong with the social underclass, entered the shop making full use of the term, "the great unwashed".

'I, ever the professional hostess offered him a simple greeting, "Good morning, please take care when perusing our wares as all breakages must be paid for." Warm, but enough to make him aware his influenza wasn't welcome.' She rustled up a few pastrami baguettes and brought them to the table before continuing, she said, 'After a completely unacceptable amount of time browsing the shop, this gentleman – and I say that in the loosest sense of the word – approached the counter with not one, but three compact discs of the collected works of Chris de Burgh.

'I hadn't realised he was that popular an artist.

'I mean everyone and their great aunt Beatrice has waltzed to *Lady in Red* but does he really have the appeal of the greats?

'Elvis Presley still reaches number one in the charts – the most we can expect from Chris de Burgh is he'll one day set foot in *I'm a Celebrity Get me Out of Here.*'

'And how exactly does this relate to the curious case of the snotty customer?'

Our Doris gave me the Look and said to me, she said, 'I did go off at something of a tangent but what you must remember, our 'arold, is that I am a storyteller and can tell the story in any which way I choose. If you didn't know that by now I would be greatly concerned as to whether you had finally descended into senility.

'Anyhow, this social degenerate approached the counter. I charged him the customary pound per disc and he took a five pound note from his wallet – a five pound note he promptly sneezed on before handing it over.

'He will have known how angry I was – I didn't offer him a bag, nor did I say, "bless you". Once he went on his merry way I pressed the emergency bell and went to thoroughly disinfect my hands.'

By teatime our Doris complained of a scratchy throat, she coughed a few times during Holby City and went to bed early.

By Wednesday she had flu.

We're both so far past sixty-five we know what a flu jab is like. Our Doris refuses to go after she discovered that Janice Dooley of Little Street goes to the same practice and she will not receive a flu jab when she can't be sure just how Miss Dooley pays for her prescriptions.

Now we both regretted the decision.

I ended up spending Wednesday as a regular Florence Nightingale. I wouldn't have minded if I hadn't already made plans – our Doris should have attended a WI crisis talk with the committee and I planned to catch up with my series link of Mrs Brown's Boys. I can't have it on when our Doris is around because she's taken a personal affront against Ireland. She says as it keeps sending its cast-offs to England in the forms of Louis Walsh, Jedward and, worst of all, Pandra O'Malley.

Instead of watching television I got to ferry chicken soup, hot Vimto and Kleenex to our Doris, checking every few minutes to make sure she hadn't choked to death on her own phlegm.

Erin and Edith arrived just as I'd got our Doris off to sleep. It took the afternoon drama and half a bottle of rum but she were soon snoring for the cheap seats.

I lead them both into the kitchen. They looked as though they'd just walked through a muck midden, their expressions were that glum. Edith kept glancing at Erin all accusatory ready to play Inspector Morse and have Erin as the main suspect.

I said to them, making fast work of brewing tea, I said, 'I'm guessing the crisis talk didn't go too well.'

I've known Edith since we were children, in that time I have seen her throw junk mail at postmen, scorn mothers who allow their kids to cry in public, and tell Arnold Merryweather that his obesity did not give him a free pass to wear jogging bottoms to church. When Edith is angry she lets you know she's angry, and she fired such a ferocious glare at Erin.

She said to me, her tongue practically lathered in venom, she said, 'Of course it didn't go well, Harold. Doris went on stage and made more of a display of herself than Mary Berry does a Victoria sponge. We are a charitable Women's Institute with a great social responsibility and she soiled all our names because she decided to play in the gutter with the likes of this young lady.' Edith shot Erin another side-eyed glare and removed her gloves.

Erin sat down at the table and said to Edith, she said, 'You can say what you like, Mrs Simpson, I've heard it all before.'

I wish our Doris had Erin schooled in conversation rather than mathematics because Edith looked ready to hang her on the back of the door as she said, 'Well it clearly bears repeating because it doesn't sink in. Doris and I have been friends since our gingham days, Miss Beaumont, she is well-versed in the doctrines of polite society she should know better than to go airing dirty laundry to the likes of the Partridge Mews Gazette.'

'Mrs Copeland isn't a jellyfish – she has a spine and a voice and she wished to speak out against Pandra O'Malley.'

Edith sat down beside Erin and said, 'She has responsibilities.'

I were grateful the kettle boiled at that moment, I poured the water that quickly it spilled over onto the counter but I didn't have time to wipe it up, I needed to get the tea to the table before nuclear war broke out near our Doris's sideboard.

I realised Erin hadn't heard of tact as she said to Edith, she said, 'I don't deny you're Mrs Copeland's friend but as a friend shouldn't you be sticking up for her? The paper had her as a witch ready to raise the devil – did you offer any support?'

'Doris knows I care.'

'Good for her because all I know is that you hide behind excuses of politeness to avoid saying you didn't do enough.'

I got the tea to the table but I knew it were too late. Edith glared at Erin and said to her, she said, 'Doris is facing expulsion from the WI, an institution she has been part of for most of her adult years. You may think I don't care but I am not sure who she will be without the WI. If she'd followed my advice she wouldn't have that issue.'

Erin scoffed. 'Your advice was to do nothing, at least my way we took action.'

'You fought slander with slander and made fools of yourselves. Can you in all honesty say you helped Doris out of the goodness of your heart, or was it merely revenge against the WI for wronging you?'

'I didn't do this because of some campaign to change my son's name. I did it to help a friend.'

'So you keep saying.'

They sat in silence, making quick work of the tea and biscuits I'd arranged.

We sat there for a while, saying nothing, when our Doris rang the bell I'd left on her bedside cabinet. Lord knows I should have realised she wouldn't be able to sleep through such racket.

She wanted to speak to Edith.

I stayed in the kitchen with Erin, hoping the quiet wouldn't remain as awkward. I needn't have worried, once we heard the door close upstairs the words spilled out of Erin like her mouth was a soda stream as she said to me, she said, 'I'm sorry, Mr Copeland, I had no idea that the WI would think about getting rid of her. I mean, she's the chairwoman for crying out loud.'

I offered her another biscuit and said to her, I said, 'These women are in a different league. We don't question their ways because we've no idea what they're going on about half the time. Mrs Aldrin emigrated to New Zealand in nineteen eighty-eight because of a tiramisu mishap and I've still no idea what was wrong with it.'

'Have they never heard of loyalty?' Erin said.

I'd have answered had Edith not stormed down the landing with all the subtlety of a rhinoceros. She didn't offer any parting words as she turned down the hall and left. The rate our Doris keeps offending folk we may need to reinforce the hinges on the front door because Edith did not hold back as she slammed it shut.

We finished our drinks and went to see our Doris.

Our Doris looked like someone had drizzled icing on her face and left it to dry, a confectioner's Elizabeth First, as she sat regal, her skin pale and sweaty. Her eyes may as well have been closed they were that puffy. Every few minutes she would hack a cough from the very depths of her lungs – some sort of reminder of my wedding vows. Forget in sickness and in health I was married to the living dead.

Usually our Doris won't allow guests into the bedroom, she worries it might give off the impression we're swingers, but for a few special occasions she has allowed a select group of close personal friends an insight into a room where I get to hear the sounds of a safari for free every night.

Our Doris snores.

I thought that over time her subconscious would take hold and she'd refine the snoring to some heavy but bearable breathing.

No.

When our Doris snores she goes for the gold. I've tried getting off to sleep first but inevitably I will be awoken by snores reminiscent of Chester Zoo in surround sound.

The bedroom was styled by our Doris. She had the curtains specially made by a girl on the Gawsworth Road, the fabric is John Lewis and cost that much I have to use off-brand denture adhesive.

There's pine furniture, wardrobe, dresser and the like. The salesman wanted us to go with a shabby chic motif and was told under no uncertain terms that if our Doris wanted distressed furniture she'd have introduced it to his haircut.

Our Doris wanted a bedroom that impressionable Arighi Bianchi would hire her as a window dresser. There's floral wallpaper with colours that match the curtains that match the bedding that I'm sure matches a blouse of our Doris's – maybe they had material left over, it's more than my life's worth to speculate.

Now, our Doris sat swathed from head to toe in florals, ever the dandelion, as she said to us, she wheezed, 'Mrs Simpson and I have had a disagreement, do not remove her from the Christmas card list but do remind me to regift that hemp hand lotion to Mrs Poe's Lawrence.'

I said to her, I said, 'What did you do, our Doris?'

She gave me the Look, or some snotty semblance of it as she said, 'I am incapacitated, our 'arold, I can't be expected to remember who was in the wrong.'

'Did she say anything about the WI?' Erin asked.

Our Doris snivelled and edged the duvet further over her face, looking like I did when my Mum came after me with the olive oil.

I said to our Doris, I said, 'What did you do?'

The duvet just reached her lower lip when she finally decided to speak. The words were little more than a whisper, something akin to a squeak as she said, 'I told her that the WI is dead and I refused to apologise to Pandra O'Malley and she is well and truly beggared if she thinks I have a nice word for Janice Dooley of Little Street, I have tact not miracles.'

Here she embarked upon a coughing fit, and I weren't surprised, no one can go on for that long with flu and expect no consequences.

I said to her, I said, 'Erin says as you could be excluded, shouldn't you say something?'

Our Doris conceded and said, 'I could but my mother taught me better.'

Next day I caught the flu. We did what all septuagenarian parents do when incapacitated, we rang our Angela.

She arrived almost immediately, a tea tray piled with breakfast in her arms. She's a good lass is our Angela, she has her mother's high maintenance without the temper.

Once we'd eaten she got the doctor around who

confirmed that yes we did indeed have flu and was there a reason we failed to have our jabs.

Our Doris said to him, she said, 'Would you ask that of a Jehovah's Witness?'

The doctor looked nonplussed as he asked, 'Why?'

Our Doris, though riddled with snot, still had strength to argue, she said to him, she said, 'It is my own business why I chose to forego a flu jab this year and I'll thank you to respect that.'

There comes a time in every person's life when doctors stop talking to them like an adult and adopt this patronising tone, as though you've only egg sandwiches left at the picnic. This doctor had clearly decided that our Doris and I were that far up the ladder of senility as to warrant talking to us as though we were toddlers after lollipops as he said to our Doris, he said, 'Your daughter mentioned something about a disagreement with another patient that may have triggered your decision.'

Our Doris's cheek twitched, a visible tic, a sign I'd become accustomed to when she's on the verge of anger but not ready to take the whole plunge. She said, 'Our Angela has always been a tad dramatic. I suggested she go on stage but she hasn't really the calves for it, I suppose RADA's loss is our gain.'

Angela stood by the door, her arms folded, looking every inch the mother hen. Sometimes I wonder if she's schooled herself against our Doris's attacks, she were that calm as she said to her mother, she said, 'You know you won't go because of Miss Dooley, Mum.'

'I'll thank you to remain silent on these matters, our Angela, I'm your mother I've not gone like Mrs Dignan with the bath mat just yet.'

The doctor interfered here, he said to our Doris,

he said, 'Our local pharmacies now offer free flu jabs for those in an at risk group.'

'And how am I to know it's a flu jab? They tell me they're injecting me with a vaccine when it could be anything from testosterone to Angel Delight.'

I fell asleep after that.

When I woke up our Doris were shuffling and scuffing and sniffling on her side. I stayed on my side, if I lifted my head the world spun until our Doris's wrinkles all merged into one. I said, 'What're you doing, our Doris?'

I couldn't move off the pillow so I only had trust to go on as she said to me, she said, 'Nothing.'

And I used the phrase hated by many and loved by all when I said to our Doris, ever suspicious, I said, 'It doesn't sound like nothing.'

We could have argued. Ordinarily we would have argued, if only to pass the time of day – after fifty-five years of marriage there's not much left to say. We discussed fetishes in the seventies, realised we'd never bring mint imperials into the bedroom – we never did find that last one – and after that you're stuck for conversation. Married couples all over the world have realised that arguments are the key to maintaining a healthy relationship, they also make for great foreplay, not that I'd mention this to our Doris, she still thinks the erogenous zones are from an episode of Star Trek.

We didn't feel up to arguing. Instead our Doris let me in on her fidgeting, she said, 'If you must know, our 'arold, I'm working on my correspondence with key members of the WI. There are whispers that Pandra O'Malley is worming her way back and I've let myself fall behind in this race. I knew no good would come from Halloween, I don't know why I let you talk me into it.'

I spent the next few hours dozing as our Doris scribbled beside me, as frenetic as a flea on speed. Our Angela kept checking on us. There wasn't any sign of the flu affecting her, she doesn't tend to get ill does our Angela, not since she had an allergic reaction to tomato puree in nineteen ninety-one.

I planned to spend the remainder of the day in bed, guzzling Lemsip and bandaging my nose with Kleenex. Our Doris had other plans. Without my knowing it she had invited Pandra and Edith over.

Our Angela appeared and said to me, she said, 'You might want to make yourself decent, Dad, we've got company.'

There was no time to reply, the two of them edged in the doorway behind her, Pandra clearly hoping to catch us on the verge of death.

Our Doris said to her, she said, 'Pandra, here I was thinking I only had a touch of the flu and you appear, a spectre of death if ever there was one.'

I managed to sit myself up only to watch as their faces fell. I said, I croaked, 'It can't be that bad.'

'Dad, you look like someone painted a corpse's face with chalk.' I'd never seen our Angela so shocked, and that includes the time she discovered the truth about George Michael.

I turned to our Doris and said to her, I said, 'What do you think?'

I couldn't tell if she gave me the Look, the flu had glued her left eye shut, giving her this look of John Wayne in True Grit.

She said to me, she said, 'If I were you, our 'arold, I'd be more concerned that guests saw fit to barge into our bedroom, uninvited and every bit as unwanted as a dachshund with explosive diarrhoea.'

'Mum!'

'Oh, do hush, Angela, they're seeing me in my nightclothes, the time for tact is long gone.' Our Doris blew her nose with all the gusto of an asthmatic saxophonist and stared Edith dead in the eye. She said to her, she said, 'Mrs Simpson, please tell me as to why you saw fit to bring this lumbering windbag into my home.'

Edith met our Doris's gaze with equal fire in her eyes and said, she said, 'After our conversation yesterday I invited Mrs O'Malley to see you so as you could clear the air. You do remember the conversation?'

Our Doris said, 'I have yet to reach such realms of senility. I'd remember that travesty you call a blouse any day of the week – it gives such frightful nightmares.'

Edith pulled her lapels closer together and said, 'I'd be worried if I were you, Mrs Copeland. You know as well as any that we only recognised my mother's dementia when she started entertaining guests in her nightclothes.'

I thought that our Doris might throw the bedside lamp at Edith. She said to her, she positively growled, 'That's not dementia, that's promiscuity.'

Edith hid a gasp behind her hand and said, 'Are you suggesting my mother was a lady of ill repute?'

'Only as much as you're suggesting I'm going around the twist.'

Our Angela attempted to divert the topic of conversation, she said, before Edith could say anything else, she said, 'Mum, Edith is your friend, why are you treating her like this?'

'Angela, you wouldn't understand. You never

wanted to be part of the WI.'

'If this is what being part of the WI means I clearly made the right decision. We all know what went on in the Gazette and the church hall, but there's only so much we can accept before wondering whether you're a complete and utter lunatic.'

There was tension between Edith, Pandra and our Doris, that's to be expected, but the air grew that thick between our Angela and her mother I questioned whether our Doris taught her as well as she thought.

I said to them, I said, 'We are ill. I haven't felt this bad since the pneumonia, so if you're going to fight, fight, but please shut the heck up.'

A chorus of apologies filled the room but I felt our Doris seethe beside me. It could have been anger, it could have been a fever, whatever it was she burned more than a vindaloo broiled on the surface of the sun.

I've said it before and I'll say it again, being married to our Doris is like being married to Mount Vesuvius, cracks and all.

Our Angela stood, arms folded, cheeks purpling, beside Edith, now more than ever conscious of her lapels. Pandra had no one to interject, to jump in and stop her stoking our Doris's temper. She said to our Doris, she said, 'I am sorry, Mrs Copeland, I took things too far. Being chairwoman means a lot to me and I got ahead of myself.'

Edith and our Angela froze and stared at Pandra in what can only be described as sheer astonishment. I were already wheezing but the rest of the air fled my body in complete disbelief at Pandra O'Malley's stupidity.

Pandra's words ignited the fuse in our Doris's brain and her mouth, ever the cannon, unleashed fury upon Pandra, well as much fury as someone with flu and a community order can unleash as she said to her, she raged, 'I thought I'd said all I had to say at the church hall but one look at your face proved me wrong. Do you think that being chairwoman means nothing to me? Do you think that I've been idling my life away for seventy-three years and just happened upon the role? That I have done no work whatsoever to support my election as interim chairwoman of the Women's Institute.

'You have brought enough animosity and conflict into my home to last a lifetime - I'm sorry you felt that threatened by me that you chose to drag my name through the dirt from whence you came. In the last few years I have faced women I thought were the lowest of the low but you surpassed even them, at least Janice Dooley has something going for her, at least she has charisma.'

The day had arrived.

The day no resident of Partridge Mews ever expected to see, the day our Doris complimented Janice Dooley of Little Street.

Edith spoke up then. She said to our Doris, she said, 'I think it's time Mrs O'Malley and I took our leave but let me offer some advice as your oldest friend, don't become a caricature of yourself, Doris. You cannot treat everyone as though they're beneath you and expect them to keep accepting it. I truly believe that becoming chairwoman is the worst thing to ever happen to you.'

Our Angela lead them out and I watched our Doris deflate beside me. She dabbed at her eyes with her Kleenex, slumped against the pillow and said to me, she said, 'She's right, our 'arold, I've no idea what I'm doing anymore.'

I said to the air, I said, 'Come back, Violet Grey, all is forgiven.'

Beside me, our Doris began to cry.

A few days down the line she felt well enough to move about, leaving me to wallow in my own filth. My immune system doesn't work as well as it used to – as I struggled to keep my breathing steady through The Archers, our Doris vacuumed downstairs and made a cheese and tomato quiche.

I bet it's because I'm two years older. They say nothing about it when you're young, make out like two years is nothing and then you're sixty-five having a knee replacement and your wife at sixty-three years of age, is not only the main breadwinner in the home, she's never had the shame of walking into the post office and setting off all the alarms.

Edith might have fallen out with our Doris but she didn't stop Alf from visiting. He turned up at one o'clock in the afternoon with a bottle of rum and a Daily Mirror he'd hidden in his sleeve. He said to me, he said, 'Bet you wish you'd gone in for that flu jab now, don't you, 'arold?'

I said to him, my face numb from blowing my nose, I said, 'If it ends up killing me do me a favour and get to my shed before our Doris.'

Alf got that smarmy smirk on his face, all hush hush, wink wink, as he said to me, he said, 'And why might I do that?'

I quickly put any thoughts towards illicit misdeeds to bed by saying, I said, 'It's not pornography, it's socks.'

'Socks?' Alf asked, all disappointed – he'd found a few pork scratchings in his pocket so was picking at those.

I said to him, I said, 'There might be the odd newspaper but it's mostly socks, our Doris keeps giving mine away.'

'Our Edith had the same idea about my coats until I kept getting them caught on fences.' He shrugged before coming over all serious and saying to me, he said, 'Speaking of our Edith, what's going on between our wives, 'arold?'

I said, 'You best open that rum because it's a long story, Alf.'

'When have I ever needed an excuse to open a bottle of rum?' he said.

I told Alf everything I knew about the arguments, the fake Bake Sales, and the supposed Satanism, and by the end of the conversation we were well and truly pie-eyed.

We'd emptied the bottle and a few hours down the line I awoke to the shrill cry of our Doris as she screamed, ''arold, what's he doing in our bed?'

I looked over to see Alf in bed with me.

He snored that loud I hadn't been able to tell the difference between my best mate and my wife.

Our Doris caught sight of the empty bottle and said, she said, 'You could've done the decent thing and been a homosexual, but no, you had to be a drunk. Wake him up and get him into the spare room, I can't send him back to Edith in this state.'

She bustled off and I held onto the hope that if our Doris was on first name terms again, things might be looking up.

Things are never simple. I have spent seventy-five years waiting for a quiet life and now I question if it will even arrive with death, if our Doris won't follow me into the afterlife and complain about Mary Magdalene's drapes.

Most of the snot had left my system by next morning and Alf still slept in the spare bedroom – it must be said for Alf, when he steals he doesn't just bring the cheap stuff.

I went down to the kitchen, every bone in my body aching. Our Doris sat at the table, her expression somewhere between glum and psychotic.

I said to her, I said, 'What's the matter, our Doris?'

She said to me, she said, 'Sometimes I question why I bother, our 'arold, why I ever thought about bettering myself because there's no enjoyment – I'm a clown with no jokes.'

I said, 'You haven't the nose to be a clown, you're too … distinguished.'

'Distinguished?'

'You know your nose is very much part of your face.'

'Well I didn't think it would be on my foot. Honestly, 'arold, I wonder what I ever saw in you.'

'You've seen enough of my body in the last fifty-five years. It always amazed me you didn't ask to sit in on my colonoscopy.'

'You must be feeling better, spreading crude around the kitchen like Marmite.' She got up to make breakfast and I knew it was my duty as a husband to offer some reassurance, some soothing words to assuage her hurt.

I said to her, I said, 'You do this because you're Doris and there's no one else knows as much about the social etiquette of puff pastry as you.'

She had the kettle boiling as she said, 'But is it all useless, our 'arold?'

'You might not make it on Mastermind but it'd be a shame to waste all that knowledge.'

She didn't say much as she made breakfast but I'm pretty sure there was a spring in her step, like a billy goat, or a space hopper.

Later that day we received a visit from the committee. I watched them traipse up the drive, three women who wouldn't have looked out of place at a morgue. They were dodderers, every few steps seemed to take hours and they had an inability to walk without scuffing the soles of their Hotter plimsolls against the paving stones.

Our Doris greeted them at the door, she must have been feeling better, the way she waffled on, she said to them, she said, 'Good afternoon, ladies, this is a most unexpected visit. Though I'm never one to turn away guests, I must warn you that 'arold and I are currently prey to a particularly virulent strain of influenza, I trust you've all had jabs.'

She lead them through to the living room and began the introductions. They were all interchangeable to me, vice-chair Mrs McBride could have easily been Mrs Patel the secretary who you wouldn't be blamed for thinking was Mrs Cribbins the treasurer.

Mrs McBride was the first to speak, she said to our Doris, clutching at her handbag like a lifejacket, she said, 'I'm afraid this is a rather delicate matter, Mrs Copeland. Perhaps we'd be better talking in private?'

The other two nodded like spaniels after treats but our Doris were having none of it as she said, 'I'll just pop the kettle on,' and disappeared into the kitchen, leaving me with three sallow windbags – I'd have more luck talking to bagpipes.

Feeling groggy, I chose to bite the bullet and said

to them, I said, 'So you're turfing out our Doris then?'

The ladies caught their shock before it had chance to reach their eyes and once again it was up to Mrs McBride to speak as she said, 'We're here on WI business and last I checked you weren't a woman, Mr Copeland.'

'No, but I've never a known a man want to see his wife get shafted.'

'I must say you're being rather confrontational.'

I opened my mouth ready with a retort but Mrs Mcbride was saved by our Doris walking in with the tray because I were on the verge of using words she won't even forgive Chaucer for writing.

Once the tea things were assembled on the coffee table, our Doris sat down in her chair. It was only then I realised that she had anticipated this visit. She looked every inch the Margaret Rutherford as she gave the ladies a look that could only be described as withering, it were all cold, as though to meet her gaze would result in the onlooker being reduced to a pile of ash. Our Doris wore her lavender Per Una suit with the court shoes that expensive I never bothered looking for a label.

She'd applied make-up to cover the flushes of fever and her lips shone. I tell you there's something enchanting about a woman's lips shining – as long as it's purely cosmetic, if it's slobber even I'd steer clear and I can eat custard cold.

And she wore her jewellery.

Our Doris usually sticks with the engagement, wedding and eternity rings but this time she'd accessorised with the diamond studs I got her for our fortieth anniversary, and to top it all off, the crowning glory, not a tiara, but the white gold necklace.

She was every inch the queen and we were merely voyeurs to her glory.

'I believe the tea should be sufficiently brewed. Mrs Patel, I brought you an extra jug of milk, I know how weak you like your beverages.' I felt like a young lad again, our Doris had me scared and thrilled, my heart were beating that quickly I couldn't be sure if it were infatuation or cough mixture. Our Doris played mother, offered biscuits around – Florentines we'd planned on saving for Christmas visitors – and made sure to check how everyone liked their tea before serving. She'd served us all drinks in the cheap M&S selection she bought from the charity shop, choosing Royal Winton for her tea, green and gold design, one lump of sugar, milk.

'Now,' she addressed Mrs McBride, 'how can I help?' Although we all knew the tea too scolding to drink, our Doris sipped it and exhaled a plume of smoke to punctuate her sentence.

Mrs McBride must have been a bit rattled. She set her saucer on the coffee table and said to our Doris, she said, 'Mrs Copeland, we are here because we are understandably concerned about the behaviour that you have recently displayed. It is not in line with our code of conduct – not only have you been convicted of harming another human being, but you chose to air the dirty laundry of your fellow women in a public arena. We feel that we have no choice but to ask you to step down as interim chairwoman.'

Our Doris tittered, somewhat reminiscent of the Wicked Queen before saying to Mrs McBride, she said, 'May I remind you that I was chosen as interim chairwoman because of the regret I displayed for my actions. You and I both know that the WI has seen a rise in the number of members since I became chairwoman – do you believe those members would remain should I be forced out?'

Mrs Patel intervened here, struggling to chew her Florentine thanks to a rather bad set of dentures. She said to our Doris, she said, 'Although there has been a rise in members they aren't necessarily the type of woman we like to see within our ranks. The Partridge Mews Women's Institute has always been a respectable group and now we are faced with women such as Erin Beaumont, who, admittedly a nice girl isn't really our sort.'

Our Doris sat forward in her seat, a mongoose ready to rip off the snake's head, as she said to Mrs Patel, she practically growled, 'Miss Beaumont is a close friend of mine and I'll thank you not to infer she isn't respectable. How you could say such a thing is beyond my comprehension, Edna Patel, you've seen more gutters than rainwater.'

Mrs Cribbins, having scoffed a few Florentines and already on her second cup of tea, finally spoke up, she said, 'We have seen some monetary increase due to the inclusion of those from more unfortunate backgrounds, but that does not mean we should lower our standards.'

'You lowered your standards when you married husband number six, Norma.' Our Doris breathed and reclined in her chair, she closed her eyes for a moment, opened them and said to them all, she said, 'I aired the dirty laundry of a few women, so what? I have had much worse said about me in seventy-three years, I can tell you.'

It was Mrs McBride's turn to speak again, at this point I was happy for the show – Warwick Davis was having another bash at a quiz show on ITV and it wasn't up to much – she said to our Doris, she said, 'Mrs Copeland, you must understand, you've developed a very acerbic character we feel doesn't represent the WI in the best light, would you at least consider stepping down and allowing another, more reputable candidate take on the role?'

'No.'

'Mrs Copeland –'

'Please do allow me to talk, it would make it so much easier for all of us.' Our Doris allowed them a moment to speak before continuing, she said to them, she said, 'You forget that I am Mrs Doris Copeland, I once held a dinner party for eight with nothing more than a beef joint and three litres of chardonnay, I know a thing or two about difficult circumstances. I was chosen by Violet Grey to finish her term as chairwoman and I will continue to do so until such a time as the next AGM, at which point you are well within your rights to vote for my potential successor, but I refuse to concede to Pandra O'Malley, a woman that in touch with her Irish heritage she married a potato.

'Need I remind you all that I have helped you all in one way or another over the years and you can allow me some common courtesy at this time. I have kept secrets – you have seen the radical change in my behaviour, what with all my current personal stresses, disregarding my illness, I just might gossip as much as Pandra. She informed Edith Simpson that with all of you in her pocket she's had to find somewhere else for her keys.

'No, I will remain interim chairwoman for the time being. Please feel free to finish your drinks, but my husband is quite unwell and I must take care of him.'

They didn't bother, choosing to look from one to the other before Mrs McBride bid our Doris farewell and they fled, handbags between their legs.

I said to her, I said, 'That were brilliant, our Doris.'

She beamed at me and said, 'Oh, I know, our 'arold. I think I'll invite Edith and our Angela over for dinner – we can order from the Indian, what do you think?'

I didn't have time to answer.

Alf showed up at the door looking as bad as we did on the flu and said to our Doris, he said, 'I think that's a great idea, Doris love, but I'll need some Pepto-Bismol before I embark upon a Balti.'

7

FiREWORKS

Our Doris has arranged a winter wonderland to apologise for her recent behaviour.

She sprung it on me last Tuesday. I'd just got back from the Hare and Horse to discover her in the cubbyhole with Erin, thumbing through phonebooks as though folk still found them useful.

I said to our Doris, I said, 'The reason we ended up in this mess is because you decided to host an event.'

She gave me the Look and said to me, she said, 'I'd mind my tongue if I were you, our 'arold. This winter wonderland will exhibit the very essence of Christmas, there will be a Father Christmas, the likes of which has never before been seen in Partridge Mews. I've yet to decide whether he will be garbed in green, red or white but it does depend very much on the colour scheme. There will be elves, reindeer, craft stalls, a more esteemed version of street food, and a carol service, in both an exploration of Christianity and consumerism.'

Erin stared at our Doris open-mouthed before

saying, she said, 'I just wanted a proper Christmas for Reuben, he's not had one before.'

I said to her, I said, 'When it comes to our Doris, Christmas is always proper.'

Our Doris beamed at this and said, 'I've produced a timeline of six weeks to pull together a truly festive extravaganza.' As if by magic, she unveiled a sheaf of typewritten pages and, with a flourish, handed it over.

Awe-struck, I said, 'This must be an expensive do.'

She said, 'You can't put a price on Christmas.'

'You can,' I said, my eyes stuck on the amount of tinsel we'd need. Our Doris doesn't ordinarily go in for tinsel, she must be getting on the edge of senility because she'd decided we needed forty feet of the stuff in various shades, as appropriate. I said to her, I said, 'What does as appropriate mean? Where are you holding this wonderland?'

She'd clearly wanted me to ask this question – her smile widened that much I thought her teeth would split her cheeks. She sat down and said to me, hands clasped across her chest, she said, 'I have arranged with Clementine Partridge of Greenfields Hall to use their former ballroom.'

'Oh,' I said.

This wasn't the response our Doris wanted. She gave me the Look and said to me, she said, 'Do you fail to understand the air of prestige the hall will bring to my winter wonderland? Not only have I managed to single-handedly gain entry to Greenfields, a place that hasn't opened its doors to the public at Christmas since nineteen seventy-three, but the fact that Miss Partridge has allowed me free rein over the event emphasises that she has faith in the current interim chairwoman of the Partridge Mews Women's Institute – what better advertisement, could I ask for?'

I went to make a brew and left our Doris to her own devices.

It was her fault I'd been to town so early in any case because it is impossible to buy a gift for our Doris. She spends the entire year dropping hints about what she wants and when I think I've figured it out she decides the vacuum I bought is too gaudy, and a further example of the class divide, emphasising we put expensive appliances above the lives of the less fortunate. Either way, our Angela was grateful for a new Dyson.

I must've searched for nigh on three hours with not a glimmer of fortune in sight. There were a pair of diamond earrings at the jewellers that may have gone down well but I could hear our Doris in my head telling me that a woman over the age of sixty-five should never purchase new jewellery. She should have completed her collection with a few extravagant pieces that become staple accessories for her best outfits, plus it makes the business of wills more difficult if you return to the solicitor every birthday to add a new bangle.

With this in mind I ventured to the pub, supped a lone pint, and returned home where I found my wife, the great bane of my wallet, planning a winter wonderland.

The first thing we had to do was interview Father Christmas. After a few telephone conversations with the editor of the Partridge Mews Gazette, and the threat she'd mention their smear campaign against her to the Press Complaints Commission, they placed an advert in the newspaper asking for an older gentleman with strong knees and preferably a beard to meet us at the church hall on Saturday afternoon.

We'd expected drunks.

We hadn't anticipated the amount of drunks there are in Partridge Mews. I hadn't realised how many drunks, waifs and strays our town holds, even Dennis Perry made an appearance and he's been on a tag for eighteen months after he mistook a goldfish bowl for a jar of pickled onions at the GP. They lined up outside the church hall like it were the dole queue, filled with this mixture of excitement and fury – you could tell by the sheer build of them that if someone jumped the line they'd be decapitated before they had chance to say, 'ho, ho, ho.'

I said to our Doris, I said, 'I didn't think there'd be that many men interested in playing Father Christmas.'

Erin cut across and said, 'You'd be surprised by the amount of men who jump at the chance to dress up.'

The church hall was set up like a court room. Me and Theo sat with our Doris and Erin behind a trestle table, waiting to judge our Santa Clauses. We'd been made to dress up for the occasion. It didn't take much persuading to get Theo into his three piece suit, our Doris had it tailored to his measurements as a birthday present and he's been waiting for the chance to give it an airing. It's navy, pinstriped, gives him the look of someone off The Apprentice.

Our Doris handed us all clipboards and said to us, she said, 'Now I want you to be as harsh as possible, do not let people off lightly. We all saw Brian McMillan out there and we need not forget the business at Salford Quays.'

Theo nodded, unable to lose the grin. He's like his grandmother, you give him one ounce of power and he thinks he's in charge of nuclear weaponry.

Once we were fully assembled, Thermos full of coffee beneath the table, our Doris checked the time and summoned the first act.

And thus began the most painful four hours of my life and I've sat through Steel Magnolias. We needn't have worried about Dennis Perry or Brian McMillan, both turned out to be the most favourable of the drunks – at least they were able to string a sentence together. Curly Donahue lost his trousers, Mrs Yates protested against our sexist undertaking by standing in the middle of the room for five minutes and discussing the latest Woman's Weekly, and a few of them only came in because they wanted to find out why there was a queue.

After watching the majority of the town's old codgers cough up phlegm whilst forgetting the name of Santa's reindeer, we managed to whittle the list of applicants down to five. In his efforts to appear inclusive, Theo campaigned for Little Barry Upperdyke to be present but our Doris has always had a thing about overbites.

The cream of the crop, our five Father Christmases, stood before us, each more bedraggled than the last. Ernie Jackson made it by the skin of his teeth and only because Erin felt she owed him a favour.

Some of them wouldn't even win awards for trying.

I said to our Doris, I said, 'They think because they've tucked in their shirts it's a costume – Ernie's worn that red fleece since Linda left him in two-thousand-and-seven. I'm telling you, our Doris, send them all home we'll think of something else.'

I didn't realise I'd raised my voice until Ernie

interjected, he said, 'Actually, 'arold, not to dampen the moment, because as an argument that were up there with the best but Linda, you remember my former partner, Linda? Yes, well, in actual fact, it was two-thousand-and-nine. I didn't want to spoil the mood but it hasn't just quite really been nine years.'

Our Doris gave me the Look before saying to the men, she said, 'Please forgive my husband's tactless outburst there, but I must say I agree with his pronouncement.

'You are a shambles.

'I have directed theatre troupes of toddlers with little to no bladder control and they were a sight better than you. Honestly, I am a woman of few words but you were well and truly awful.

'My only wish – just one wish – is to spread some festive cheer this Christmas with the help of a spectacular Santa Claus. Instead I'm left with the extras from Auf Wiedersehen Pet.'

At that moment something completely unexpected happened. The sound of jingle bells filled the hall, echoing off the ceiling alongside the beat of boots against the lino. With an explosion of ho, ho, ho, the double doors flew open and Father Christmas entered the church hall.

He was the greatest we'd seen all morning, his beard had that Daz white sheen, and his big black boots glowed with polish. His belly was huge, and his ankles were scrawny, and he was unmistakeably Alf.

He walked over to join the line and said to us, he said, 'I hope I'm not too late, I heard they'd got a special offer on Grouse down Tesco and you know how Edith likes a tipple.'

The other five may as well have fled at this point

because when Alf stood beside them he emphasised all of their failings. Their beards were little more than scraggly and grey, like an Irish wolfhound trapped in the rain.

Our Doris hid her smile behind a cough before saying, she said, 'Mr Simpson, I'm most pleased that you chose to attend today. Although the rest of you made some attempt at embodying the Christmas spirit, you're still closer to goblins than elves. When compared against Mr Simpson – a man known for his sheer untidiness – it's really no contest. I can express nothing but sincere gratitude that you auditioned but none of you showed me the charisma, verve and wonder necessary to truly encapsulate a man as esteemed as Saint Nicholas.'

We watched them leave. Dennis Perry called it a fix, whilst Ernie questioned whether the Hare and Horse still served dry-roasted peanuts.

Our Doris said to Alf, she said, 'You'll need to be properly briefed on the decorum of Father Christmas – you and Edith are invited for dinner tonight, please arrive no later than half past six. I fear amends must be made.'

Alf looked shell-shocked as he stammered, 'Does that mean I've got the job?'

'Of course you've got the job, Mr Simpson,' Theo said, that hyped up on coffee I'm surprised he didn't hallucinate, 'you're the best we've seen.'

'Where'd you get the outfit?' Erin asked.

'Evie down the charity shop let me have it. I said as I wanted to help out and she found it with some old copies of the Daily Star.' Alf reached deep into his pocket and removed a pork pie. Melton Mowbray. He wiped off the fluff and dug in, flecks of pastry crumbling into his beard and I knew that if our Doris wanted to train him in decorum, and keep him clean she'd have a struggle on her hands.

That evening I felt all excited. My heartbeat juddered as though the Grand Old Duke of York and his ten thousand men were marching their way up my ribcage. It were the anticipation, the sheer hope that our Doris would make it up with Edith.

'It's not right when you're arguing,' I said to our Doris over afternoon scones. 'You and Edith have been friends since before I developed an interest in girls.'

Our Doris gave me this look, not the Look, just a touch of a quirked eyebrow and said to me, she said, 'And just what were you interested in beforehand?'

I shrugged, scooping up a glob of jam with a stray sultana, and said, 'I don't know, my yo-yo probably – I never did find out what went on with Mrs Kettlewell.'

'Did you take a sudden blow to the head, our 'arold? I cannot begin to comprehend what you're talking about.'

'It doesn't matter,' I said, 'what matters is that you and Edith patch things up.'

Our Doris said, 'I'm glad to have your approval, our 'arold, though it certainly wasn't asked for.'

We let the conversation dissipate and I went to clean my teeth. That's the problem with strawberry jam, it has a terrible habit of depositing seeds in your dentures.

A few hours down the line and I stood at the front door. Our Doris sent me to wait after I interrupted her mashing potatoes. She said to me, the Look ever prominent, she said, 'I might've misplaced the Elmlea, it isn't dementia, it's the stress of being married to you for fifty-five years.'

And she slammed the kitchen door.

I imagine it was the stress that made her do it. She doesn't ordinarily slam doors as she says such behaviour isn't befitting of an upper-middle-class household, a statement that was made before she tried cooking a three course meal whilst applying mascara.

Alf and Edith arrived, he greeted me with an 'How do, 'arold?' and I got a chance to look at his suit. Edith must've forced him into it because he certainly never went willingly – if his collar got any higher it'd be a noose.

I said to them, I said, 'I've been put on door duty as punishment.'

Alf's eyes widened in that conspiratorial fashion famous in the mischievous elderly as he said, 'What did you do?'

Out of nowhere rose this booming yell, the dulcet tones of my spouse, sounding as though her vocal cords had been made walk over hot coals. She said, a proper banshee at this point, she said, 'It's more what he didn't do – making our guests wait outside in the middle of December. Honestly, it's like his common sense went the same way as Fairy liquid.'

And this is when the realisation hit.

Our Doris wandered down the hall and reached the door only to discover she was wearing the exact same outfit as Edith.

They looked each other up and down like cats over fish guts, from their matching tops to their shoes they could've been twins.

I felt on the verge of a heart attack, praying for nuclear warfare, questioning if I should hide any throwable objects when our Doris and Edith burst out laughing.

Edith said, 'I must say, Doris, you have remarkably good taste in jackets, you must put me in touch with your stylist.'

They laughed more as they stumbled down the hall, giggling like schoolgirls. Our Doris said, she said, 'I've been a fool, Edith.'

'I won't deny that, you represent the women of Partridge Mews and they're being blooming dozy as of late.'

Alf and I stood, amazed as they began to potter around the kitchen like nothing had happened. I said to him, I said, 'Alf, I've not even got the front door shut.'

He clapped me on the shoulder and said, 'They're our wives, we don't question their inner machinations.'

'Machinations?'

'I learnt that off Countdown. Any ale going?'

Over the next few days Edith became a fixture at the house, helping our Doris with her preparations. Me and Alf took to hiding out at the allotment, we borrowed his grandson's laptop, a back-up generator and a Clint Eastwood boxset.

I came home one evening to discover our Doris talking to a reporter. She hadn't hit him with a table lamp so I guessed things were going well. I said I'd brew up and our Doris said, she said, 'There you are, our 'arold, I thought Mr Han would leave having never had chance to meet my illustrious husband.'

If she were using adjectives she was either showing off or she'd been at the sherry. After an easy life, I applied my best posh accent and said, 'You know how it is down the allotment, busy time of year – everyone wanting carrots.'

'You grow vegetables then, Mr Copeland?' Mr Han said, pen poised, his phone recording every word.

Our Doris gave me a look to say if I ruined this she'd have my giblets for gravy. She said to Mr Han, taking control of the situation, she said, 'Although 'arold is a most esteemed horticulturist in Partridge Mews he chooses to employ his skills in the growth and circulation of plants with a more floral nature. His talk of vegetables is merely the help he gives to his fellow allotment users as they strive – as we all strive – to make Christmas a truly wondrous occasion for all.'

I made the drinks.

Our Doris and Mr Han sat at the kitchen table. She often brings unknown guests there in case they're unsure of the etiquette surrounding carpets.

Mr Han said, 'Really I'm only here to discuss the retraction. The editor would have come himself but he sprained his ankle on a Viennetta.'

Our Doris gave her best simpering smile and said, 'Such an unfortunate misadventure. A Viennetta – even the most upper class dinner parties struggle to see it as even an ironic dessert.'

I can't say I didn't smile. There's something about watching our Doris at work that brings a grin to a man's face. I stood and watched as Mr Han's neck and cheeks came out in blotches of red, the fear set his eyes to pinholes like a mouse staring a viper dead in the face.

He said to our Doris, gulping that hard I'm surprised he didn't swallow his Adam's apple, he said, 'I can't really comment on that Mrs Copeland. Mr Stoppard works hard and should he wish to indulge in a less-than-upper-class treat every now and then it is his prerogative as a citizen of these British shores to do so.'

I saw the tell-tale twitch of our Doris's eyebrows before she said, 'Had I known you were such an advocate for ice cream cake I'd have arranged a meeting in the freezer section of Waitrose.'

'There's the thing,' I said, 'Would Waitrose stock Viennetta? Or would they be concerned about the possible societal implications of displaying foodstuffs of such lower class standing?'

Our Doris gave me the Look and said, 'Please excuse my husband, he does like to let the conversation deteriorate. I trust the retraction will also draw attention to my winter wonderland, there will be a traditional Father Christmas, and a tremendous firework display to rival Bonfire Night at Buckingham Palace.'

I went a bit flabbergasted, unable to get my mug to my mouth as I said to her, I said, 'Fireworks, our Doris?'

'That's right, our 'arold. I'm ever so glad you haven't slipped into deafness like many of your peers.'

Mr Han got this almost malicious look in his eyes as he said, 'Does the thought of fireworks concern you, Mr Copeland? Perhaps you have some repressed childhood trauma due to your time in the war.'

Our Doris's Look went nuclear. I said to Mr Han, I said, 'My only concern is time, but I know my wife and she has a way of making a spectacle at short notice.'

The truth was I couldn't have been more terrified if I tried. Our Doris and fireworks have never really got on – she lost both eyebrows when she got too close to a Catherine Wheel in nineteen seventy-eight. There've been incidents with sparklers and bonfires, it got that bad we've even taken to avoiding Burns Night. That's why I can't help but see our Doris and fireworks as anything but another stress on the road to a heart attack.

Eventually Mr Han went on his way, leaving me to ask her, I said, 'What the bleeding heck are you thinking, our Doris?'

She said to me, the threat of the devil in her eyes, she said, I was thinking of what to serve with the roast ham for dinner, mashed or baked potatoes. It's one of the perils of being an exceptional housewife.'

'I'm talking about the fireworks.'

'I know what you're talking about, I am your wife. You've no need to fuss, I've hired trained professionals to prepare and supervise the display. Our biggest concern is elves – we can't very well hold auditions, look how well it went last time.'

I shrugged, an idea percolating. I said to our Doris, I said, 'How about Miss Moonflower and co.?'

'I hardly think they'll want to help.'

'It would be in their best interests. The Gazette are posting a retraction, more folk are on your side.'

Our Doris nodded. 'Mrs Cribbins did say "good morning" to me the other day.'

'See? Ask the elves, they'd be fools to say no.'

They were fools.

Two days later Miss Moonflower sat in the lounge, throwing back the French Fancies like they were Bombay Mix. She looked our Doris dead in the eye and said, 'I just don't think it would be beneficial to our cause if we were to perpetuate stereotypes.'

Our Doris reclined slightly, relaxed. No one ever wants to see our Doris relaxed. It means she's comfortable, it means she'll tear the heart from your chest without thinking otherwise. A relaxed Doris is a dangerous Doris.

She said to her, she said, 'The way I see it, you don't have any other choice. Though I defiled your name with the images of yourself in rather indecent circumstances, I brought attention to your group of eccentric layabouts and for that you should be somewhat grateful.'

Miss Moonflower seethed. Her shoulders rose slowly, as though demonic wings elongated from beneath her cloak. She snarled, she actually snarled, if she wanted to give off the appearance of being otherworldly or tapped in the head then she had succeeded. She said to our Doris, she said, 'You cannot be serious. I only questioned your religious leanings, you strove to completely destroy all of my future career prospects and possible relationships.

'Do not feign senility and behave like you didn't understand the damage your actions would cause. You're canny, Mrs Copeland, and your words carry power.' Miss Moonflower punctuated her speech by guzzling coffee.

I'd hidden myself behind the Argos catalogue. With Edith back on side the search for our Doris's gift had been reignited. We'd considered candles but thought they were too bohemian. Edith mentioned bespoke toiletries but the idea of buying our Doris a bath bomb made me break out in a hot sweat.

I imagined how the conversation would go. She'd say as I suggested she was untidy, and had reached an age she didn't know the rules of modern cleanliness. If I bought her a bath bomb, forget cruelty free, our Doris would use it as a knuckle duster.

Which is how I came to be sat there during the exchange between our Doris and Miss Moonflower that would undoubtedly become more uncomfortable. In fact, our Doris looked almost perturbed, as though recollecting a particularly painful throat infection.

She sipped her tea, a sure sign she was thinking. When she has something important to say she likes to calculate, mull over the words until she has everything correct. I thought I'd die when the screwdriver went through my hand and she took five minutes to phone for an ambulance.

After a few more minutes of awkward silence, in which I considered buying her a Playstation for Christmas, our Doris spoke, she said, 'Miss Moonflower, you are right. I do understand the power of my words and my position in society.

'I abused that position.

'There's nothing I can do but apologise for my behaviour. I should have known better than to allow my hurt to fuel my actions. I didn't and now we're both maligned by our town.

'I hope to use the winter wonderland to regain some favour – it is foolish to hold people's opinions in such high stead but I am a fickle, seventy-three year old woman and I know the way this world works. I understand completely when you tell me you won't be part of the show. If I were you I wouldn't be associated with me, either.'

It was a miracle.

Miss Moonflower stopped eating.

She battled our Doris in a staring contest for the ages before saying, she said, 'If we do this you have to help rebuild my name.'

Our Doris offered a smile, ever the lioness and said, 'The WI can make all of this go away.' She'd never looked more like Don Corleone.

With Miss Moonflower on side things really took off. She brought the rest of her posse around for costume fittings and lessons in decorum. Our Doris vetoed any ideas about them speaking in Elvish.

Our Doris's only concern was Alf. To look at him

you'd think he coined the term 'the great unwashed'. It's not that personal hygiene eludes him. Alf maintains that although he may forget to change his underwear, he washes his face every day.

His lessons with our Doris had been no picnic. We met down the Hare and Horse when the WI disappeared to Manchester for the Christmas markets.

He was pale. He said to me, he said, 'I think your Doris is trying to kill me, 'arold.' He necked three quarters of his pint, wiped his mouth on his sleeve and proceeded, 'I only thought I'd do her a favour, put on a red suit, jingle a few bells and you're laughing, but 'arold ... 'arold, she must think we're recreating Miracle on 34th Street the way she's going on.'

Lynda from behind the bar brought over a couple of mince pies. We thanked her and I said to Alf, I said, 'What exactly has she got you doing?'

He looked from me to the mince pie and said, 'Take this mince pie – a Christmas tradition – your Doris sees it as a threat. This little, sugar-coated pastry is on par with Guy Fawkes.'

'Only when eaten incorrectly,' I said. Our Doris taught me the proper way to consume a mince pie years ago, but it did make me grin to see someone going through it as well.

Alf stared at me agog. 'It is a mince pie,' he said, 'you bite it, chew, and swallow, who cares about a few crumbs?'

'Our Doris,' I said, though he knew the answer.

'Aye, your bleeding Doris. Do you know what her problem is? Everything. First, she says the pastry is treacherous because it crumbles. Crumbles, 'arold, I tell you – she says take small bites so as to not get the filling all over myself, the filling she says is too sticky and causes untoward issues during polite conversation. If you don't make a mess when eating a mince pie you're doing it wrong.'

In an act of defiance, he bit the pie in half, chewed with his mouth open, and allowed the pastry and mincemeat to catch in the wool of his jumper.

I went and bought the next round.

Somehow, over the next few days, Alf seemed to mellow. He still bristled whenever our Doris mentioned the muck on his boots but he kept his mouth shut, fifty years of marriage had taught him how to keep his mouth shut.

Meanwhile, our Doris had almost finished putting everything together for her winter wonderland. She'd employed Theo to share the event on social media, even going so far as to invite the strange folk who'd followed her around when she began her community service. I said to her, I said, 'You do realise this is like inviting a stalker into your home, our Doris.'

She said to me, she said, 'I can't imagine that you'd possibly understand, our 'arold. It is a sign that I have forgiven them for their past mistakes.'

Theo looked up from his laptop and said, 'Nan said they'd taken more flattering photos than the Gazette ever had.'

Our Doris gave Theo something not dissimilar to the Look and said to him, she said, 'I told you that in the strictest confidence, Theodore.'

He raised his coffee and said, 'You called them paparazzi. I'm telling Grandad before someone finds you dead in a ditch.'

'I must say you're overreacting, what imbecile would get it into their head to murder the interim chairwoman of the Partridge Mews Women's Institute?'

'Anyone who's ever been to one of your talks on the position of pickled onions in modern kitchens,' Theo said. He'd grown a bit more bumptious when talking to his grandmother had our Theo. I don't know whether it's because he's approaching his final year at high school, that it's instilled this strange confidence in him that he thinks he can insult his grandmother and she won't deck him. It doesn't matter either way, he's still our Doris's golden boy – sometimes I think Theo could rob a bank and she'd blame their lack of security first.

I hid a grin behind my newspaper and said, 'Apologise to your Nan, Theo.'

He shrugged and said, 'Sorry Nan.'

Our Doris said to him, she said, 'Do not apologise for being concerned, Theo. Honestly, I don't know what your Grandad is thinking – I don't know why I didn't recognise the legitimate fear that my celebrity status makes me something of a target for the more-unhinged members of society.' She made some comment about hiring more security for the event and disappeared into her cubbyhole.

I said to Theo, I said, 'Do you know something we don't?'

He gave me this look of questioning that looked equal parts pitying and gormless, and said to me, he said, 'What do you mean?'

'Do you think that someone is likely to try and hurt your grandmother?'

He thought about it for a moment before saying, 'I shouldn't think so. She can be a bit of a pain but I don't think anyone would try anything drastic.'

I agreed with him and went back to my newspaper.

Perhaps we should have paid more attention.

The day of the winter wonderland arrived and our Doris had me drive her up to Greenfields at three o'clock in the morning to make sure everything went to plan. Our Doris had given that much time, money and effort to the event I'm surprised she didn't fly to the North Pole in search of the real Saint Nicholas. She'd dressed herself like this strange mix of Theresa May and the Snow Queen, all in blue, from her tweed skirt to her blazer, even her scarf had touches of pale blue in it. How she'd managed to coordinate an outfit to suit the theme, I'd never know.

Greenfields Manor is a huge manor house on the edge of town, fit for one of those old crimes, one look at the sandstone building gave off this aura of their being a body in the library. A few Christmas trees stood in the drive, bedecked in icicles and fairy-lights, baubles and tinsel, looking every inch the regal tree you'd expect somewhere this upmarket. Someone had built a grotto, front and centre, the trees towering over them, giving an almost forest illusion – I just hoped they'd left room for Alf to hide his pork pies. He and our Doris came to an agreement, he could bring food with him as long as he ate it away from the grotto without his beard on.

Miss Moonflower and the elves agreed to mill about the wonderland, offering beverages and making sure any children knew where to find Father Christmas. No wonder Gadsden and Taylor's sales went up when our Doris worked at the factory, she knows a thing or two about marketing does my wife.

The next few hours were spent in a haze of being pushed this way and that by craftspeople looking for the fair, asking me to cart boxes for them because I clearly wasn't up to much – I wasn't but that's beside the point, I'm seventy-five years old. I got a good look at the stalls in any case.

Our Doris hired a few food vans meaning I snuck away for a bacon barm and a mug of tea, leaving some young lass named Simone to figure out how best to display her artisan dreamcatchers.

At half-past nine folk were waiting at the gate. Our Doris had taken her own advice and hired security – I don't know why, she's more vicious than half the bodybuilders she employed. They were jovial enough, I took them some breakfast over and they growled at a few folk who tried to get through early.

I don't know whether they were there because they'd forgiven our Doris, or because of the winter wonderland, either way seeing the children all excited at the prospect of Father Christmas, his reindeer, and his elves was enough to warm the heart. I hoped they wouldn't be disappointed.

Once the gates opened, our Doris's winter wonderland became bedlam, excitable folk rushed around, not realising they had all day. Eric Brocklehurst joined a queue for the sake of it, only to discover it lead to the toilets. Edith, who'd been supervising to ensure no funny business, told him off for being a lemming and pointed him in the direction of the beer tent.

I didn't see our Doris for the rest of the day. I wandered around the craft fair trying to find a gift for her, thinking if I used words like artisan and bespoke she wouldn't mind a necklace made from bottle caps.

Our Theo found me and said as he'd seen his grandmother giving an interview to BBC Manchester but by the time we'd got there she'd disappeared on to the next endeavour. I bought Theo lunch and asked him what he thought I should get our Doris for Christmas. He said to me, his mouthful of cheeseburger, he said, 'I don't know, she's your wife.'

'Well what have you got her?'

'Nothing.'

I said to him, I said, 'She's your grandmother.'

He nodded and said, 'Exactly – she's my grandmother. All I have to do is show up. You're her husband, if it isn't the perfect example of undying love you may as well put a mattress in your shed and hope for the best.'

Once he finished his lunch, he disappeared to find our Angela. She might have been able to help, but there was always the chance she'd tell our Doris I hadn't managed to find a present on my own. It's not that our Angela a snitch, it's just easier to tell our Doris straight out than wait, she once decapitated a Coalport figurine when I followed the advice of a Boots sales assistant in nineteen ninety-five.

The rest of the day passed by. I borrowed a copy of the Times of a security guard and read it in my car.

Eventually it came time for the fireworks display.

I met Edith, our Angela and Theo to join the throngs of people meandering into a field for the fireworks. We stood at the front of the crowd, pushed against the barrier.

Our Doris stood inside with Erin and Reuben. The fireworks waited to be lit behind her, their crew in the wings.

The press took photographs alongside some lads with camera phones who looked like they'd stepped right out of a documentary about inner-city poverty.

Our Doris stepped forward, and raised a microphone to her mouth, I've no idea where she got it. She addressed the crowd, ever the orator, she said to us, she said, 'Good evening, I hope you've all had a wonderful day, I won't keep you for long. I'm told that Father Christmas and his elves have met so many making their way onto the nice list, including young Reuben behind me. Today has proven to me just what Partridge Mews can achieve when it sets its mind to something and I am more than pleased to be part of this community. I just wanted to say, "thank you" and wish you all a very merry Christmas.'

She caught my eye and made her way over to the barrier. A crewmember came to retrieve the microphone

It didn't make it.

Out of nowhere, Miss Moonflower snatched the microphone from our Doris and faced us all, her face curled into something resembling a gargoyle. The cloak was out in full force, worn over the costume our Doris had chosen, she still had the green slippers.

Something like shock slipped across our Doris's face before she caught herself and flew into a nuclear-level Look. She said to Miss Moonflower, raging, she said, 'What in the Lord's name do you think you're doing?'

Miss Moonflower said something that may have been Elvish but sounded more like she'd swallowed her tongue.

Our Doris said, 'In English, please.' She had her hands on her hips, never a good sign.

The crowd grew more aggravated. They'd been promised a fireworks show and Mrs Pritchard-Singh worried she wouldn't get back in time for Casualty.

Miss Moonflower said to our Doris, she said, 'I have something to say.'

'Perhaps it could wait. Everyone is here for the fireworks, they don't want to see a melodramatic young woman with too much time on her hands rant about the plight of goblins in the Western hemisphere.'

'I am an elf,' she protested.

'I don't care what you are, we can talk about this in private.'

'Like you did at the church hall?'

Our Doris rolled her eyes, probably not the best move when facing an angry elf. She said to her, she said, 'I thought we'd moved past that, Emmeline.'

Miss Moonflower roared and pulled something from her pocket. Well, she attempted to pull something from her pocket but that's the problem with cloaks, it's easy to get your hand caught. As she struggled, she said to our Doris, she said, 'I should have known you were an enemy when you showed up in the library that day, Mrs Copeland. You are an awful specimen of a human being and I am the only one who can put an end to your reign of tyranny.'

'Doris!' Erin grabbed Miss Moonflower's hood and dragged her to the ground.

Edith cheered.

Erin yelled at our Doris to get back but it didn't matter.

Miss Moonflower had found what she wanted. She jumped to her feet and ran across the field, lighter in hand, and set the flame to nearest firework.

The firework that happened to be closest to Reuben.

He faced the sparks and I watched all colour drain from our Doris's face.

She vaulted back over the barrier, as though practising for the Olympics. Her Hotter shoes had done their job, the speed at which they carried her to Reuben.

She grabbed his middle and spun around.

Our Doris flung him at Erin as the firework set off.

'Nan!' Theo ran to our Doris.

No one saw the firework explode in the sky. All eyes were on our Doris's hair, her perfectly Silvakrinned perm now burning on top of her scalp.

I'm ashamed to say I froze on the spot. My heart was in my stomach. Fear I didn't think possible filled my entire body as I stared at my wife of fifty-five years and all the forbidden thoughts rose to my mind. Thoughts of cold mattresses, an empty house, remembering birthdays and cooking for one.

My lungs were fit to bursting.

Erin grabbed a bucket full of water and threw its contents over our Doris's head. She got her to the ground as the crewmembers and paramedics ran into the field.

She told them to continue with the fireworks.

They took her into the house and gave her a cup of strong, sweet tea. I sat across from her and said to her, I said, 'Are you sure, our Doris?'

'Of course, I'm sure, our 'arold, I paid for them. I'm not about to let Miss Moonflower ruin anyone else's evening.' She slurped her tea and said, 'How bad does it look?'

'You look like someone set your head on fire. It's patchy, and you'll be saving money on a hairdresser for a while.'

Erin and Theo came running it at that moment, both eager to wrap their arms around her. Once Theo finished hugging his Nan, Erin grabbed her and I thought she wouldn't let her go she held on that tight, like a leopard climbing a tree trunk. She said to our

Doris, she said, 'Mrs Copeland, thank you, I just, I don't know what I'd have done if anything had happened to Reuben.'

Our Doris patted Erin's shoulder and said, 'He's all right, isn't he? Not too traumatised about being catapulted across a field like a rugby ball, I hope.'

Erin sat down beside our Doris, she said to her, she said, 'He's fine. I left him with Angela, he wanted to see the fireworks but I couldn't stand out there. I think she understands – she seemed more than happy – maybe I should have let her come, you are her Mum after all.'

Theo said, 'I've texted her.'

I said to Erin, I said, 'Yes, and she knows not to worry about her mother. Our Doris has faced worse things than having her head set on fire.'

Theo smirked. 'It's amazing it hasn't happened before,' he said, 'the amount of hairspray she wears, walking past someone smoking in the street is a risk.'

We sniggered somewhat but it was half-hearted. After the paramedics cleared the way for our Doris, the police stepped in to remove Miss Moonflower. They were taking her to the hospital first, a decision that had Edith wrangling her way into the ambulance in case she tried to make an escape.

There was a banging about in the hall, a jingling of bells, and a bleary-eyed Alf wandered into the room. He said to us, he said, 'What's all this noise for? Can't a man kip in peace around here?'

I sat and watched as he blinked, his eyes alighting on our Doris's patchy scalp, wisps of hairs like wiry straws growing from the slight blisters. His mouth fell open and he said to her, he said, 'Blimey, Doris, what the bleeding heck happened to you?'

'Miss Moonflower,' she said.

He stood there, his mouth opening and closing, like a goldfish with a speech impediment before he said to our Doris, he said, 'I knew she couldn't be trusted. The only elf I've known to try and kill Father Christmas. I sent her out to get the drinks and all she brought back was green tea. Green tea? I tell you, have you ever met a drinker of green tea who wasn't around the twist?'

Alf sat down to hear the full story.

A little while later, our Angela appeared. She handed a sleeping Reuben to Erin and said to us, she said, 'It's all over the internet – those weirdoes livestreamed it to Facebook or something. Honestly, Mum, one day I'll be able to leave you alone without you getting into mischief. It's Burns Night nineteen eighty-three all over again.'

'Don't be so melodramatic, our Angela.' Our Doris slurped her tea before saying to me, she said, 'I'll need some headscarves, our 'arold.'

That's when Theo chose to pipe up with, he said, 'This evening's got a silver lining then, hasn't it, Grandad? Now you know what you can get Nan for Christmas.'

I glared at our Theo and said, 'That was a secret told in the strictest confidence.'

Once again our Doris wouldn't see me admonish her grandson as she said to me, she said, 'Edith already told me, our 'arold. This happens every year, am I really that difficult?'

Everyone glanced around at one another, before I was brave enough to say, I said, 'You are, love, but that's why we stick around.'

And we did.

8

BAKED

Our Doris won't let losing her hair hold her back. There were a few weeks where she didn't want to leave the house but she soon changed her mind when Pandra O'Malley stepped up her election campaign.

She came into the living room fashioning a Laura Ashley scarf into a turban. Since the accident she'd had a few attempts at using hatpins and assorted hairclips in her efforts to look more Marilyn Monroe than Nora Batty. Today's scarf had a pattern of butterflies, they had an almost whimsical look about them, delicate, completely in keeping with the torrential frown that currently occupied the central folds of our Doris's face.

It's a common complaint of the elderly, no matter your expression there's a wrinkle to really hit the message home, one grin and it looks like your cheeks are trying to swallow your ears. Our Doris glowered and said to me, she said, 'You'll never guess what that fool Pandra O'Malley has gone and done now.'

I said to her, I said, 'I imagine you'll tell me.'

She stalked over to the mirror on the chimney breast and said, 'I remembered I'd loaned my black and white polka dot pashmina to Edith and I thought it would make a rather fetching take on the classic bandanna. I'd pair it with the hat I wore to Susie's wedding, of course you're not likely to remember, but still, that is one of the perils of being married to a man who's more interested in aspidistras than the state of your headdress.'

I have to say I were somewhat astounded. Only moments earlier I'd been sat, minding my own business, watching Holly Willoughby navigate her way around a watermelon, when our Doris ploughed in with a look sour enough to rot lemons. I said to her, I said, 'Did this story have a point, our Doris?'

She gave me the Look and said, 'It did, actually, our 'arold, thank you for asking, you know how I like to ramble, I wouldn't want to interrupt you ogling a woman young enough to be your daughter, would I? Now, Edith told me that Pandra O'Malley is resurrecting her plans to hold a bake sale. A bake sale? This time she better not get any funny ideas about defrauding the community.'

'I suppose you'll enter, won't you? You won't just gad about making a mess of the kitchen like last time?'

If the Look could have got any more nuclear it would've been apocalyptic. After Miss Moonflower set fire to our Doris's head, got arrested, and subsequently awaited trial, I liked having our Doris around. There'd been this sense of fear that constantly filled my head. I'd lie awake at night knowing that I'd been too close to losing her. It was like having a cricket in my heart, constantly jumping around, making it difficult to catch my breath.

Then a week passed.

Once we hit the one week mark I wanted our

Doris to return to her normal way of life, attending committees, writing letters, and making sure that Mrs Turnpike got her newspaper on a Thursday morning when her daughter went to work early.

She didn't.

Our Doris became a hermit. Although the Partridge Mews Gazette had written an article about how a well-meaning, charitable woman, a pillar of our community, faced off an attacker who almost killed a toddler, our Doris didn't respond.

Not in the usual way, in any case.

Ordinarily, she'd write a long tale of her exploits. Instead she simply telephoned the editor and told him she had decided to take some time away from the public eye and would appreciate if they didn't focus too much on a small blot on what had otherwise been a rather successful event.

I'm not a horrible husband, I'm sympathetic to the fact that having your hair burned off by a psychotic elf is likely to leave a person feeling somewhat downtrodden, but our Doris has never felt sorry for herself before, and that includes the time she broke her ankle at the roller disco in nineteen eighty-six.

I certainly wasn't prepared to idle around the house making sure she was all right. She'd taken to hiding in the back bedroom watching price-drop auctions on the old television.

I said to her, I said, 'I don't know why you bother with that channel, our Doris, I thought you said as it was an ostentatious display of lower-class consumerism.'

She gave me the Look and said, 'I have been through a trauma, our 'arold, I like a bit of light relief.'

'Then watch Bargain Hunt,' I said, 'anything but

cash-drop TV.'

She didn't listen.

When Erin suggested that our Doris might enjoy a trip to Chester she was shot down faster than Billy the Kid.

Even our Theo tried to cheer her up by digging out the rock music and spinning her around the lounge but she complained of vertigo and that was the end of that.

Honestly, it isn't natural for her to stay in so long. After her hip replacement she had me wheel her around to Edith's every day to make sure she didn't miss any gossip. Now, she'd accept visits but wouldn't even consider stepping out the front door. Miss Moonflower had done a number on her and it caused such anger to rise in my veins I questioned how high your blood pressure could get before being considered a nuclear warhead.

It isn't healthy for our Doris to linger around the house.

Which is why I was hopeful that Pandra O'Malley's bake sale would cause our Doris to get out of the house. She paced across the carpet like Road Runner lost on a roundabout and said to me, she said, 'This isn't going to be like last time, our 'arold, because Erin isn't invited. Unless, of course, she chooses to enter something of her own making. She has found herself a position within the WI and I am not about to infringe upon it. No, I will prepare a British staple, a classic, and enter it into the bake sale.' I must have looked a bit astonished because she added, 'You're gawping. Don't gawp, it makes you look like a goldfish who's forgotten how to breathe underwater.'

I said to her, I said, 'It's just that you sounded

something like sensible, our Doris.'

'And that must be the most insensible thing you've ever said in fifty-five years of marriage, including the time you were "too tired".' She swanned out of the room like an empress leaving a ballroom and went into her cubbyhole to scour the recipe books. She'd end up with her grandmother's recipe whatever she chose to bake, it's what she does.

She's always had a thing for baking, has our Doris. When we first started courting, I put on a stone and half by the sheer amount of cakes and pastries she and her cousin made. It's no wonder Mavis went on to open a café. She might be an awful hostess, her hospitality is close to abysmal, but she knows how to concoct the best custard tart this side of the River Bollin.

With our Doris affecting some sort of normalcy I escaped to the Hare and Horse.

Alf hadn't been there long when I arrived but he still managed to neck his pint in time for my round. I said to him, I said, 'You know I would've bought you a pint anyway.'

He shrugged and said, 'It's good to show folk you've still got it, 'arold. It's not every day you can down a pint without threat of an angina attack.'

'You don't have angina.'

'Then you can go all out and buy us a couple of packets of pork scratchings.' He went and sat down, leaving me to bring everything over. It's not that Alf's inconsiderate, he just has this air of the perpetual ragamuffin, and once you have a reputation you don't want to let anyone down.

Once I sat down, he said to me, he said, 'Go on then, bake sale, what's happening?'

I said to him, I said, 'She's in her cubbyhole looking up recipes. I'm hoping it gets her out the house – I swear if she stays in much longer she'll start knitting. Our Doris isn't the type of woman to start knitting, she'd stab me faster than knit one, purl one.'

Alf spoke through a mouthful of pork scratchings, slobbering down his chin as he said, 'She hasn't got the knitter's temperament has your Doris, she's more suited to military combat, training soldiers and the like.'

'You're not wrong there, I'm sure the WI is only practise for the real thing.' I supped my pint and sighed. There's always something about that first taste of bitter as it travels from your lips to your stomach that calms you down, much more than the Daily Mirror crossword in any case.

Lord, did I need calming down.

Our Doris might not have noticed but having her around the house had begun to cause me untold stress.

I have a routine, a routine that revolves around the TV Guide but a routine nonetheless and when I wanted to watch a rerun of The Sweeney our Doris would wander into the lounge and suggest I read that Lee Child she bought me for Christmas. In the past I'd have said I'd lost my reading glasses, but she caught on to that years ago and had me switch to varifocals.

It felt like decades since I'd met Alf for a quiet drink without having to worry about who might threaten our Doris's life. I said to Alf, I said, 'Is your Edith entering a cake then?'

He cracked and crunched a few more pork scratchings in his mouth, yowling around the pieces stuck in his teeth as he said to me, he said, 'No, she's not prepared to support Pandra O'Malley. If she had her way I think she'd have her pilloried.'

'It's as good a reason as any I suppose.'

Alf had to pick the pork scratchings from his mouth, using his nails to scrape between his teeth like a monkey pecking for fleas. He said to me, sucking on his index finger, he said, 'What do you think Doris'll bring to the sale?'

'I've no idea,' I said, draining a few more inches of ale, 'she says she's going to go for a British classic.'

Alf removed half chewed remnants of previous meals from his mouth, stared at them on his fingers, before wiping them down his tongue. He said to me, he said, 'She always says she's going to make a British classic, it's one of her things, it could be a chocolate éclair and she'd call it British because she made it in a British kitchen.'

'She would that,' I said.

'She's wily,' he said.

'She's not a coyote.'

Alf looked to be thinking about something, an endeavour that's always something to watch, the way his forehead seems to devour his eyes, the same eyes that wander about the sockets like tourists who've lost sight of the Eiffel Tower. After he tapped his hands along the table, looking to be playing an invisible piano, he came out of his trance and said to me, he said, 'I bet she makes a Victoria Sponge.'

I considered it for a moment before ultimately shaking my head and saying to him, I said, 'No, not after last time.'

'It wasn't Arnold's fault.'

'I'm not saying it was,' I said, 'but how he ever thought it was a dishcloth is beyond me.'

'I think he did it to get out of ever volunteering to wash up again. It backfired anyway – he has hearing aids now.'

We finished our drinks. I said to Alf, I said, 'Do you fancy getting the next round?'

He beamed, his eyes glittering, either from cheek or flatulence, I'm not sure which, and he said to me, he said, 'If I were to go up there and pay for drinks, it would shatter the fragile equilibrium of this small community. You know that – it's the reason Dougie Usborne never wears flip-flops.'

'You've got a point there,' I said, 'are you all right for pork scratchings?'

'There's that many stuck in my gob, I'll be set till supper.'

I went and bought the next round. I'd managed to have a bit of a think at the bar so that when I returned I said to Alf, I said, 'I think I know what type of cake our Doris will make for the bake sale.'

Alf had downed half the pint before smearing his mouth on his sleeve and saying to me, as excitable as a dachshund in need of the lavatory, he said, 'What is it?'

'Carrot cake,' I said.

'Carrot cake?'

'Carrot cake,' I repeated.

Perhaps I should've broken the news in a kinder fashion. Alf slumped down in his seat, deflated, as though I'd run over his best Action Man. He said to me, he said, 'Are you sure it's carrot cake? Might it not be a chocolate cake? Or even better, a Black Forest Gateau?'

I shook my head and said, 'It has to be carrot cake. She'll want something that allows the illusion of being healthy so she can say that she cares about the welfare of our community and is aware of the sugar crisis and rise in obesity. There's no way our Doris would make anything other than a carrot cake.'

'I suppose,' Alf said, 'but don't ask me to eat it. I've never been able to stomach carrot cake – not after our Edith caught on to Vanessa Feltz's last diet.' He shuddered, he visibly shuddered at the memory.

It isn't often that I regret saying something at the pub. Often it's forgotten by the time I've got home, but as Derek O'Malley approached from the bar I realised we had been heard, that this wouldn't be forgotten, and that our words would be directly fed back to his wife. I felt bile rise in my stomach, melting my intestines, leaving them to gurgle from either indigestion or the unfathomable tension.

Alf broke the silence, saying, he said, 'How do, Derek?'

Derek smiled, he positively beamed as he said to me, he said, 'You definitely think that illustrious wife of yours will be making a carrot cake for the sale then, 'arold?'

I nodded once, a sign that he needn't continue, we knew exactly how this would end. 'It's practically a certainty.'

'Aye,' Alf said, 'like the fact your mother never taught you not to flaming eavesdrop.'

I'm surprised Derek didn't rub his hands together as he said to Alf, he said, 'Now don't be like that, Alf, you know what it's like being a husband of the WI. We can't band together, we have to stick by our wives or face the consequences.'

I seethed, I clenched the edges of the table and said to him, I said, 'Have you heard of showing some honour, Derek? Some compassion to your fellow man? Our Doris could have been killed. This bake sale could be the first thing to get her out of the house in weeks and you're about to set her back all for the chance of keeping your wife happy? The chance to please that bloody parasite of a woman?'

Derek stammered, his eyes wide. It's not often I get angry. Any sort of outburst is usually settled because I can't have it getting back to our Doris that I've been unsociable in public, but this was different. He said to me, he said, 'You have to understand she's my wife –'

'Aye,' I said, 'just like our Doris is my wife, and if you think I'm going to let a potato-scrubbing, louse-infested, fraudster take the WI away from her you've another thing coming, Derek O'Malley.'

'That's two things you've said to offend my wife, one more and we'll have to take this outside.'

'What's the point in taking it outside?' I said, clearly not thinking as I rose to my feet. 'How about I show you just how we used to deal with men like you back in the day?'

'I won't have any fighting in my pub, Mr Copeland,' Linda called from behind the bar.

'It's not a fight, love, don't you worry,' Derek said.

I must've thought myself a bit of the Bruce Willis as I said to him, I said, 'It's not,' and punched him.

I knew I'd gone too far when Derek stumbled back, hand to his cheek. I'm lucky he didn't ring the police, just left the pub without another word.

Linda asked me to leave, said I was barred until the end of the week, and only because she knew Derek could be a swine.

I wasn't worried about any of this, I was worried about our Doris.

My fist smarted but it was worth it.

As we left the Hare and Horse, Alf beamed, it was like he was back in short trousers and had just discovered where Denise Hemsworth hid her toffees. He said to me, he said, 'That were brilliant, 'arold, absolutely brilliant. I never thought you had it in you. Blooming heck you must be mad, you must be completely and utterly off your bleeding rocker.'

'I feel sick,' I said.

'That'll be the adrenaline. We best get you home, tell Doris before anyone else gets chance.'

Our Doris was unconcerned. When we arrived at the house, I took her and Alf into the kitchen and busied myself making a pot of tea. I told her everything that had happened, and she sat there, back straight, unwavering, filling me with the sort of fear that wives for centuries have instilled in their husbands.

Once I finished telling her the tale she said, 'And before you clouted Mr O'Malley he'd been convinced I would be bringing a carrot cake to the bake sale?'

I said to her, apologetic as a puppy who's made a mess of the carpet, I said, 'It seemed the obvious option. You'd want to create something that folk would see as healthy, even though it isn't, and it had to be a British classic.'

Our Doris smiled, she actually grinned and patted Alf on the arm before saying to him, she said, 'My husband can be a fool at times, Alf.'

He blinked a few times, fearful, and said, 'What's that got to do with anything?'

She poured us all cups of tea and said to me, she said, 'Of course I'm not going to make a bleeding carrot cake. Although it would seem like the most obvious option, I want to have something to sell, who in their right mind would buy a carrot cake when there's a whole host of better confectionary to choose from? Even the most obese Weight Watcher would choose a slab of chocolate cake over carrot cake any day of the week.'

'So you're not making a carrot cake?' I said.

Our Doris shook her head. 'No.'

'I punched Derek for nothing then?'

She shook her head again. 'Oh, I think it was the best thing you could have done, our 'arold. It would have added an air of believability to the performance. You can't go around laying your fists on folk at every opportunity but if it's an O'Malley I'm not sure I can complain.'

'What cake will you make then, Doris?' Alf asked.

She tapped him on the hand and said to him, she said, 'I can't possibly say, Alf. If our 'arold finds out, there's no telling who'll be next on his hit list.'

I thought I'd finally got my wife back, that she'd managed to escape any throes of sadness. I slept soundly that night, confident that in the morning I would wake up and discover our Doris in the kitchen, back to her old tricks. Indeed she was, she made us both breakfast and I went with Alf to check on the allotment.

I should have understood that things have a tendency to go bad in Partridge Mews, that there's enough in-fighting we may as well be the Labour Party making dinner plans.

We reached the allotment to find Richard Peg sat in a deck chair, staring across an empty patch that only the other day had been flourishing. I said to him, I said, 'What's going on here then?'

He came out of what can only be described as a stupor to say to me, he said, 'It's that Derek O'Malley – good going on that eye, 'arold, he had a right shiner, and it's only well-deserved. His Pandra got on to the missus and she had me sell him my carrots. She made out like they're for a dinner party with soup for starters. Soup, my right eye, we all know what happened at that pub and he can sod off if he thinks I'm helping him out again.'

'He paid you the going rate though,' I said.

Richard nodded. 'That he did – they weren't ready, 'arold. She could've waited a few more days. How many carrots does she think you need for one cake?'

I shrugged and said, 'I shouldn't worry about it, Richard.'

'Our Nancy says the greengrocer's sold out of carrots as well. Where's she going to keep them all is what I'm wondering.'

'I wouldn't question her thinking,' Alf said, 'she's WI, there's no knowing what's going on in that head of hers.'

If only carrots were all we had to worry about. Our Doris hadn't played rock music in a while, even when Theo brought it around to make her feel better she kept it that quiet so as not to disturb the neighbours. Yet as we turned into Shakespeare Avenue, Alf and I became all the more aware of a pulsating noise that seemed to shake the car. I pulled into the drive and realised just whose voice roared above the terrifying blare of drums. Our Doris was somewhere in the house listening to Meat Loaf at full blast.

Alf thought it might be serious and decided he'd make the tea this time.

I found our Doris in the back bedroom, staring at a price drop auction with tears in her eyes. I said to her, I said, 'I never thought cubic zirconia would get you that way, our Doris.'

I was glad Alf stayed downstairs.

Our Doris attempted the Look but ended up floundering. She sat on the bed with the duvet cover pulled around her so that she looked like some sort of floral tortoise. Our Doris has never looked more meek. Even when her Aunty Phyllis shouted at her for marrying a snob with less personality than a lettuce leaf, she stood her ground. Something was wrong, something that had stopped our Doris from standing tall in the face of adversity.

I said to her, I said, 'What's the matter?'

She shook her head and pulled the duvet further over her head, and said to me, she said, 'It's not right, our 'arold, it just isn't right. I never wanted any of this to happen – I know that I'm not the most agreeable person, that I can be a bit high-strung, but I never expected someone to hurt me like that stupid girl did.'

I knelt down in front of her, it's no easy feat with my new knee. I said to her, I said, 'Miss Moonflower? She's on remand, isn't she?'

Our Doris shook her head and said, 'She was until this morning. For some reason they let her off lightly. They say she showed remorse but she looked smug as anything when they sentenced her.

'Reuben could have been killed but because she said she was sorry she's got away with a little bit of community service.'

I pushed down any sense of anger and said, 'You never mentioned a trial.'

'I couldn't face you being there, our 'arold. I told Erin not to say anything when the letter came last week. It was all over quite quickly. I said my piece. Miss Moonflower apologised and that was the end of that.

'Erin said she'd come over but I told her not to bother. I can't be doing with people all over the house all the time.' Our Doris shrank further into the duvet and I knew that this wasn't my wife talking. She looked nothing like herself. She'd become some sort of victim, and I didn't know what to do.

I reached out for her, to hold her in my arms like any husband ought, but she covered her face. She told me to leave her alone.

Despite what she asked I got Erin to come around. I hadn't seen her much recently. Apparently her college work, mixed with caring for Reuben and spying for our Doris meant she didn't get much chance to sit down and chat.

Alf stuck around. He'd called his Edith and told her about all the goings-on. She arrived a few minutes after Erin, bearing sandwiches and a flask full of hot cocoa, made to her own recipe.

Once we all sat at the kitchen table, I said to Erin, I said, 'What went on at the court then?'

Erin looked tired herself as she said to me, she said, 'Her lawyer said as Mrs Copeland had a good case against Miss Moonflower, what with the previous harassment, but they brought up all that stuff about the church hall and it was enough to sway the decision I think. Miss Moonflower had already pleaded guilty so all that was left to do was to sentence her and they said as it was her first offense and she'd had some provocation. Honestly, Mr Copeland, it was hard to watch, they made out like it was all Mrs Copeland's fault.'

There was a moment of silence as the music ended, a shimmer of hope, soon obliterated by the roar of Bon Jovi. I said to them, I said, 'This is going to be the death of me, I can tell you.'

'Maybe I should have a word with her,' Edith said.

'I'm not sure it would work, love,' Alf said, his lips smeared with hot cocoa.

I met her eyes and said to her, I said, 'She doesn't want any visitors. I don't know what to do, Edith.'

Edith's brow creased, her eyes filled with something like fury. She pursed her lips and said, 'All of this because of the WI, 'arold. I wonder that it's worth it.'

Days passed and still our Doris didn't leave the back bedroom. Our Theo brought some headphones around as a means of noise control but she didn't let him stay near her for longer than two minutes.

It had shaken him. He said to me, he said, 'You need to do something, Grandad. Nan's not like this.'

I said that I knew and sent him home to his mother.

He was right.

Our Doris stumbled around upstairs wearing her duvet like a housecoat. I took her meals but she wouldn't touch them. I thought about getting a doctor out, but word travels fast in Partridge Mews and before she got a prescription folk would have it in their heads that she'd slipped into some form of senility.

Alf returned on the fifth day. He looked a bit sheepish as he said, 'How is she?'

'I had her probation officer around the other day,' I said, 'he wondered why she'd missed her hours at the charity shop. She wouldn't let him see her. He says as if she misses many more days she'll be back up in court.'

Alf allowed my words to process for a moment before heading towards the stairs, he said to me, he said, 'Don't bother making us a brew right now, come upstairs, I want to try something.'

I followed him to the back bedroom but stayed by

the door. Our Doris sat on the bed, headphones on, still loud enough for us to hear Jailhouse Rock.

There were an air of concern about Alf as he placed his hand on our Doris's shoulder. She jolted up and faced him, her eyes red as though she'd rubbed at them with chilli peppers. Adopting this air of superiority, she said to him, she said, 'I'll thank you but I'm not taking visitors today, Mr Simpson.'

Alf switched the stereo off at the wall and stared at her, his gaze imperious. Our Doris made to protest but he said to her, he said, 'I came here to have a word, Doris, and you don't want it getting around that you ignored the basic rules of hospitality by being a bad housewife, no matter the circumstances.'

Our Doris gawped at him. She considered his words for a moment before removing the headphones from her ears, that red they were practically luminescent. She bowed her head and said, 'Please excuse my current state of dress, I had no idea we would have guests. I had very explicit instructions about that.' She spun around and gave me the Look – a sign of good things, I hoped.

Alf sat down beside our Doris and said to her, he said, 'The way I see it, I've no room to talk about the state of one's clothing, I've had the same pair of socks since nineteen ninety-seven. Thermals from John Lewis.'

'They do have some good socks,' our Doris said. She wasn't wearing a headscarf, meaning we could see the white tufts of hair peppering her scalp, she patted at them, seemingly trying to force them into some sort of shape.

'The thing is, Doris,' Alf said, 'I've been thinking a lot lately of that business with Ruby. I didn't press any charges because I didn't want it getting around that some young piece had managed to outwit me. I might gad about town acting at the rascal, like nothing could hurt me, but the fact of the matter is that it left me absolutely terrified.'

'Oh Alf,' she said.

I don't know why Alf had wanted me to hear any of this but I remained there, stood at the bedroom door, looking in on them both.

He continued with his story and said to our Doris, he said, 'You knew that I wasn't myself – you and 'arold set me on the straight and narrow, but it doesn't mean you stop being scared. Miss Moonflower did something much more horrendous, I know that, but we both know you've faced worse things.'

Our Doris dabbed at her eyes with the edge of the duvet. She said to Alf, she said, 'It's not just that, Alf. She's going to participate in the bake sale. Her being there just emphasises the point that no matter what I do she'll always be there.'

'Like a mole,' he said, nodding, 'like some poxy little mole you get on the back of your knee. It doesn't need worrying about until it begins to irritate you.'

She nodded and said, 'Alfred Simpson, when did you become so philosophical?'

He offered a slight smile and said to her, he said, 'You're not just 'arold's wife, Doris, you're one of my closest friends, and it doesn't matter what we've joked about in the past, I'm not going to let some young slip of a girl leave you hiding in a bedroom like the mad woman in the attic.'

Our Doris sniggered slightly and the dread disappeared for a moment. This time I left them to it and went downstairs to make the drinks, we all deserved a cup of tea.

The next few days passed by in a whirlwind. With our Doris back on her feet she began to make all the necessary preparations for the bake sale. She invited Erin out for a meal in town, leaving me to look after Reuben.

I think our Doris wanted to test the waters, see how much she could cope with. She needn't have worried. She was soon back home bemoaning the state of the restaurant, saying they clearly had no concept of modern menus if they thought apple crumble a suitable alternative to ginger pudding and custard.

Neither of us knew how to tell Alf how grateful we were. Our Doris informed Edith exactly what had happened, reiterating everything he had done, knowing he would receive unimaginable gifts from his wife. She always likes knowing when he does anything respectable, it happens rarely enough.

In the days approaching the bake sale our Doris squirrelled herself away in the kitchen. She still hadn't let on what she was making and I didn't concern myself too much, I knew she felt better about things, and I also had a few episodes of The Sweeney to catch up on. I'd considered finding some of my old videos of Charlie Dimmock but I wasn't up to the task of complete infatuation.

Eventually, the day of the bake sale arrived. Our Doris kept her cake hidden beneath a cloth in the Tupperware so as no one could garner any ideas as to what she'd made. We made our way to the church hall, meeting Pandra at the door. She glared at me and said to me, she said, 'I had half a mind not to let you in after the way you treated my husband, Mr Copeland.'

Our Doris smirked and said to her, she said, 'Half

a mind, Pandra? I should think that brings it to about full capacity.' And she wandered inside. Both our Doris and I know from previous experience that Pandra wasn't allowed to exclude anyone from entering the church hall, on direct orders from the vicar. He says as it doesn't give the right message about Christianity.

Our Doris dressed for the occasion. She wore her peach blazer and skirt, with her white court shoes – she's always maintained that white is a dangerous colour for a woman to wear as she never knows just what she might step into. Before we left the house I'd pointed out she'd forgotten her headscarf but she said as she wanted Miss Moonflower to know the damage she had caused.

And Miss Moonflower did know.

She stood placing her own cake on the table amongst all the other creations the people of Partridge Mews had put together for the event. We still weren't sure what the bake sale was fundraising for, but the vicar wandered around the hall so we imagined it was definitely a legitimate cause.

'Emmeline,' our Doris nodded in her direction before setting her Tupperware on the table between a three-tiered chocolate cake and a pineapple upside-down cake.

'Mrs Copeland,' she replied, leaving something brown and crusting on the table, it certainly didn't look like a cake and I doubt there'd even be enough for a mouthful. She wandered off in the direction of the crowd.

I said to our Doris, I said, 'Are you all right?'

She said to me, she said, 'Of course I am, our 'arold. She's just one woman – shall we have a cup of coffee? I could do with a sit down.'

As Alf had said, Edith didn't enter the bake sale. They arrived half an hour later, joining us as we reviewed the cakes on offer.

Pandra had managed to wrangle a few of the WI members into selling them. Mrs Cribbins struggled a bit without her glasses, but she did well enough.

'I didn't think much to Ida's fruitcake, did you?' Edith said.

'No,' our Doris said, 'it reminded me a lot of houses in the seventies. Pebble-dashed.'

After a few minutes of walking past the many carrot cakes of Pandra O'Malley Alf said to our Doris, he said, 'Come on then, which one's yours?'

'I haven't seen it,' she said, 'it must have all gone.'

Out of nowhere the words of Pandra O'Malley spoke, like a phantom, or some other mystical creature you can't wait to get rid of. She said to us, she said, 'Perhaps it simply went missing. You know how it is, Mrs Copeland, there are so many cakes and sometimes we lose track of them. Especially when our minds are at full capacity.'

We turned to catch her sneering at us, arms folded, looking ever the headmistress.

Alf said to her, he said, 'Where's the husband, Mrs O'Malley? Still running scared.'

'It's none of your business where he is. He's hardworking, unlike some of the men I could mention.' Her eyes settled on Alf and I imagine that was the final straw for Edith because I have seen Edith Simpson angry before but I have never seen her so ferocious she could tackle the Hulk.

She roared, I'm sure she roared as she said to Pandra, she said to her, 'How dare you, you good-for-nothing, little harlot. You've always been power hungry but to hide a cake at a bleeding bake sale that you organised is nothing short of petty. So Mr Copeland punched your husband in the eye, so what? At least he's a real man, defending his wife. You husband is nothing short of a worm, and why should anyone be surprised when he is married to a god-awful blowfish like you?'

Everyone in the church hall stood frozen to the spot as Edith grabbed the closest thing to her and thrust a Victoria Sponge at Pandra O'Malley.

It slammed into her face with all the force of a torpedo, splattering cream and jam and cake all over her face, matting her hair.

Edith didn't stop there. Alf struggled to hold her back as she stormed further up the table and said, 'Then you go around town buying up carrots simply because you hear there's a slight chance Mrs Copeland might make a carrot cake. Again, this is your event, surely you should know it will be successful without having to stoop to such lows. Have some confidence, woman.'

Next, she threw a carrot cake. Then another. 'I'm sorry, you don't really seem to be enjoying that one, Mrs O'Malley, it'd be best to just get rid of the lot, wouldn't it?' She took hold of the table's edge and in one swift movement, upended it.

The vicar scuttled over, never raising his voice enough to stop Edith's tirade.

Still Pandra stood, clearly shellshocked. Edith surged towards her, took her arm, and pulled her in the direction of the table. 'Now you're going to show me just what you did to Mrs Copeland's cake or I am going to make you taste every single one of these cakes. Maybe you'll do us all a favour and slip into a diabetic coma.'

'Edith, that's enough!' our Doris shouted.

Throughout all of this my eyes had been on Edith. I hadn't thought to check on our Doris. She gave her closest friend the fiercest Look I have ever seen in my life, worse than any she's ever aimed at me.

Edith stood, a firm hold on Pandra's arm as she faced our Doris and said to her, she said, 'I can't cope with this anymore, Doris, I am fed up with this woman's constant sniping. If no one else will teach her a lesson then I will.'

'By destroying cakes that other people went to the trouble of making?' Doris asked. 'Alf tell her.'

'Don't you dare, Alfred Simpson,' Edith said.

The vicar stood beside me now and said to us, he said, 'I think you all best come with me. Somebody better explain themselves.'

The five of us looked at each other and turned to follow the vicar out of the church hall. I spotted our Doris's Tupperware as we left, someone had tried to hide it behind one of the radiators. I made a diversion and took it with me, I had a feeling we might need some cake, no matter the variety.

9

INTERVENTION

Our Doris and the rest of us found ourselves in the vicar's living room, ready for him to chastise us about the bake sale. He'd taken Pandra upstairs to show her where she could wash the carrot cake out of her hair, leaving me, Alf and Edith to sit on the sofa across from our Doris who immediately sat herself down in an armchair facing the window. Everything about the vicar's furniture suggested chintzy, floral upholstery with lace antimacassars, I felt like I'd stepped into my grandmother's living room. She died in nineteen fifty-eight.

I'd placed our Doris's Tupperware on the coffee table between us. She hadn't spoken a word since we left the church hall. I hoped she was biding her time, thinking of something intelligent to say to bring us to our knees. Hoping to break the silence, I said to her, I said, 'I found your cake, our Doris.'

She continued to stare straight out the window as she said to me, she said, 'That's nice, our 'arold, you should keep it away from Edith, she may think it's a torpedo.'

'That's not fair, Doris,' Edith said, 'I was defending you.'

'You were making a mockery of me. You were saying to every person in that church hall that I only know how to solve things with violence. I am not completely unhinged, not so senile that I immediately begin to throw things should I not get my own way,' she said.

Edith settled back on the sofa and offered a simple, 'Sorry.'

Over the last few weeks I'd seen our Doris despondent. She'd only set foot out of the back bedroom a few days before thanks to Alf's efforts. I couldn't pretend I wasn't worried. Our Doris's emotional state could almost be described as a tightrope, it doesn't take much to push her over the edge.

Out of nowhere she said to us, she said, 'A year ago I was a respected member of this community. Since I took on the role of interim chairwoman I have met nothing but condescension, folk have questioned my mental state, and one young man thought it perfectly acceptable to run over my handbag with his bicycle and faced no consequences.

'He faced no consequences because since I fought Janice Dooley of Little Street the people in this town have started seeing that I am a normal human being with my own flaws. Being sentenced to community service as though I were a common teenage hooligan means that I can never be taken seriously.

'In the past I always solved things with words. I joined the WI in the nineteen-seventies and it was a gateway to my becoming the woman I am today. People looked at me differently, it gave me a certain power that others didn't have – a knowledge of the ways of polite society that I have seen torn apart. My letters to the Gazette were sought after because I taught women a thing or two about how to keep their homes and what service was suitable to use. I may have been mocked in the streets but they looked up to me. Now, if I send a letter to the editor it is rarely printed. They look to paint me as this figure who is lost in the past, who yearns for the days of yesteryear, who refuses to embrace modernity.

'I've never needed my friends to stand up for me before. I had such notoriety that if someone said something against me I could bite back and have the WI on my side. Now my husband seeks to punch the husband of my running mate and my closest friend chooses to throw baked goods at Pandra O'Malley for no other reason than she's proven herself to be a formidable opponent.

'I have never sought to solve things with violence before, and I am most appalled that any of you think that would be my way. I am not some common yob who uses their fists because they do not have the intelligence to settle scores with the air of the civilised.'

There was such a silence once our Doris finished speaking even pins would refuse to drop. I've no idea whether she thought about what she said before she said it, but she left me feeling like I did back in my short trouser days. Alf and Edith can't have been feeling much better – Alf stared at his feet, twiddling his thumbs and Edith gulped that much it were like watching someone with a thistle caught in their tonsils.

The door opened and Pandra O'Malley entered, towel around her shoulders, with a scowl so fierce she could give the gargoyles a run for their money protecting Notre Dame. She sat in the chair opposite our Doris, crossing her legs with all the rapidity of a lobster snapping its claws. She said to us, she said, 'I knew you'd do something to ruin my day. It's just so bleeding typical.'

None of us responded.

The vicar brought in the tea, carrying it on the tray alongside a plate of biscuits, bourbons, chocolate digestives, custard creams, he must've emptied the tin in his efforts to calm the situation. I said to him, I said, 'I'm not sure a custard cream and a brew is going to solve this one, vicar.'

He offered up a smile and said to me, he said, 'You've not tried my tea yet, Mr Copeland, trust me I think it'll do the trick. Besides, you're none of you leaving this house until we've solved this problem.'

There were glances around the room and I said, 'I best have a bourbon then.'

Now our vicar has always been smart. He came to Partridge Mews about fifteen years ago, young, full of fresh ideas and with a modern haircut that he's kept up even though it's started to recede. At that moment though, he chose to do something so incredibly stupid I began to question my faith in his sermons. He reached for the Tupperware on the table, and said to us, he said, 'This must be one of Mrs Copeland's cakes. I've never known someone with more pristine Tupperware – perhaps we might have a few slices with our drinks.'

For the first time in her life our Doris gave the vicar the Look. She's always saved it for the more deadly of crimes but right now her glare could have sent him into the fiery depths of Hell and I'm not sure he'd know until he felt a warmth in his cassock. She said to him, our Doris said, 'I don't wish to be unholy, vicar, but if you so much as lay a finger on that cake then I will write a letter to the bishop stating as you made unwanted advantages towards my baked goods.'

The vicar stopped in his tracks and stammered, he said, 'My apologies, Mrs Copeland, I just thought since we weren't unable to sample your wares at the bake sale you may wish to give us a slight taste test.'

'You thought wrong.'

'Oh,' he said.

'Yes,' she said.

Clearly not one to be thwarted by a shark biting off his leg, the vicar said to our Doris, he said, 'I must say that I've never known a bake sale to cause such animosity before.'

Edith piped up here and said to him, she said, 'You're the one who chose to support Pandra O'Malley in her endeavours, even after she thought to try and defraud the church only months ago.'

'That's an outright lie,' Pandra protested, 'I wouldn't take money from the church, I would have taken it from the people of Partridge Mews. Besides, Mrs Copeland saw to it that I didn't hold the first bake sale so I see no reason to bring it up.'

'Only because it shows you in a bad light,' Alf said. He faced our Doris and said to her, he said, 'Sorry, Doris, but you might not be happy with our Edith for throwing cakes at her but I do have something to say to her if you don't mind.'

The vicar interjected here and said, 'I'm not really sure that's wise, Mr Simpson.'

'And I'm not really sure you're supposed to accept stolen pork pies for those food baskets for the homeless, but we've never said anything about it before, have we?' Alf waited for the vicar to nod before he turned on Pandra O'Malley and said to her, he said, 'I don't know you enough to know whether you were dropped on your head as a child but I'm beginning to question whether that's the reason you act like you've a cattle-prod wedged up your backside.'

A few crumbs of carrot cake toppled from Pandra's head like cinnamon-scented dandruff as she said to us, she said, 'I find it funny that you're all here defending one another and I have nobody. Can't we wait until my husband gets here? Though I can't imagine he'd want to spend two minutes in the same room as Mr Copeland.'

'Then he's not a real man,' I said. The words were fuelled with an anger so fiery it was as though I had a river of boiling tar resting in my intestines. I said to Pandra, I said, 'If this were thirty years ago, I'd have punched Derek and no one would have said another word about it. It's the way things were. Men sorted things out between men and their wives didn't get involved. This might seem like an attack, in some ways it is, I do not care about the fact that you want to be chairwoman of the WI, what annoys me is the way you have treated my wife. The same way your Derek doesn't stand for people offending his wife, I refuse to let anyone make a mockery of our Doris, and if you think you can continue to do so then we have a problem.'

Pandra glowered at our Doris and said to her, she said, 'They're all leaping to your defence but you've nothing to say, Mrs Copeland.'

I saw a glimmer of something in our Doris's eyes, a slight twitch of her lips as she said our Doris said, 'Would you care to pour me a cup of tea, please, vicar? All this hot air is making my mouth rather dry.'

The vicar set about making her a drink and handed it over.

She evaluated the china, I saw her counting the petals of the flowers, murmuring to herself. It's a trick our Doris has perfected over the years, to elicit a sense of fear in folk, and I knew she wanted the vicar fearful now, that fearful that his eyes were wide as he said to her, he said, 'Is something the matter?'

She said to him, she said, 'It's nothing to worry about, vicar, I merely chose to inspect your china. Royal Albert, I think? I'm most sorry to say that I've never been the biggest proponent of their work, it always seems a little derivative of the finer china makers renowned throughout the British Isles. Though, who am I to judge?' She pursed her lips and blew slightly over her cup, every movement precise, as though she were a spy surveying the territory.

Pandra couldn't stand it, she flew forward and said, 'I'll have a cup of tea, too please, vicar, I've no problem with Royal Albert, I'm just happy that someone took the time to serve tea in china cups – it's not something you see often nowadays.'

'I can imagine so, in the places you frequent,' our Doris said, 'though in the finer establishments it is much the norm to make sure that your guests receive an adequate, indeed, exceptional dining experience with the most exquisite bone china.'

Pandra accepted her cup of tea, whispering her thanks to the vicar. After that we helped ourselves. Edith poured the tea, handing a cup to Alf who handled it with all the care of a bulldozer.

Once we'd all got our drinks we returned to the silence. The last few weeks had seen my life filled with uncomfortable quiet. I glanced around the room and wherever my gaze landed, be it the crinoline ladies on the mantelpiece, or the photographs of the vicar and his family spotted here and there so as you couldn't avoid them, I was unable to avoid the unutterable discomfort of that silence.

Instead, I decided to speak to the vicar. He'd knelt down behind the table, it didn't seem right this being his house but we're a considerable age older than him and I wasn't about to complain. I said to him, I said, 'I think we might need to start now. We could end up being here for the next six months otherwise.'

He nodded and said, 'I would be most appreciative.'

Still the silence continued, save for Alf's crunching of custard creams.

I said, 'Are you going to start then?'

'I'm not sure I've got anything to say, Mr Copeland,' he said, looking all the more gormless, a face that doesn't sit right on a vicar.

'You said you were bringing us here to solve a problem. Tell us your problem, ask questions and the like – I thought this were some sort of intervention.' I've seen enough episodes of Jeremy Kyle in the last decade to know what an intervention looks like. Of course I don't watch it when our Doris is around the house, she's never got on with Jeremy Kyle, thinks as he allows more lower class people on his show than you ever found on Trisha Goddard.

'An intervention?' The vicar seemed to consider my words for a moment, looking ever the dog anticipating a ball, before his face brightened up and he said to me, he said, 'Yes, that does sound a rather interesting idea, doesn't it? An intervention. I could say as we'd set up a counselling service, earn a bit more money for the Scout's trip to Prestatyn.'

'I'm sorry, vicar, but I don't think we're in need of an intervention,' our Doris said, her cup balanced on the palm of her left hand.

'I'll agree with Doris on that one,' Pandra said.

Our Doris nodded. 'Quite,' she said, 'I think that Mrs O'Malley is a complete waste of my time and energy and she agrees that she's a no-good layabout. The argument ends there, in my opinion.'

Pandra set her now empty cup on the table and said, ignoring the rest of us, she said, 'If I'm such a waste of time, why are you going to all this effort?'

'Finally, a question of which I have no answer.'

'Do you want to know what I think, Doris?'

'I can't say it has ever interested me before.'

'I think that if you didn't have someone to argue with then your life would be utterly meaningless. You'd simply gad about the place baking cakes and telling people they've been using salad forks wrong for decades.' Pandra sat back, a smug grin settling on her face, something akin to the Cheshire Cat, or a baby after burping.

The vicar looked between them both and said to us, he said, 'This is just the kind of animosity I was talking about. You may think these things don't reach my ears but there are members of this parish who are most concerned with the way you're getting on with one another.' He turned on Edith at this point. 'And Mrs Simpson, your behaviour at the bake sale today is completely out of character. If I hadn't seen it with my own eyes I would never have believed it of the woman who nursed the Guides after the last communal curry night.'

Edith, visibly chastised, held her head high and

said to him, she said, 'It is true that ordinarily I would not behave in such a fashion as you saw earlier today. However, there were extraneous circumstances.'

'Perhaps you'd care to enlighten us.'

She nodded in the direction of Pandra and said, 'I've never before met anyone I've thought would look better with a carrot cake planted on their thick head.'

Alf and I couldn't help ourselves. We burst out laughing, a pair of rabid hyenas chortling to ourselves until we choked. Alf clapped Edith on the shoulder and said to her, he said, 'Good on you, Edie, you tell her.'

That's the thing about Alf and Edith, they always bring out the worst in each other. When they first started courting, most of their dates took place down the courthouse because Alf couldn't help acquiring gifts for Edith and she couldn't help bragging about them. She always knew how to get around the judge, though. It always helps to have a solicitor for a father.

It'd be easy to question whether Alf only married Edith for her legal connections, but he's always bought her lilies for Valentine's Day – roses are overdone, and lilies are freely available, folk leave them all over the cemetery.

Pandra interrupted our frivolity to say to the vicar, she said, 'See, this is what I have to deal with day in and day out. The constant bullying from Mrs Copeland and her cronies is enough to drive even the most Christian of women to murder.'

Our Doris said to her, she said, 'Do you believe that you have ever behaved in a fashion befitting a Christian woman, Mrs O'Malley?'

Pandra began to stammer, scattering words, searching for a response.   She tugged at the frayed hems of her M&S blouse, as though she might be able to find something to say in the seams.

'It's like looking at a poor imitation of a lady,' our Doris said, eyes pierced, lips pursed as she went on, she said, 'Once the rumours began to circulate of your candidacy you changed your appearance and I can't say it has been for the better. You cannot deny that, Mrs O'Malley. At first I thought that we had a polite acquaintance with one another, that this would be a friendly competition, that you were a worthy adversary, but you chose to play dirty.

'I have said my piece more than enough but I want to know where you got the idea to behave in such a fashion, to drag my name through the dirt to the point that I am a laughing stock in my hometown.

'Please, Pandra, enlighten me, just why did you choose to hurt me like this?'

I couldn't help staring open-mouthed at our Doris. She doesn't like me to gawp, but to hear her speak so freely left me unaware of just what my body was doing.

Pandra stared our Doris down and said to her, she said, 'You act like I'm the one who set your hair on fire.'

'I don't care about my bleeding hair. I don't care about any of it. I want to know just what I did to deserve this malice, Pandra.' Our Doris looked mildly unhinged as she pleaded with Pandra. She doesn't often go in for pleading, has a way with words that usually has folk agreeing to any of her demands, no matter how farcical. Besides, pleading doesn't suit our Doris's face, her wrinkles are that deep and wide it's like watching canyons stretch across her forehead.

After a few moments of staring into our Doris's eyes, Pandra said to her, she said, 'I simply followed your example, Mrs Copeland. There's no secret that I want to be the chairwoman of the WI.'

'What do you mean, my example?'

'There are a great many women in this town who have found themselves denigrated by Mrs Doris Copeland. You're quite free with the insults when it suits your own means, yet you're quite unable to cope when those same words are turned on you.'

Our Doris slumped back in her chair and ran a hand through the barely-there tufts of hair on her scalp, wincing when she happened upon a blister. Her body seemed to collapse in on itself, she were practically insubstantial, as though a gust of wind could blow through the living room and deposit her on the left-hand side of Timbuktu.

I said to her, I said, 'Are you all right, there, our Doris?'

She said to me, her words little more than a whimper, she said, 'She's right, our 'arold.'

I don't know what came over me as I said to the rest of them, I said, 'I'd like to talk to my wife in private, if you'd all kindly beggar off.'

'I'm not sure that's the wisest course of action, Mr Copeland,' the vicar said.

Edith rose to her feet and said to him, she said, 'It'll only be a few minutes, vicar. You can show us around your garden, you had a question about gladioli, I believe. Perhaps we could offer some assistance.'

'I'm staying here, I know nothing about gardening,' Pandra said, shooting a glare in our direction.

Edith offered a simpering smile and said to her, she said, 'Come now, Pandra, we've all done some digging in the past, haven't we?'

She stood up and they left, shutting the door behind them.

I sat forward on the sofa and took our Doris's hand in mine, not allowing her to let go. I said to her, I said, 'Of course she's right, our Doris. I've no idea where you got it into your head that you can sit around and feel sorry for yourself. I did not marry some weakling who didn't know how to laugh in the face of adversity.'

Our Doris met my gaze and said to me, she said, 'I don't understand it myself, our 'arold. I'll feel almost like myself again and someone will offer a snide comment. Ordinarily I'd have a retort ready in the back of my mind, but now each insult weighs on my mind.'

'Why?'

She gave me the Look and said to me, she said, 'Why do you think?'

I shrugged and said, 'We have been married fifty-five years and I've still no idea what goes on in that brain of yours so why don't you let on and tell me.'

Our Doris knocked back the remainder of her tea and set the cup on the table. She said to me, she said, 'Ever since Violet Grey left Partridge Mews, I've questioned whether any of this is really worth it, our 'arold. She and I were the only members of the WI who had any notion about dinner parties and polite society. We came from a different world. No one in this day and age cares about the correct way to prepare butternut squash for more than twelve people.'

I said, 'And that's why you're feeling sorry for yourself?'

'Not just that,' she said, helping herself to a custard cream.

'What else?'

'As soon as I became interim chairwoman I questioned whether I'd be any good at it. I knew that there'd be a microscope on me immediately as I hadn't been properly elected – Violet fed my name to a few of the committee and they thought it would be a good idea, an opportunity for them to say they support women from all walks of life.

'And at first they were supportive. I had some good ideas and made an impression. Then I introduced Erin to the women and it was as though I had done the worst thing imaginable. All because she has lived on the council estate her entire life, because she's a young mother.

'A few years ago I was exactly the same. I am one of the women who forced her to change Reuben's name. We are truly awful, people, our 'arold and the more I remain part of the WI, the more I become aware of that fact.

'It makes me question what they thought of me before I joined the WI. I had working class parents. Now I wonder if my entire adult life has been built on a lie, if the only reason they allowed me to join is because I married well.'

She bit the custard cream in half to punctuate her speech.

I must admit I were a bit flabbergasted. I sat there staring at our Doris unsure of what to say. Of course, I'd always known that when we married folk had started to look at us a bit differently but I assumed it was because our Doris returned from our honeymoon with a perm. I thought about my words for a few more moments before saying to her, I said, 'Do you remember my mother?'

'I might be a bit upset, our 'arold, but I've not dipped into senility whilst I've been at it. Do you honestly believe I could forget your mother? You call me domineering.' She rolled her eyes at me and finished her biscuit.

'Exactly, my mother was a force to be reckoned with. When we got engaged she said that she'd have to teach you a thing or two about puff pastry.'

'Because I prefer shortcrust, I know.'

'And what did you say to her?'

Our Doris smiled slightly and said, 'I said to her, I said, "I might not speak like there's a potato stuck up my nose, but I'm not completely inept when it comes to baking." I thought she'd kill me but from that day onward she took me under her wing and she taught me everything I needed to know about society. She paid my first subscription to the WI.'

'And now you're doing the same for Erin. What would my mother have done if anyone said something against her daughter-in-law?'

'She'd have told them to go forth and multiply in no uncertain terms,' our Doris said.

I nodded. 'Right, and you can do the same, our Doris, because my mother didn't teach you to fall down at the first hurdle. If it weren't you these women were talking about, it would be the next one to come along because without gossip there's really not much for a pensioner to do bar watching Cash in the Attic.'

I'm not sure whether my words had the desired effect but our Doris sat up a little straighter in her seat. She said to me, she said, 'I do love you, you know, Harold Copeland.'

'After fifty-five years, I should bleeding well hope so,' I said, 'now, shall we get that lot back in here?'

'I'll have another custard cream before Alf gets a look in.'

Once our Doris regained her composure, I

brought the other four back into the living room. I allowed them to catch their breath before saying to Pandra, I said, 'I'd like to say sorry for punching your Derek in the face, Mrs O'Malley, it was uncalled for and I should have let our Doris's work speak for itself before going in all guns blazing.'

Pandra looked almost startled, her eyebrow quirked, and said to me, she said, 'It's him you should be apologising to. I'm his wife, not his keeper.'

I said, 'I'll say the same to him at the first opportunity, don't you worry about it.'

'Why you couldn't apologise earlier is a mystery, Mr Copeland, but if you're truly sorry I suppose I can forgive you.'

'That's very big of you.' I turned to Edith and said to her, I said, 'Is there anything you'd like to say?'

She had her arms folded, looking like a hen forcing out a particularly large egg, and said to me, she said, 'If you think I'm about to apologise to her then you've got another thing coming, Harold Copeland.'

Almost out of the ether, our Doris spoke. She said to the air, to no one in particular, she said, 'I'm sorry.'

'Pardon?' Pandra asked, smirking.

Our Doris breathed deeply, met Pandra's gaze and said to her, she said, 'I can offer nothing but my most sincere apologies at the harsh words spoken by myself and others in relation to your behaviour, Mrs O'Malley. I have no room to judge. Being the interim chairwoman of the Partridge Mews Women's Institute comes with a certain amount of honour. I have been the face for women in this town for much of the last year and it is quite unfortunate that I have used this platform to belittle and diminish the work of my peers. For that, I can say nothing more than sorry.'

The vicar practically threw himself to his feet, his grin widening to the point he looked to be entirely made of teeth. He said to us, he said, 'Bravo, Mrs Copeland, that speech is worthy of commendation. We often refuse to look at our own failures during a confrontation.'

'Don't pander to her!' Pandra exclaimed. 'She has wronged us all.'

'And I have apologised,' our Doris said, 'whether or not you choose to forgive me is your decision but I shan't lose any more sleep over it.'

She said to our Doris, she said, 'Then I guess I'll accept your apology as well, though if you think it will force me to drop out the election you have another thing coming.'

Our Doris nodded and said to her, she said, 'I'm rather looking forward to the outcome, aren't you?'

I nudged Edith in the side and said to her, I said, 'I think it might help our Doris's cause if you apologise.'

'Fine,' she said, rolling her eyes hard enough to crack her skull. She stood up, faced Pandra, and said to her, ever the head girl, she said, 'Mrs O'Malley, I am sorry I threw those cakes.'

'You didn't just throw them, Mrs Simpson, you threw them at me.'

'If your past baking experience is anything to go by, they could have been contaminated. I may have just saved the entire bake sale from a gastrointestinal epidemic the likes of which haven't been seen since the Black Death.'

'Are you saying I'm a bad cook?'

'I am,' Edith said, with a nod. 'You should add it to your curriculum vitae.'

'Is this your idea of an apology?' Pandra asked.

'It's all you're getting.' With that Edith sat back down, nabbing a chocolate digestive for herself as she went.

Alf beamed and said, 'This must be the first time I've never had to apologise to anybody.'

I said, 'It wouldn't hurt to say sorry, Alf.'

The vicar looked at him expectantly but Alf wasn't forthcoming. I'm that used to Alf doing wrong I'd anticipated him apologising just to get it out the way beforehand, but he stuck to his guns and sat there picking his nails.

I said to the vicar, I said, 'I think that's about it, really, vicar. Our Doris is never going to get on with Pandra, but at least they've apologised.'

He seemed about to say something when our Doris leant forward and picked up the Tupperware with her cake inside. She lifted the lid off and said to us, she said, 'I thought I'd bring a British classic to the bake sale, something that spoke class in abundance. Then I heard that Pandra invited Miss Moonflower to take part – of course this is her prerogative, and should she have set fire to anyone else's hair I'm certain my first idea would be to put her in charge of an oven – I won't lie, I became somewhat despondent, I hid myself away in the back bedroom acting something of the lemon.

'By the time I came downstairs the bake sale was too close to travel in search of specialist ingredients, therefore I chose to make a cake that I believe emphasises how people no matter their differences can create something of a relationship.'

With a flourish, our Doris unveiled the cake.

A Battenberg, the most beautiful I had ever seen in my days, sat within the confines of the Tupperware. My taste-buds shocked to life. I were salivating as I said to her, I said, 'That's my favourite, our Doris.'

She said to me, she said, 'Of course it is, I followed your mother's recipe.'

10

MY FAIR DORIS

Our Doris is looking at holiday brochures.

She's decided we've enough money saved for what she has planned. Not that she'll tell me the destination, just sends me into the living room to fall asleep in front of Dickinson's Real Deal.

When she first mentioned going away I thought it were a great idea – a few nights in Whitby, real fish and chips, paddle in the sea. Then she said as she wanted to go abroad and see something of the world.

I said to her, I said, 'Are you suffering an end-of-life crisis, our Doris? Since when have you wanted to see the world?'

She gave me the Look and said, 'I'm suffocated here, our 'arold.'

'Suffocated by who?' I asked.

'Sometimes I question whether you listen to a word I say. Due to recent events, I believe it would save my sanity to take a short break away from Partridge Mews.'

'But what about the WI election?'

Our Doris wrestled a few more holiday brochures from her bag and said to me, she said, 'That's months away, they're not going to hold it before the AGM.'

It turned out they planned to do exactly that. I'd just got back from the corner shop when she sprung it on me. I mean I'd barely stepped over the threshold when she lunged at me, eyes wild, as furious as a badger after a lamb, and her words were that high-pitched even dogs would struggle to hear them as she said to me, she said, 'You'll never guess what they've gone and done now, our 'arold.'

I said to her, I said, 'I only went out for a carton of milk, our Doris.'

She followed me into the kitchen with energy that frenetic it wouldn't be misplaced in a cockatoo. I started making a brew whilst our Doris began her pacing. It were like having a bleeding horse in the kitchen, the way her Gabor court shoes tapped against the lino. She growled, she hissed, ever the Doctor Dolittle, as she said to me, she said, 'I just had Mrs McBride on the phone, she says that the committee has chosen to bring the election forward so as not to inconvenience any members who won't be available for the AGM.'

'Isn't everyone expected to attend those?'

Our Doris nodded with such force it's a wonder she didn't dislocate her spine and said, she said, 'There's a man able to see the flaws in their logic. I know exactly why they brought it forward – they want me out.'

I weren't dumb enough that I'd failed to realise their intentions but I also wasn't dumb enough to admit this to our Doris. I said to her, I said, 'That can't be it surely.'

She wafted her hand in my general direction,

dismissing my comments, and said, 'Don't simper with me, our 'arold, I can't stand it when you're simpering. Give me your honest opinion, what do you think they're planning?'

The kettle finished boiling as I said to her, I said, 'They're hoping to oust you from the WI.'

'I should imagine they're doing more than hoping. I suppose it's only right that after decades of being faithful to the Partridge Mews Women's Institute they should unceremoniously throw me out like last week's cheese soufflé.'

I said to her, I said, 'We just have to get folk on side, our Doris.'

'You'll have a hard job there, our 'arold, I don't know if you've noticed but I'm something of the harridan.'

I met Alf at the Hare and Horse a few hours later. I'd only been barred for a week, but I'd taken Linda a bouquet of flowers in apology for punching Derek. Alf said to me, he said, 'I could've got them a damn sight cheaper than that.'

I handed him his pint and said, 'I'm not apologising with flowers from the unsuspecting dead.'

'Everyone knows that graveyards are the poor man's florist.' He knocked back his pint and said, 'I imagine your Doris has heard all about the election then?'

'She's taken it as well as you can imagine.'

'Did she throw any plant pots?'

I shook my head and said to him, I said, 'No, she's avoiding violence at the moment.' We'd had her probation officer around earlier in the week. He'd heard about mine and Edith's activities in relation to the bake sale and was worried that our Doris had orchestrated the attacks to avoid a prison sentence.

Once I'd assured him I'd acted of my own volition he told our Doris that she'd completed the hours required in her community service, though the manager of the charity shop said she could remain a volunteer should she so wish.

Our Doris let him out of the house and vowed to abstain from violence for the remainder of her days on the planet. I imagine she must've had some blow to the head but I said nothing. I've never known someone change their ways at seventy-three, usually that's an age you can get away with hitting folk.

Alf slurped his bitter, this hollow vacuum sound, before setting down his glass and saying to me, he said, 'Our Edith threw a plant pot, a few plant pots. Our garden looks like we've had an accident with crazy paving.'

'Oh,' I said, wondering just when mine and Alf's wives decided to switch personalities. Of course, they've been friends since ragdolls, it's likely a few of their attributes have rubbed off on one another. Alf and I were put on the same course of carrot sticks and hummus in the early two-thousands when they saw it mentioned on GMTV.

Alf said, he said, 'I left Martin cleaning it up and sent Edith around to your house. If I go home and find Pandra O'Malley's head on a spike I won't be surprised.'

'Our Doris will talk her around. She said as she didn't want any more violence – she's not likely to lie to a vicar is our Doris, he's the one authority she will listen to.'

'Do you think your Doris has a chance of winning the election?' he asked.

I said to him, I said, 'There's a better chance of you buying the next round.'

'That bad?'

I nodded. 'I'm getting a holiday whatever the outcome.'

Next day, a letter from our Doris appeared in the Partridge Mews Gazette. It detailed the rampant ageism that had the town in its grips, causing many of the more mature residents to feel unnecessary strife from their younger and more impressionable peers. She listed how she had been treated by store assistants at the supermarket who, despite her protestations, always deemed her wrinkles as a sign that she was on the edge of dementia and sought to follow her around like lost children after the Pied Piper. Our Doris listed everything wrong with the town's attitudes towards the older generation, going so far as to state that although younger people think it perfectly respectable to offer her a seat at church she can't help but see it as a level of condescension. Their parents may have taught them it is the polite thing to do but she refuses to take a seat from someone who hasn't learned how to properly pull up his trousers.

She didn't mention the WI.

When I brought it up she said to me, she said, 'Of course I didn't mention them, our 'arold, I don't want to overtly suggest that the organisation is corrupt. They may see it as slanderous and force my ejection from my role. I merely wish for them to understand the lengths I will go to in order to protect my position within the Women's Institute.'

Later that afternoon, Erin appeared, a rucksack heavy with folders and notepads slung over her shoulders – our Doris nearly collapsed under the weight of it as she helped Erin extricate herself. She said to her, she said, 'Have you had any lunch, dear?'

Erin shook her head and said to her, she said, 'I haven't had chance, Mrs Copeland. I nearly had to tie Reuben to a lamp-post and hope no one nicked him.'

Our Doris, busying herself in the fridge at his point, turned to her, fear etched into her eyes and said to her, she said, 'You never did, did you?'

'No, I'd have missed the class first. His Dad had him at the last minute, I think he wants to show off to his new girlfriend, not that I mind, maybe she can stop him eating wax crayons.' Erin slumped down at the kitchen table, her head in her hands. She hadn't washed her hair in a few days from the look of things, just scraped it back into a ponytail and hoped for the best. Her eyes were ringed with hollows deep enough to be rabbit holes.

I said to her, I said, 'You look worn out, Erin.'

'Have you ever tried to study for an exam in the middle of the night whilst your son runs around thinking he's training for the Power Rangers? And you have no will left to stop him because you're wondering just what you would do if you accidentally sent a nonagenarian to a Zumba class and she had a heart attack?'

Our Doris, quickly assembling a turkey salad said to Erin, she said, 'What's that got to do with social work?'

'It happened a few months back in Wren's Lea. A social worker got her cases mixed up, she lost her job and everything.' Erin sighed and went on, she said, 'Not that it matters, I graduate next week, I've just been doing some extra work on CVs and that sort of thing.'

'Next week?' our Doris said, eyes that wide she

might've overdosed on Botox.

'Yeah, next Wednesday, why? You are still coming, aren't you?'

Our Doris stopped slicing lettuce and hurried out of the room, scuttling to her cubbyhole. I watched as she moved sheaves of papers across her desk, dropping phone books and holiday brochures until she found her diary.

I hadn't seen her use her diary in weeks, most of her social engagements had dried up, I can't remember the last time we were invited out – we imagined most of the usual hosts had either gone on holiday or died, but now I wondered at whether it had something to do with the election.

She tore through pages at such a speed until she came to the next week.

And her face fell.

She ran back into the kitchen, as fast as her new hip could carry her, and stared at the calendar beside the fridge. Her face grimaced with anger, such fury as has never before been seen in a provincial upper-middle-class household, and said to us, she said, 'It's the same bleeding date. Who in their right mind thinks to organise an election on a Wednesday? Why not hold the event on a Tuesday night when we actually meet.' She turned on Erin and said to her, she said, 'Who else have you told about graduating?'

Erin looked to stammer a response, clearly no idea what our Doris was going on about.

'Now hold on a minute, our Doris,' I said, 'Erin's not the only person graduating next Wednesday, it could be any from a huge number of folk who've let the committee know.'

'So you agree with me?' she said, 'you agree that

they found out just when Erin's graduation was, knowing that I wouldn't attend the election, so that they could usurp me in my absence.'

'The election?' Erin said, 'I thought that wasn't until June.'

'Did no one ring you?' I asked.

'Of course no one rang her, our 'arold,' our Doris practically howled in her anger, she were seething as she said to us, she said, 'they won't contact Erin or any of the girls who may perhaps vote for me.'

Erin sat up straight and said, 'Mrs Copeland, you don't have to come to my graduation. You've been part of the WI a lot longer than you've known me – they have to come first.'

Our Doris went back to chopping lettuce. 'We're coming to your graduation, Erin. We'll just have to improve our strategy.'

'I'll ring our Theo,' I said. He'd be at school but he's always known how to keep a clear head in a crisis. During the potty-training crisis of two-thousand-and-two, he was the one who's quick thinking saw him urinating in the changing room of the British Home Stores.

I picked our Theo up from school, we collected his laptop, and took him back to the house. Erin and our Doris had already been at work, telephoning WI members who hadn't made their decision about who to vote for.

He said to our Doris, he said, 'Right, Nan, what are we doing?'

'It's up to you, our Theo, I'm not sure Instagram will work this time. After everything I said about the ageist culture it may seem too hypocritical to use such a modern social networking site.' Our Doris sat down at the kitchen table.

Theo set up his laptop next to her and said, he said, 'I think that's where you're wrong. See, if they see that you're using the site it emphasises just how in touch with modern trends you are.'

Erin interjected here, and said, 'Most of us girls from the estate haven't heard anything about the election. If you mention the election on there, I could share it with them, and then we don't have to worry about all the posh ones voting for Mrs O'Malley.'

Our Doris listened to what they said, a smile creeping across the face, looking ready to battle Batman. She said to them, she said, 'And that's precisely why I brought you both here.'

'I just came for lunch,' Erin said, 'you sprung the election on me. I only wanted to tell you about my graduation.'

'You're graduating?' Theo said.

'There's no need to seem so surprised, Theo, I've put in the work.' Erin went back to looking through the numbers in our Doris's phone book.

Our Theo shook his head and said to her, he said, 'That's not what I meant – it just seems a bit quick is all.'

'I took an introductory course,' she said, 'I'll start an apprenticeship soon.'

'Oh,' he said, 'I think I'll make a brew whilst the internet loads, want one?'

I said to our Doris, I whispered, 'We'll have to watch that one.'

'Why, our 'arold, whatever do you mean?' she said, a smirk on her lips.

'I think our Theo's grown a bit enamoured with that Miss Beaumont over there,' I said, making sure they couldn't hear me.

Our Doris batted me on the shoulder with a phonebook and said, 'Honestly, our 'arold, you will gossip. You should keep your mind on the task at hand.'

'Fine,' I said, glad of the diversion, I said, 'Why don't we go door to door?'

She beamed and said to me, she said, 'Look at that, our 'arold, when you get your mind out of the gutter you have some good ideas.'

Our Theo began his internet campaign almost immediately. Once Erin's friends in the WI were told about the election, they began calling our Doris – first to offer her words of support and tell her as they were thinking of getting their friends to join so as they could vote in her favour. Our Doris said they seemed almost disappointed when she informed them they wouldn't be allowed to vote as they hadn't been members long enough.

I said to our Doris, I said, 'It must be heartening though.'

She agreed and the next day we began our own campaign, travelling to members houses throughout Partridge Mews.

We first stopped by Mrs Patel's.

She invited us in, though she offered lukewarm lemonade as she doesn't believe in hot beverages before three o'clock in the afternoon – I thought as she's had plenty of brews in our house before lunchtime but I kept my mouth shut. It wouldn't help our Doris's cause should I complain about the lack of tea and hospitality in a household with two en-suites.

Mrs Patel took us through to the lounge, a claustrophobic den with its red curtains closed, refusing to allow even a ray of natural light in. Every surface in the room was filled with ornaments, china dolls, porcelain statues, brasses that thick with dust they mustn't have been polished since nineteen eighty-nine.

She sat in an armchair and had us sit in a sofa that small that we were wedged in it, my arm almost entangled in our Doris's handbag.

Our Doris said to her, she said, 'We're here today, Mrs Patel, to issue you with an appeal.'

'Let me stop you there, Mrs Copeland. If this is about the election then I cannot possibly invite you to speak. I am a member of the committee and as such it wouldn't be right.' Mrs Patel fluttered her eyelashes, hands clenched in her lap.

And that's when I spotted the flyer.

I said to her, I said, 'What's that up your sleeve, Mrs Patel?'

She clamped her hand around her cardigan and said, she said, 'How dare you look up a woman's sleeve, Mr Copeland? I'm surprised you would make such a statement with your wife sat next to you.' She settled for a moment, allowed herself to breathe and said, 'Though I will accept all apologies, I am nothing, if not a forgiving woman in such a trying time.'

'Save it, Edna, what's up your bleeding sleeve?'

Mrs Patel removed the flyer from her sleeve and set it on the table between us, blank side facing up, and said, 'It's merely a novelty handkerchief our Sanjeev brought back from Indonesia.'

Our Doris reached for the flyer and said to her, she said, 'It seems rather shiny to be a handkerchief.' She turned it over and the rage returned to her eyes faster than a boomerang. Pandra O'Malley's face stared up from the flyer, she had her arms folded, hair coiffed

– as coiffed as she could manage – and a list of things she could deliver that our Doris couldn't. She'd gone as far as to have it put on the flyer, 'Mrs Doris Copeland promises to raise the integrity of the WI, yet she lost it in the first place.'

'Mrs Copeland, I can explain,' Mrs Patel said.

Our Doris said to her, she said, 'How dare you sit there, claiming you cannot listen to any appeals as it wouldn't be right, when you've already made your decision?' She stood up, squeezing herself away from me, and said, she positively yelled, 'If you want Pandra O'Malley, bleeding well have her, but don't lie about it. Questioning my integrity when you have less integrity than boiled cabbage.'

She stormed out of the house, leaving the door swinging behind her. I managed to catch up to her halfway down the street. She surged away purposefully, arms swinging faster than an army cadet.

I said to her, I said, 'It's only one woman, our Doris, there's many more we can bring around.'

'I shouldn't have to bring anyone around,' she said, 'fair enough if these women were still my friends, but they've turned their backs on me.'

'I know,' I said.

'I'm not going down without a fight, our 'arold.'

I said to her, I said, 'I didn't expect you to. Shall we go to the next house?'

We did, and she showed us Pandra's flyer, as did the next person, and the next. The tenth person had the flyer in her front window alongside the 'Beware the Yorkshire Terrier' poster. In fact, the only person to show any interest at all in our Doris's campaign was Tabitha Quail who couldn't vote as she had a trip to Reykjavik planned.

The entire time we traipsed around town, I worried that we would run into Pandra O'Malley, so that when we did it was like staring the Grim Reaper dead in the eye. She met us in the middle of Bronte Lane and said to us, she said, 'Fancy seeing you two, here. I thought you might be home taking selfies, or whatever it is you need to do nowadays to bear some semblance of relevance. And yes, Mrs Copeland, I am talking to you directly.'

Our Doris stood straight, shoulders back, enough hair that she didn't look like a turnip sprouting, and said to Pandra, she said, 'Here I thought we'd put all animosity behind us. Though my mind isn't as off-kilter as yours, I must commend you, I would never be brave enough to wear capri trousers with ankle boots.'

'I should think not, your style has a suitably vintage flair to it. You're the only person I know to wear shoulder pads outside the nineteen-eighties.'

Our Doris offered a curt nod and said, 'This has nothing to do with the forthcoming election. Frankly, I've always found it charming you thought you could command such authority as chairwoman when you've barely any command over your ... I'm sorry you probably call it hair, I'm afraid I've seen more moisture in tumbleweed.'

'Says the woman whose hair is only now growing back.'

'I had an unfortunate accident with a firework, is your hairstyle an accident as well? It looks like it needs intensive care.'

That's when I realised that folk had stopped in the street to watch the both of them, that there were curtains being opened and cars were slowing down as they went past. I should've known there'd be some interest with our Doris and Pandra O'Malley sharing insults like children share chewing gum.

Pandra went on, she said, 'You'll never make it as chairwoman because the only way you command respect is by insulting people. Do you remember the Christmas Pageant of nineteen eighty-two? I asked you if you thought I worked well as Mrs Claus and you said that I was the perfect size for the role being as I had the bust measurements of a VW Camper Van.'

Our Doris looked at her, all gone out, and said, 'That wasn't an insult, that was constructive criticism, you were gargantuan. I merely expressed concern that one of my close friends looked as though she was about to star in King Kong.'

'I was not that hairy,' Pandra said.

'Only because I set you on to Nair.'

'This is what I mean, you can't go a sentence without insulting someone.'

'It wasn't an insult, it was a statement.'

'That insulted me.'

'You chose to get insulted, that certainly wasn't my intention,' our Doris said, as smug as a headmistress with a resoled slipper.

I said to them, I said, 'Are you two going to keep at this? If so, I'm off to the pub – it's like watching terriers over a bowl of stew. I've had enough.'

Our Doris gave me the Look and said to me, she said, 'And who are you to get involved now, our 'arold?'

I did something I didn't know I was capable, I fired our Doris's Look right back at her and said to her, I said, 'You can look at me however you bleeding like, our Doris, I am sick to the eye-teeth of it. Folk are going to vote either way, and you slinging insults at each other like an episode of Coronation Street is nothing short of childish.'

'Your wife started it,' Pandra said.

I turned on her and said, I positively yelled, I said, 'I don't care who bleeding started it, Pandra. Why don't you beggar off to whichever sewer you were raised in and leave us to get on with our day? We understand, you're not going to back down, you're an old biddy with a score to settle, you're Irish, did I forget anything?'

Pandra shook her head and said, she murmured, 'I best be going then, hadn't I?' And she scuttled off like a choirboy caught with the communion wine.

Our Doris fumed behind me, and said to me, she said, 'What in the good lord's name do you think you're doing, our 'arold? Talking to me like that in the middle of the street.'

'We're going home, our Doris,' I said, 'and we're going to look at holiday brochures because we know how this election is going.'

We arrived home to find Erin on the doorstep. She'd been crying. Our Doris rushed over to her and said to her, leading her inside, she said, 'Come on, girl, let's get you inside and you can tell us what's the matter.'

I made the drinks and we took them into the living room. Our Doris allowed Erin to sit in her Arighi Bianchi chair, the chair I'm not allowed to sit in unless I leave any unpalatable odours behind. Once she'd tidied her face up a bit, she said to our Doris, Erin said, 'I don't think you should come to my graduation, Mrs Copeland.'

Our Doris had Erin's hands in hers and said to her, she said, 'Why ever not?'

'You've been fighting to be the chairwoman since

before Mrs O'Malley announced her candidacy. As interim chairwoman you should be there during the vote – I was speaking to Mrs McBride, if you don't attend the meeting they're likely to strip you of your title.'

'I know they will,' our Doris said, 'but you needn't worry about that, Erin. I've been there for every essay and exam you've had to sit, I'm not about to miss out on your graduation.'

Erin's face brightened up. She smiled at our Doris, though she was still a bit teary and said to her, she said, 'Are you sure?'

And then our Doris said something I thought I'd never hear from her lips. Even when the Partridge Mews Women's Institute disagreed with her stance on piccalilli, she had accepted their decision and hid jars in the cupboard under the sink. Yet, now she sat there and said to Erin, nodding, our Doris said, 'The WI can go whistle.'

I can't say I didn't grin.

That night our Doris and I discussed holiday destinations. We'd just finished watching Endeavour on catch-up when she brought the brochures into the living room and said to me, she said, 'I've looked at our savings, our 'arold, and really the world is our oyster, so where have you always wanted to see?'

She'd forgiven me for shouting at her in the street. I've no idea why, but I wasn't about to question it. I thought about her question, cradling my mug on my chest. I said to her, I said, 'I wanted to see Machu Picchu when I was twenty-four but I don't know if I've waited too long. They wouldn't insure Michael Eaton when he wanted to go go-karting in Malaysia, do you think they'd insure me for climbing up a mountain in

Peru?'

Our Doris said to me, she said, 'I could always ask the travel agent, say as I wouldn't be fussed if you got altitude sickness. Besides, it's a mountain, if you suddenly drop dead we can just push you over the edge.'

'There is that,' I said, 'how about you? Where do you want to go?'

'There's a three month cruise around the world I had my eye on.'

'Three months?' I almost jumped out of my chair, just glad my reflexes were quick enough for me to grab my mug. I leant forward and said to her, I said, 'We can't just beggar off for three months, our Doris, what about the house?'

'Since our Angela has a key, and she stands to inherit the place, I should think that it's in her best interests to keep an eye out,' she said.

I tried to look somewhat inquisitive as I said to her, I said, 'Just how long have you been planning this holiday, our Doris?'

She hid her face behind her brochure and said, 'Not long at all really, it is merely an idea that has been percolating in the back of my mind. I thought that since we've never been further than Guernsey as a married couple, we could see the most in what is really a rather short amount of time.'

'You decided to wait until you were seventy-three before realising this? I wanted to go to Peru fifty years ago, our Doris. It was supposed to be our honeymoon.'

'Well it wasn't, now what do you think?' she said.

I said to her, I said, 'You better not take any life insurance policies out against me in the near future is what I think.'

'You've nothing to worry about there, our 'arold. I did that years ago.'

I said, 'I hope the lifejackets are easily located.'

That night I went to bed fearful. I don't think any man in their right mind would want to spend three months on the open seas with our Doris.

A few days down the line and we assembled ourselves alongside the other parents, partners and friends of the students in the auditorium of the local college. Our Doris dressed especially for the occasion in a new wool skirt from John Lewis, alongside Marc Cain blouse and a lemon-coloured blazer she said she found in the wardrobe but I'm pretty confident she showed me in the window of the boutique a few weeks earlier.

I stuck with the navy suit, there's no point changing the habit of a lifetime.

We found two seats together and sat down. I said to our Doris, I said, 'I'm sure graduating from college wasn't this big an occasion when our Angela did it.'

She said to me, she said, 'Everybody graduates nowadays, remember when our Theo left junior school and our Angela had to go out of her way to find a gown and cap for a ten year old?'

'I'd forgotten about that,' I said.

Our Doris hadn't been herself all day. We both of us knew why. It wasn't that she was downtrodden, that she had the weight of the world on her shoulders, in fact she seemed almost calm about no longer being the chairwoman. It's just that she looked a little bit like those folk in supermarket car parks who can't find their cars.

I said to her, I said, 'Are you all right, our Doris?'

'I think we'll take Erin out for a bite to eat after this, our 'arold. The Hare and Horse still serves food, doesn't it?'

I said as it did and we quietened down to watch Erin graduate. First came a long speech from Mrs Porter, the headmistress, who talked about the students overcoming adversity in the face of the modern working environment and how they had proven their worth. I tell you, Mrs Porter was that much of a windbag she'd do well at Hogmanay.

Eventually, after more speeches from teachers of different subjects, they allowed the students to accept their diplomas. Due to her surname, Erin was one of the first. We saw her for all of thirty seconds as she walked across the stage, shook someone's hand and then disappeared down some steps. This meant that we got to spend another half an hour, watching students follow in her path, completing the same rituals, the only change in routine when a young lad tripped on his gown and bruised his chin.

When it was all over we met Erin by the front gates. She'd already changed into a Doris-approved dress, Karen Millen, purchased from the charity shop.

I said to her, I said, 'Where did the gown go?'

'I borrowed it from another girl, I'm not forking out all that money just to go and grab a piece of paper,' she said.

'Isn't that your diploma?' I asked.

She shook her head as we made our way over to the car. 'No,' she said, 'you hand that in once you're finished and they put it in a box for the next ceremony. The real thing comes in the post. It's more for show than anything.'

I said to our Doris, I said, 'Did you know about this?'

Our Doris said to me, she said, 'If you're going to

say how I could have gone to the election because the graduation was meaningless then you can keep your mouth shut, our 'arold. Erin and I were making a statement.'

'Really,' I said, 'and just what was that statement?'

'All you have to do is drive, you can hear my statement later.'

When we reached the Hare and Horse we found a celebration already underway. Pandra O'Malley and Derek sat near the coal fire, surrounded by a few select members of the Partridge Mews Women's Institute. They had an empty bottle of prosecco on the table, all of them giddy as toddlers with Haribo.

I said to our Doris, I said, 'We don't have to eat here – we could go to the Harrington.'

She wandered over to the bar and said to Linda, she said, 'I would like to purchase two bottles of your finest champagne, please.'

'Celebrating as well, are we, Mrs Copeland?' she said. 'They've been at it for over an hour – she's giving me a ruddy headache with all her cackling.'

Our Doris hid her smile and took out her purse. 'I'm sorry to say I'll be sending one of the bottles over to Mrs O'Malley's table. The other is for Erin – she graduated today. Of course, you're more than welcome to toast her with us.'

Linda beamed at Erin and said to her, she said, 'That's brilliant news. You lot go and sit down, I'll bring the bottle right on over.'

When we sat down Erin said to our Doris, she said, 'Champagne, Mrs Copeland? Isn't that a bit, I don't know, extravagant? I only passed an introductory course.'

'We celebrate all successes in this family, Erin.

Reuben's with his father for the rest of the evening, which leaves you free to enjoy yourself.'

Linda brought our bottle of champagne over, she poured a few glasses, including one for herself. Our Doris said, she said, 'Thank you, Linda. Now, I would appreciate it if we could raise our glasses to a young woman who has proved to me that it is never right for one to forget their roots, no matter how unfashionable.

'Over the last few months, Erin has shown me what it means to be a woman of the twenty-first century, and I couldn't be more proud of her today. Erin, I can offer you nothing but gratitude for showing me how hard-hearted I had become.

'Please raise your glasses to Miss Erin Beaumont.'

'To Erin,' I said.

Our glasses met in the middle of the table. I looked from Erin to our Doris, seeing tears twinkle in their eyes. We drank our champagne – I've never had a taste for it myself, but our Doris has always been one for ceremony.

Erin said to our Doris, she said, 'Thank you, Mrs Copeland.'

Our Doris handed her a handkerchief and said, 'You've nothing to thank me for. If left to my own devices I'm confident I'd have become nothing more than a bitter old crone.'

'Congratulations, Erin,' Linda said, draining her glass. 'Shall I take the other bottle to Pandra, now?' she asked.

Our Doris said, 'That would be most appreciated.'

Linda nodded and took the bottle over to Pandra, who accepted it with a look that can only be described as consternation on her face.

I said to our Doris, I said, 'That was really big of

you, our Doris.'

She said, 'It's damage limitation, our 'arold, and don't you forget it.'

We were in the middle of our meal when Pandra approached the table. She came alone, mildly inebriated – not completely addled, but still having to hold the tables to make sure she stayed upright. She said to our Doris, she said, 'Just what is the meaning of the champagne, Mrs Copeland?'

Our Doris stood up to greet her, a smile on her face. She said to her, she said, 'I thought I might congratulate you, Pandra. Though I am against making assumptions, since I saw you celebrating I assumed that you must be the new chairwoman of the Partridge Mews Women's Institute – it's an award that calls for champagne, does it not?'

Pandra said, 'They're having a party in my honour at the church hall tonight.'

Our Doris nodded and said to her, she said, 'I thought they might. Would it be completely awful of me to request something from you? It is a rather small request, really.'

I imagine Pandra's face was supposed to be questioning our Doris's words, however, she'd ingested that much alcohol it looked more like her face had melted. She said to our Doris, she said, 'What would the request be?'

'A concession speech. I merely wish to address the ladies.'

Pandra considered it for a moment before saying to our Doris, she said, 'I should be able to stretch to that.'

'Good, now I am most apologetic for taking up so much of your time. Shouldn't you be getting back to

your table? Derek will wonder just where you got to.'
Our Doris sat down before Pandra could answer, and
downed the rest of her glass of champagne, her hands
trembling more than a waltzer.

Later that night we made our way to the church
hall with Erin, Alf, and Edith, whose rage with the WI
knew no bounds. She had already leaked the story that
Mrs McBride once stole from the donation plate at
church when she needed change for parking. It turns
out that she has a lot of secrets about Partridge Mews,
and isn't afraid to share them. Alf said to me, he said,
'It's like being married to a landmine, waiting for it to
explode.'

I said, 'Welcome to my world,' as we reached the
church hall and walked inside.

They'd clearly been planning this for months, no
matter what they said. Banners hung from every beam
in the ceiling congratulating Pandra on her success. The
trestle tables had been unleashed once again, piled high
with food and wine, and cans of ale. The ladies of the
WI and their husbands sat at tables, white cotton cloths
hiding all manner of stains and sins.

We sat close to the microphone. Our Doris chose
the seats, she wanted folk to know she was there. She'd
changed into her aquamarine dress and put on the
white gold jewellery. She'd decided to go out on her
own terms and I must admit, I were a bit proud.

After the buffet, Mrs Cribbins approached the
microphone. She coughed before saying to the hall, she
said, 'I'm afraid Mrs McBride was unable to attend
tonight's proceedings due to reasons of a personal
nature. She asks that we continue as we would
ordinarily, and says she hopes to forget all the sorry
business in good time.

'But enough of that.

'Tonight we are here to celebrate our new chairwoman, Mrs Pandra O'Malley, who we hope will return the Partridge Mews Women's Institute to its former glory, free of unsavoury opinions and a fresh idea of what it means to be the face of our organisation.

'Before we begin, however, I believe our former chairwoman, Mrs Doris Copeland, has a few words she wishes to share.' She met our Doris's gaze with a look that can only be described as contempt and said to her, she said, 'Would you like to approach the microphone?'

Our Doris garnered a smile and stood up. She smoothed down the front of her dress and walked with purpose towards Mrs Cribbins, nodding her head in either deference or pure hatred.

Facing the rest of the hall, our Doris said to us, she said, 'Thank you, Mrs Cribbins. I can only hope that should Mrs O'Malley seek to restore the WI to its former glory she looks to you, a woman whose ideas and opinions we thought eradicated with the culmination of the second World War.'

There were sharp inhalations all around at our Doris's words. Mrs Cribbins made to step forward, only for our Doris to hold up her hand, seemingly freezing her in place. She said to her, she said, 'You needn't worry, I haven't much else to say.

'The truth is I asked Mrs O'Malley for the opportunity to speak because I felt it only right.

'I have been a member of the Partridge Mews Women's Institute since the nineteen-sixties. There have been many chairwomen, but none has ever caused as much controversy as me. I must say that fills me with a sense of pride – to stand at the head of an organisation, knowing you're the most hated woman in the room takes courage I never knew I had.

'Either way, I am no longer the interim chairwoman.

'I have also decided that I no longer wish to participate in the WI.

'Over the last year this organisation has caused more arguments within my family and circle of friends than I thought possible. I have given much more of my time and effort to being interim chairwoman than I have my family, and I've realised that none of you are really worth it.

'The majority of you represent what is wrong with society today and I refuse to be part of it any longer.

'I am grateful to the WI of old, who taught me what it means to be a woman. However, I long to spend more time with my family than a bunch of spiteful women who care more about the quality of quiche than they do their peers.

'That is why I implore you, women of the Partridge Mews Women's Institute, to go forth and multiply.'

Our Doris stepped away from the microphone and took a determined tread across the church hall. We soon trailed after her, shielding her from the calls and snide comments of the audience who served to prove her right.

Once we reached the car park, Edith said to her, she said, 'That took some nerve, Doris, are you sure you want that to be your lasting impression?'

Our Doris continued walking down the road and said to her, she said, 'I'm sure, Edith. I hope you realise I wasn't talking about you in there.'

'Of course she realised,' Alf said, a grin streaking across his face showing a great many foodstuffs trapped in his gums. 'We won't let them get to you, don't you fret.'

She faced Erin and said, 'I think they'll try and oust you next.'

Erin shrugged and said to her, she said, 'I won't bother going, if you don't mind – you paid the subscription, after all.'

We ended up going our separate ways.

Our Doris and I were silent as we walked home.

We went straight through to the kitchen. She sat at the table, removing her jewellery as I put the kettle on.

After she removed her earrings she slumped forward across the table. She said to me, she said, 'I can't help feeling like I've done the wrong thing, our 'arold.'

I sat down next to her and said, 'That's where you're wrong, our Doris. I couldn't be more proud of you. You were honest with those women and told them how their behaviour is affecting folk.'

'I feel sick,' she said.

'That's understandable,' I said, 'you just left the WI. You've been a member your entire adult life.'

Our Doris sat up, her eye shadow smeared across her forehead and said, she said, 'Exactly. Who am I without the WI?'

'You're Mrs Doris Copeland of Shakespeare Avenue, owner of the best Battenberg recipe in Partridge Mews.' I went to finish making the drinks whilst she cleaned her face.

She said to me, she said, 'What am I going to do now, our 'arold?'

I handed her a holiday brochure and said, 'I've always fancied a three month cruise around the world, how about you?'

Acknowledgements

Writers have talked about that difficult second book in the past and *Indisputably Doris* helped me figure out what that meant.

Firstly, thanks to Lindsey, for reading this book and offering reassurance when I thought the strength to write long-since past. You have guided me through my writing for many years now and it's only right that I acknowledge that here. Ours is a grand friendship and one day we will have that picnic.

Many thanks to Joy Winkler who stepped in at the last minute to help edit, and offered much advice regarding writing and helped manage the great many fears I had in relation to the dreaded sequel.

Thank you to my mother, Cathryn Heathcote, who has ferried me to events, who read the book before anyone else, and who is quite capable of coping with my rants. We'll call it an artistic temperament.

Thanks are also due to Abercrombie, Elizabeth Ellerby, Ste and Margaret Holbrook, Sandy Milsom, Phil Poyser, Jason Sandywell, Jill Walsh, and the Macclesfield Creative Writing Group for their encouragement and continued support.

Especial thanks to the many readers, audience members and librarians for their kind words, and help in bringing our Doris to the masses.

For those of you who have been here since the beginning, until next time, that is all.